RIVERSIDE COMMUNITY COLLEGE
1916

O9-CFT-181

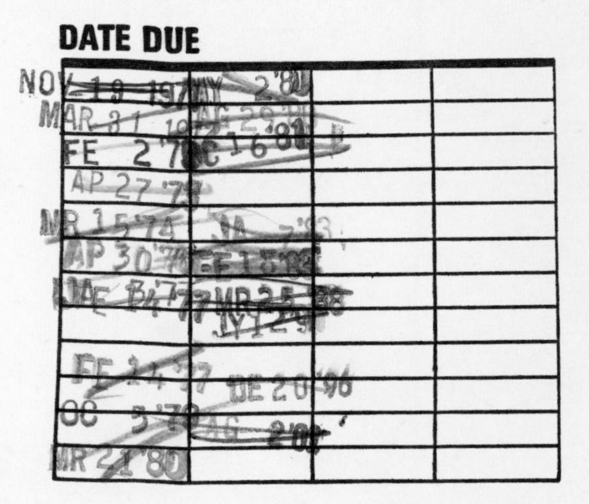
DATE DUE

ORBIT 7

Other Books
in Damon Knight's
ORBIT Series

ORBIT 1

ORBIT 2

ORBIT 3

ORBIT 4

ORBIT 5

ORBIT 6

DAMON KNIGHT'S

ORBIT 7

An Anthology of
New Science Fiction Stories

G. P. Putnam's Sons   New York

Library of Congress Catalog Card Number: 66-15585

PRINTED IN THE UNITED STATES OF AMERICA

Contents

April Fool's Day Forever

by Kate Wilhelm

On the last day of March a blizzard swept across the lower Great Lakes, through western New York and Pennsylvania, and raced toward the city with winds of seventy miles an hour, and snow falling at the rate of one and a half inches an hour. Julia watched it from her wide windows overlooking the Hudson River forty miles from the edge of the city and she knew that Martie wouldn't be home that night. The blizzard turned the world white within minutes and the wind was so strong and so cold that the old house groaned under the impact. Julia patted the windowsill, thinking there, there at it. "It'll be over soon, and tomorrow's April, and in three or four weeks I'll bring you daffodils." The house groaned louder and the spot at the window became too cold for her to remain there without a sweater.

Julia checked the furnace by opening the basement door to listen. If she heard nothing, she was reassured. If she heard a wheezing and an occasional grunt, she would worry and call Mr. Lampert, and plead with him to come over before she was snowed in. She heard nothing. Next she looked over the supply of logs in the living room. Not enough by far. There were three good-sized oak logs, and two pine sticks. She struggled with her parka and boots and went to the woodpile by the old barn that had become a storage house, den, garage, studio. A sled was propped up against the grey stone and shingle building, and she put it down and began to arrange logs on it. When she had as many as she could pull, she returned to the house, feeling her way with one hand along the barn wall, then along the basketweave fence that she and Martie had built three summers ago, edging a small wild brook that divided the yard. The fence took her in a roundabout way, but it was safer than trying to go straight to the house in the blinding blizzard. By the time she had got back inside, she felt frozen. Although a sheltered thermometer would show no lower than thirty at that time, with the wind blowing as it was, the chill degrees must be closer to ten or twenty below zero. She stood in the mud room and considered what else she should do. Her car was in the garage. Martie's was at the train station. Mail. Should she try to retrieve any mail that might be in the box? She decided not to. She didn't really think the mailman had been there yet, anyway. Usually Mr. Probst blew his whistle to let her know that he was leaving something, and she hadn't heard it. She took off the heavy clothes then and went through the house checking windows, peering at the latches of the storm windows. There had been a false spring three weeks ago, and she had opened windows and even washed a few before the winds changed again. The house was secure.

What she wanted to do was call Martie, but she didn't. His boss didn't approve of personal phone calls during the working day. She breathed a curse at Hilary Boyle, and waited for Martie to call her. He would, as soon as he had a chance. When she was certain that there was nothing else she should do, she sat down in the living room where one log was burning softly. There was no light on in the room and the storm had darkened the sky. The small fire glowed pleasingly in the enormous fireplace, and the radiance was picked up by pottery and brass mugs on a low table before the fireplace. The room was a long rectangle, wholly out of proportion, much too long for its width, and with an uncommonly high ceiling. Paneling the end walls had helped, as had making a separate room within the larger one, with its focal point the fireplace. A pair of chairs and a two-seater couch made a cozy grouping. The colors were autumn forest colors, brilliant and subdued at the same time: oranges and scarlets in the striped covering of the couch, picked up again by pillows; rust browns in the chairs; forest green rug. The room would never make *House Beautiful,* Julia had thought when she brought in the last piece of brass for the table and surveyed the effect, but she loved it, and Martie loved it. And she'd seen people relax in that small room within a room who hadn't been able to relax for a long time. She heard it then.

When the wind blew in a particular way in the old house, it sounded like a baby crying in great pain. Only when the wind came from the northwest over thirty miles an hour. They had searched and searched for the minute crack that had to be responsible and they had caulked and filled and patched until it seemed that there couldn't be any more holes, but it was still there, and now she could hear the baby cry.

Julia stared into the fire, trying to ignore the wail, willing herself not to think of it, not to remember the first time she had heard the baby. She gazed into the fire and couldn't stop the images that formed and became solid before her eyes. She awakened suddenly, like in the dreams she had had during the last month or so of pregnancy. Without thinking she slipped from bed, feeling for her slippers in the dark, tossing her robe about her shoulders hurriedly. She ran down the hall to the baby's room, and at the door she stopped in confusion. She pressed one hand against her flat stomach, and the other fist against her mouth hard, biting her fingers until she tasted blood. The baby kept on crying. She shook her head and reached for the knob and turned it, easing the door open soundlessly. The room was dark. She stood at the doorway, afraid to enter. The baby cried again. Then she pushed the door wide open and the hall light flooded the empty room. She fainted.

When she woke up hours later, grey light shone coldly on the bare floor, from the yellow walls. She raised herself painfully, chilled and shivering. Sleepwalking? A vivid dream and sleepwalking? She listened; the house was quiet, except for its regular night noises. She went back to bed.

Martie protested in his sleep when she snuggled against his warm body, but he turned to let her curve herself to fit, and he put his arm about her. She said nothing about the dream the next day.

Six months later she heard the baby again. Alone this time, in the late afternoon of a golden fall day that had been busy and almost happy. She had been gathering nuts with her friend Phyllis Govern. They'd had a late lunch, and then Phyllis had had to run because it was close to four. A wind had come up, threatening a storm before evening. Julia watched the clouds build for half an hour.

She was in her studio in the barn, on the second floor where the odor of hay seemed to remain despite an absence of fifteen or twenty years. She knew it was her imagination, but she liked to think that she could smell the hay, could feel the warmth of the animals from below. She hadn't worked in her studio for almost a year, since late in her pregnancy, when it had become too hard to get up the narrow, steep ladder that led from the ground floor to the balcony that opened to the upstairs rooms. She didn't uncover anything in the large room, but it was nice to be there. She needed clay, she thought absently, watching clouds roll in from the northwest. It would be good to feel clay in her fingers again. She might make a few Christmas gifts. Little things, funny things, to let people know that she was all right, that she would be going back to work before long now. She glanced at the large blocks of granite that she had ordered before. Not yet. Nothing serious yet. Something funny and inconsequential to begin with.

Still thoughtful, she left the studio and went to the telephone in the kitchen and placed a call to her supplier in the city. While waiting for the call to be completed, she heard it. The baby was in pain, she thought, and hung up. Not until she had started for the hall door did she realize what she was doing. She stopped, very cold suddenly. Like before, only this time she was wide awake. She felt for the door and pushed it open an inch or two. The sound was still there, no louder, but no softer either. Very slowly she followed the sound up the stairs, through the hall, into the empty room. She had been so certain that it originated here, but now it seemed to be coming from her room. She backed out into the hall and tried the room she shared with Martie. Now the crying seemed to be coming from the other bedroom. She stood at the head of the stairs for another minute, then she ran down and tried to dial Martie's number. Her hands were shaking too hard and she botched it twice before she got him.

Afterwards she didn't know what she had said to him. He arrived an hour later to find her sitting at the kitchen table, ashen-faced, terrified.

"I'm having a breakdown," she said quietly. "I knew it happened to some women when they lost a child, but I thought I was past the worst part by now. I've heard it before, months ago." She stared straight ahead. "They probably will want me in a hospital for observation for a while. I should have packed, but . . . Martie, you will try to keep me out of an institution, won't you? What does it want, Martie?"

"Honey, shut up. Okay?" Martie was listening intently. His face was very pale. Slowly he opened the door and went into the hall, his face turned up toward the stairs.

"Do you hear it?"

"Yes. Stay there." He went upstairs, and when he came back down, he was still pale, but satisfied now. "Honey, I hear it, so that means there's something making the noise. You're not imagining it. It is a real noise, and by God it sounds like a baby crying."

Julia built up the fire and put a stack of records on the stereo and turned it too loud. She switched on lights through the house, and set the alarm clock for six twenty to be certain she didn't let the hour pass without remembering Hilary Boyle's news show. Not that she ever forgot it, but there might be a first time, especially on this sort of night, when she wouldn't be expecting Martie until very late, if at all. She wished he'd call. It was four thirty. If he could get home, he should leave the office in an hour, be on the train at twenty-three minutes before six and at home by six forty-five. She made coffee and lifted the phone to see if it was working. It seemed to be all right. The stereo music filled the house, shook the floor, and rattled the windows, but over it, now and then, she could hear the baby.

She tried to see outside; the wind-driven snow was impenetrable. She flicked on outside lights, the drive entrance, the light over the garage, the door to the barn, the back porch, front porch, the spotlight on the four pieces of granite that she had completed and placed in the yard, waiting for the rest of the series. The granite blocks stood out briefly during a lull. They looked like squat sentinels.

She took her coffee back to the living room where the stereo was loudest, and sat on the floor by the big cherry table that they had cut down to fourteen inches. Her sketch pad lay here. She glanced at the top page without seeing it, then opened the pad to the middle and began to doodle aimlessly. The record changed; the wind howled through the yard; the baby wailed. When she looked at what she had been doing on the pad, she felt a chill begin deep inside. She had written over and over, *MURDERERS. You killed my babies. MURDERERS.*

Martie Sayre called the operator for the third time within the hour. "Are the lines still out?"

"I'll check again, Mr. Sayre." Phone static, silence, she was back. "Sorry, sir. Still out."

"Okay. Thanks." Martie chewed his pencil and spoke silently to the picture on his desk: Julia, blonde, thin, intense eyes and a square chin. She was beautiful. Her thin body and face seemed to accentuate lovely delicate bones. He, thin also, was simply craggy and gaunt. "Honey, don't listen to it. Turn on the music loud. You know I'd be there if I could." The phone rang and he answered.

"I have the material on blizzards for you, Mr. Sayre. Also, Mr. Boyle's interview with Dr. Hewlitt, AMS, and the one with Dr. Wycliffe, the NASA satellite weather expert. Anything else?"

"Not right now, Sandy. Keep close. Okay?"

"Sure thing."

He turned to the monitor on his desk and pushed the "On" button. For the next half hour he made notes and edited the interviews and shaped a fifteen-minute segment for a special to be aired at ten that night. Boyle called for him to bring what he had ready at seven.

There was a four-man consultation. Martie, in charge of the science news department, Dennis Kolchak, political news expert, David Wedekind, the art director. Hilary Boyle paced as they discussed the hour special on the extraordinary weather conditions that had racked the entire Earth during the winter. Boyle was a large man, over six feet, with a massive frame that let him carry almost three hundred pounds without appearing fat. He was a chain-smoker, and prone to nervous collapses. He timed the collapses admirably: He never missed a show. His daily half hour, "Personalized News," was the most popular network show that year, as it had been for the past three years. The balloon would burst eventually, and the name Hilary Boyle wouldn't sound like God, but now it did, and no one could explain the X factor that had catapulted the talentless man into the firmament of stars.

The continuity writers had blocked in the six segments of the show already, two from other points–Washington and Los Angeles–plus the commercial time, plus the copter pictures that would be live, if possible.

"Looking good," Hilary Boyle said. "Half an hour Eddie will have the first film ready . . ."

Martie wasn't listening. He watched Boyle and wondered if he'd stumble over any of the words he'd used in his segment. He hoped not. Boyle always blamed him personally if he, Boyle, didn't know the words he had to parrot. "Look, Martie, I'm a reasonably intelligent man, and if I don't know it, you gotta figure that most of the viewers won't know it either. Get me? Keep it simple, but without sacrificing any of the facts. That's your job, kid. Now give me this in language I can understand."

Martie's gaze wandered to the window wall. The room was on the sixty-third floor; there were few other lights to be seen on this level, and only those that were very close. The storm had visibility down to two hundred yards. What lights he could see appeared ghostly, haloed, diffused, toned down to beautiful pearly luminescences. He thought of Boyle trying to say that, and then had to bite his cheek to keep from grinning. Boyle couldn't stand it when someone grinned in his presence, unless he had made a funny.

His part of the special was ready for taping by eight, and he went to the coffee shop on the fourteenth floor for a sandwich. He wished he could get through to Julia, but telephone service from Ohio to Washington to Maine was a disaster area that night.

He closed his eyes and saw her, huddled before the fire in the living room glowing with soft warm light. Her pale hair hiding her paler face, hands over her ears, tight. She got up and went to the steps, looking up, then ran back to the fire. The house shaking with music and the wind. The image was so strong that he opened his eyes wide and shook his head too hard, starting a mild headache at the back of his skull. He drank his coffee fast, and got a second cup, and when he sat down again, he was almost smiling. Sometimes he was convinced that she was right when she said that they had something so special between them, they never were actually far apart. Sometimes he knew she was right.

He finished his sandwich and coffee and wandered back to his office. Everything was still firm, ready to tape in twenty minutes. His part was holding fine.

He checked over various items that had come through in the last several hours, and put three of them aside for elaboration. One of them was about a renewal of the influenza epidemic that had raked England earlier in the year. It was making a comeback, more virulent than ever. New travel restrictions had been imposed.

Julia: "I don't care what they say, I don't believe it. Who ever heard of quarantine in the middle of the summer? I don't know why travel's being restricted all over the world, but I don't believe it's because of the flu." Accusingly, "You've got all that information at your fingertips. Why don't you look it up and see. They banned travel to France before the epidemic got so bad."

Martie rubbed his head, searched his desk for aspirin and didn't find any. Slowly he reached for the phone, then dialed Sandy, his information girl. "See what we have on tap about weather-related illnesses, honey. You know, flu, colds, pneumonia. Stuff like that. Hospital statistics, admittances, deaths. Closings of businesses, schools. Whatever you can find. Okay?" To the picture on his desk, he said, "Satisfied?"

Julia watched the Hilary Boyle show at six thirty and afterward had scrambled eggs and a glass of milk. The weather special at ten explained Martie's delay, but even if there hadn't been the special to whip into being, transportation had ground to a stop. Well, nothing new there, either. She had tried to call Martie finally, and got the recording: *Sorry, your call cannot be completed at this time.* So much for that. The baby cried and cried.

She tried to read for an hour or longer and had no idea of what she had been reading when she finally tossed the book down and turned to look at the fire. She added a log and poked the ashes until the flames shot up high, sparking blue and green, snapping crisply. As soon as she stopped forcing her mind to remain blank, the thoughts came rushing in.

Was it crazy of her to think they had killed her two babies? Why would they? Who were they? Weren't autopsies performed on newborn babies? Wouldn't the doctors and nurses be liable to murder charges, just like anyone else? These were the practical aspects, she decided. There were more. The fear of a leak. Too many people would have to be involved. It would be too dangerous, unless it was also assumed that everyone in the delivery room, in the OB ward, was in fact part of a gigantic conspiracy. If only she could remember more of what had happened.

Everything had been normal right up to delivery time. Dr. Wymann had been pleased with her pregnancy from the start. Absolutely nothing untoward had happened. Nothing. But when she woke up, Martie had been at her side, very pale, red-eyed. *The baby is dead,* he'd said. And, *Honey, I love you so much. I'm so sorry. There wasn't a thing they could do.* And on and on. They had wept together. Someone had come in with a tray that held a needle. Sleep.

Wrong end of it. Start at the other end. Arriving at the hospital, four-minute pains. Excited, but calm. Nothing unexpected. Dr. Wymann had briefed her on procedure. Nothing out of the ordinary. Blood sample, urine. Weight. Blood pressure. Allergy test. Dr. Wymann. *Won't be long now, Julia. You're doing fine.* Sleep. Waking to see Martie, pale and red-eyed at her side.

Dr. Wymann? He would have known. He wouldn't have let them do anything to her baby!

At the foot of the stairs she listened to the baby crying. Please don't, she thought at it. Please don't cry. Please.

The baby wailed on and on.

That was the first pregnancy, four years ago. Then last year, a repeat performance, by popular demand. She put her hands over her ears and ran back to the fireplace. She thought of the other girl in the double room, a younger girl, no more than eighteen. Her baby had died too in the staph outbreak. Sleeping, waking up, no reason, no sound in the room, but wide awake with pounding heart, the chill of fear all through her. Seeing the girl then, short gown, long lovely leg, climbing over the guardrail at the window. Pale yellow light in the room, almost too faint to make out details, only the silhouettes of objects. Screaming suddenly, and at the same moment becoming aware of figures at the door. An intern and a nurse. Not arriving, but standing there quietly. Not moving at all until she screamed. The ubiquitous needle to quiet her hysterical sobbing.

"Honey, they woke you up when they opened the hall door. They didn't say anything for fear of startling her, making her fall before they could get to her."

"Where is she?"

"Down the hall. I saw her myself. I looked through the observation window and saw her, sleeping now. She's a manic-depressive, and losing the baby put her in a tailspin. They're going to take care of her."

Julia shook her head. She had let him convince her, but it was a lie. They hadn't been moving at all. They had stood there waiting for the girl to jump. Watching her quietly, just waiting for the end. If she hadn't awakened and screamed, the girl would be dead now. She shivered and went to the kitchen to make coffee. The baby was howling louder.

She lighted a cigarette. Martie would be smoking continuously during the taping. She had sat through several tapings and knew the routine. The staff members watching, making notes, the director making notes. Hilary Boyle walked from the blue velvet hangings, waved at the camera, took his seat behind a massive desk, taking his time, getting comfortable. She liked Hilary Boyle in spite of all the things about his life, about him personally that she usually didn't like in people. His self-assurance that bordered on egomania, his women. She felt that he had assigned her a number and when it came up he would come to claim her as innocently as a child demanding his lollipop. She wondered if he would kick and scream when she said no. The cameras moved in close; he picked up his clipboard and glanced at the first sheet of paper, then looked into the camera. And the magic would work again, as it always worked for him. The X factor. A TV personality, radiating over wires, through air, from emptiness, to people everywhere who saw him. How did it work? She didn't know, neither did anyone else. She stubbed out her cigarette.

She closed her eyes, seeing the scene, Hilary leaving the desk, turning to wave once, then going through the curtains. Another successful special. A huddle of three men, or four, comparing notes, a rough spot here, another there. They could be taken care of with scissors. Martie, his hands shoved deep into his pockets, mooching along to his desk.

"Martie, you going home tonight?" Boyle stood in his doorway, filling it.

"Doesn't look like it. Nothing's leaving the city now."

"Buy you a steak." An invitation or an order? Boyle grinned. Invitation. "Fifteen minutes. Okay?"

"Sure. Thanks."

Martie tried again to reach Julia. "I'll be in and out for a couple of hours. Try it now and then, will you, doll?"

The operator purred at him. He was starting to get the material he had asked Sandy for: hospital statistics, epidemics of flu and flu-like diseases, incidence of pneumonia outbreaks, and so on. As she had said, there was a stack of the stuff. He riffled quickly through the printouts. Something was not quite right, but he couldn't put his finger on what it was. Boyle's door opened then, and he stacked the material and put it inside his desk.

"Ready? I had Doris reserve a table for us down in the Blue Light. I could use a double scotch about now. How about you?"

Martie nodded and they walked to the elevators together. The Blue Light was one of Boyle's favorite hangouts. They entered the dim, noisy room, and were led to a back table where the ceiling was noise-absorbing, and partitions separated one table from another, creating small oases of privacy. The floor show was visible, but almost all the noise of the restaurant was blocked.

"Look," Boyle said, motioning toward the blue spotlight. Three girls were dancing together. They wore midnight-blue body masks that covered them from crown to toe. Wigs that looked like green and blue threads of glass hung to their shoulders, flashing as they moved.

"I have a reputation," Boyle said, lighting a cigarette from his old one. "No one thinks anything of it if I show up in here three-four times a week."

He was watching the squirming girls, grinning, but there was an undertone in his voice that Martie hadn't heard before. Martie looked at him, then at the girls again, and waited.

"The music bugs the piss right out of me, but the girls, now that's different," Boyle said. A waitress moved into range. She wore a G-string, an apron whose straps miraculously covered both nipples and stayed in place somehow, and very high heels. "Double scotch for me, honeypot, and what for you, Martie?"

"Bourbon and water."

"Double bourbon and water for Dr. Sayre." He squinted, studying the gyrating girls.

"That one on the left. Bet she's a blonde. Watch the way she moves, you can almost see blondeness in that wrist motion . . ." Boyle glanced at the twitching hips of their waitress and said, in the same breath, same tone of voice, "I'm being watched. You will be too after tonight. You might look out for them."

"Who?"

"I don't know. Not government, I think. Private outfit maybe. Like FBI, same general type, same cool, but I'm almost positive not government."

"Okay, why?"

"Because I'm a newsman. I really am, you know, always was, always will be. I'm on to something big."

He stopped and the waitress appeared with their drinks. Boyle's gaze followed the twisting girls in the spotlight and he chuckled. He looked up at the waitress then. "Menus, please."

Martie watched him alternately with the floor show. They ordered, and when they were alone again Boyle said, "I think that immortality theory that popped up eight or ten years ago isn't dead at all. I think it works, just like what's his name said it would, and I think that some people are getting the treatments they need, and the others are being killed off, or allowed to die without interference."

Martie stared at him, then at his drink. He felt numb. As if to prove to himself that he could move, he made a whirlpool in the glass and it climbed higher and higher and finally spilled. Then he put it down. "That's crazy. They couldn't keep something like that quiet." Boyle was continuing to watch the dancing girls.

"I'm an intuitive man," Boyle said. "I don't know why I know that next week people will be interested in volcanoes, but if I get a hunch that it will make a good show, we do it, and the response is tremendous. You know how that goes. I hit, right smack on the button again and again. I get the ideas, you fellows do the work, and I get the credit. That's like it should be. You're all diggers; I'm the locator. I'm an ignorant man, but not stupid. Know what I mean? I learned to listen to my hunches. I learned to trust them. I learned to trust myself in front of the camera and on the mike. I don't know exactly what I'll say, or how I'll look. I don't practice anything. Somehow I'm in tune with . . . something. They know it, and I know it. You fellows call it the X factor. Let it go at that. We know what we mean when we talk about it even if we don't know what it is or how it works. Right. Couple of months ago, I woke up thinking that we should do a follow-up on the immortality thing. Don't look at me. Watch the show. I realized that I hadn't seen word one about it for three or four years. Nothing at all. What's his name, the guy that found the synthetic RNA?"

"Smithers. Aaron Smithers."

"Yeah. He's dead. They worked him over so thoroughly, blasted him and his results so convincingly that he never got over it. Finis. Nothing else said about it. I woke up wondering why not? How could he have been that wrong? Got the Nobel for the same kind of discovery, RNA as a cure for some kind of arthritis. Why was he so far off this time?" Boyle had filled the ashtray by then. He didn't look at Martie as he spoke, but continued to watch the girls, and now and then grinned, or even chuckled.

The waitress returned, brought them a clean ashtray, new drinks, took their orders, and left again. Boyle turned to look at Martie. "What, no comments yet? I thought by now you'd be telling me to see a headshrinker."

Martie shook his head. "I don't believe it. There'd be a leak. They proved it wouldn't work years ago."

"Maybe." Boyle drank more slowly now. "Anyway, I couldn't get rid of this notion, so I began to try to find out if anyone was doing anything with the synthetic RNA, and that's when the doors began to close on me. Nobody knows nothing. And someone went through my office, both here at the studio and at home. I got Kolchak to go through some of his sources to look for appropriations for RNA research. Security's clamped down on all appropriations for research. Lobbied for by the AMA, of all people."

"That's something else. People were too loose with classified data," Martie said. "This isn't in the universities anymore. They don't know any more than you do."

Boyle's eyes gleamed. "Yeah? So you had a bee, too?"

"No. But I know people. I left Harvard to take this job. I keep in touch. I know the people in the biochemical labs there. I'd know if they were going on with this. They're not. Are you going to try to develop this?" he asked, after a moment.

"Good Christ! What do you think!"

Julia woke up with a start. She was stiff from her position in the large chair, with her legs tucked under her, her head at an angle. She had fallen asleep over her sketch pad, and it lay undisturbed on her lap, so she couldn't have slept very long. The fire was still hot and bright. It was almost eleven thirty. Across the room the television flickered. The sound was turned off; music continued to play too loud in the house. She cocked her head, then nodded. It was still crying.

She looked at the faces she had drawn on her pad: nurses, interns, Dr. Wymann. All young. No one over thirty-five. She tried to recall others in the OB ward, but she was sure that she had them all. Night nurses, delivery nurses, nursery nurses, admittance nurse . . . She stared at the drawing of Dr. Wymann. They were the same age. He had teased her about it once. "I pulled out a grey hair this morning, and here you are as pretty and young as ever. How are you doing?"

But it had been a lie. He was the unchanged one. She had been going to him for six or seven years, and he hadn't changed at all in that time. They were both thirty-four now.

Sitting at the side of her bed, holding her hand, speaking earnestly. "Julia, there's nothing wrong with you. You can still have babies, several of them if you want. We can send men to the moon, to the bottom of the ocean, but we can't fight off staph when it hits in epidemic proportions in a nursery. I know you feel bitter now, that it's hopeless, but believe me, there wasn't anything that could be done either time. I can almost guarantee you that the next time everything will go perfectly."

"It was perfect this time. And the last time."

"You'll go home tomorrow. I'll want to see you in six weeks. We'll talk about it again a bit later. All right?"

Sure. Talk about it. And talk and talk. And it didn't change the fact that she'd had two babies and had lost two babies that had been alive and kicking right up till the time of birth.

Why had she gone so blank afterward? For almost a year she hadn't thought of it, except in the middle of the night, when it hadn't been thought, but emotion that had ridden her. Now it seemed that the emotional response had been used up, and for the first time she could think about the births, about the staff, about her own reactions. She put her sketch pad down and stood up, listening.

Two boys. They'd both been boys. Eight pounds two ounces, eight pounds four ounces. Big, beautifully formed, bald. The crying was louder, more insistent. At the foot of the stairs she stopped again, her face lifted.

It was a small hospital, a small private hospital. One that Dr. Wymann recommended highly. Because the city hospitals had been having such rotten luck trying to get rid of staph. Infant mortality had doubled, tripled? She had heard a fantastic figure given out, but hadn't been able to remember it. It had brought too sharp pains, and she had rejected knowing. She started up the stairs.

"Why are they giving me an allergy test? I thought you had to test for specific allergies, not a general test?"

"If you test out positive, then they'll look for the specifics. They'll know they have to look. We're getting too many people with allergies that we knew nothing about, reacting to antibiotics, to sodium pentothal, to starch in sheets. You name it."

The red scratch on her arm. But they hadn't tested her for specifics. They had tested her for the general allergy symptoms and had found them, and then let it drop. At the top of the stairs she paused again, closing her eyes briefly this time. "I'm coming," she said softly. She opened the door.

His was the third crib. Unerringly she went to him and picked him up; he was screaming lustily, furiously. "There, there. It's all right, darling. I'm here." She rocked him, pressing him tightly to her body. He nuzzled her neck, gulping in air now, the sobs diminishing into hiccups. His hair was damp with perspiration, and he smelled of powder and oil. His ear was tight against his head, a lovely ear.

"You! What are you doing in here? How did you get in?"

She put the sleeping infant back down in the crib, not waking him. For a moment she stood looking down at him, then she turned and walked out the door.

The three blue girls were gone, replaced by two zebra-striped girls against a black drop. Only the white stripes showed, making an eerie effect.

"Why did you bring this up with me?" Martie asked. Their steaks were before them, two inches thick, red in the middle, charred on the outside. The Blue Light was famous for steaks.

"A hunch. I have a standing order to be informed of any research anyone does on my time. I got the message that you were looking into illnesses, deaths, all that." Boyle waved aside the sudden flash of anger that swept through Martie. "Okay. Cool it. I can't help it. I'm paranoid. Didn't they warn you? Didn't I warn you myself when we talked five years ago? I can't stand for you to use the telephone. Can't stand not knowing what you're up to. I can't help it."

"But that's got nothing to do with your theory."

"Don't play dumb with me, Martie. What you're after is just the other side of the same thing."

"And what are you going to do now? Where from here?"

"That's the stinker. I'm not sure. I think we work on the angle of weather control for openers. Senator Kern is pushing the bill to create an office of weather control. We can get all sorts of stuff under that general heading, I think, without raising this other issue at all. You gave me this idea yourself. Weather-connected sickness. Let's look at what we can dig out, see what they're hiding, what they're willing to tell, and go on from there."

"Does Kolchak know? Does anyone else?"

"No. Kolchak will go along with the political angle. He'll think it's a natural for another special. He'll cooperate."

Martie nodded. "Okay," he said. "I'll dig away. I think there's a story. Not the one you're after, but a story. And I'm curious about the clampdown on news at a time when we seem to be at peace."

Boyle grinned at him. "You've come a long way from the history of science teacher that I talked to about working for me five years ago. Boy, were you green then." He pushed his plate back. "What made you take it? This job? I never did understand."

"Money. What else? Julia was pregnant. We wanted a house in the country. She was working, but not making money yet. She was talking about taking a job teaching art, and I knew it would kill her. She's very talented, you know."

"Yeah. So you gave up tenure, everything that goes with it."

"There's nothing I wouldn't give up for her."

"To each his own. Me? I'm going to wade through that goddamn snow the six blocks to my place. Prettiest little piece you ever saw waiting for me. See you tomorrow, Martie."

He waved to the waitress, who brought the check. He signed it without looking at it, pinched her bare bottom when she turned to leave, and stood up. He blew a kiss to the performing girls, stopped at three tables momentarily on his way out, and was gone. Martie finished his coffee slowly.

Everyone had left by the time he returned to his office. He sat down at his desk and looked at the material he had pushed into the drawer. He knew now what was wrong.

Nothing more recent than four years ago was included in the material.

Julia slept deeply. She had the dream again. She wandered down hallways, into strange rooms, looking for Martie. She was curious about the building. It was so big. She thought it must be endless, that it wouldn't matter how long she had to search it, she would never finish. She would forever see another hall that she hadn't seen before, another series of rooms that she hadn't explored. It was strangely a happy dream, leaving her feeling contented and peaceful. She awakened at eight. The wind had died completely, and the sunlight coming through the sheer curtains was dazzling, brightened a hundredfold by the brilliant snow. Apparently it had continued to snow after the wind had stopped; branches, wires, bushes, everything was frosted with an inch of powder. She stared out the window, committing it to memory. At such times she almost wished that she was a painter instead of a sculptor. The thought passed. She would get it, the feeling of joy and serenity and purity, into a piece of stone, make it shine out for others to grasp, even though they'd never know why they felt just like that.

She heard the bell of the snowplow at work on the secondary road that skirted their property, and she knew that as soon as the road was open, Mr. Stopes would be by with his small plow and get their driveway. She hoped it all would be cleared by the time Martie left the office. She stared at the drifted snow in the backyard between the house and the barn, and shook her head. Maybe Mr. Stopes could get that, too.

While she had breakfast she listened to the morning news. One disaster after another, she thought, turning it off after a few minutes. A nursing home fire, eighty-two dead. A new outbreak of infantile diarrhea in half a dozen hospitals, leaving one hundred thirty-seven dead babies.

The current flu epidemic death rate increasing to one out of ten.

Martie called at nine. He'd be home by twelve. A few things to clear up for the evening show. Nothing much. She tried to ease his worries about her, but realized that the gaiety in her voice must seem forced to him, phony. He knew that when the wind howled as it had done the night before, the baby cried. She hung up regretfully, knowing she hadn't convinced him that she had slept well, that she was as gay as she sounded. She looked at the phone and knew that it would be even harder to convince him in person that she was all right, and more important, that the baby was all right.

Martie shook her hard. "Honey, listen to me. Please, just listen to me. You had a dream. Or a hallucination. You know that. You know how you were the first time you heard it. You told me you were having a breakdown. You knew then that it wasn't the baby you heard, no matter what your ears told you. What's changed now?"

"I can't explain it," she said. She wished he'd let go. His hands were painful on her shoulders, and he wasn't aware of them. The fear in his eyes was real and desperate. "Martie, I know that it couldn't happen like that, but it did. I opened the door to somewhere else where our baby is alive and well. He had grown, and he has hair now, black hair, like yours, but curly, like mine. A nurse came in. I scared the hell out of her, Martie. She looked at me just like you are looking now. It was real, all of it."

"We're going to move. We'll go back to the city."

"All right. If you want to. It won't matter. This house has nothing to do with it."

"Christ!" Martie let her go suddenly, and she almost fell. He didn't notice. He paced back and forth a few minutes, rubbing his hand over his eyes, through his hair, over the stubble of his beard. She wished she could do something for him, but she didn't move. He turned to her again suddenly. "You can't stay alone again!"

Julia laughed gently. She took his hand and held it against her cheek. It was very cold. "Martie, look at me. Have I laughed spontaneously during this past year? I know how I've been, what I've been like. I knew all along, but I couldn't help myself. I was such a failure as a woman, don't you see. It didn't matter if I succeeded as an artist, or as a wife, anything. I couldn't bear a live child. That's all I could think about. It would come at the most awkward moments, with company here, during our love-making, when I had the mallet poised, or mixing a cake. Whammo, there it would be. And I'd just want to die. Now, after last night, I feel as if I'm alive again, after being awfully dead. It's all right, Martie. I had an experience that no one else could believe in. I don't care. It must be like conversion. You can't explain it to anyone who hasn't already experienced it, and you don't have to explain it to him. I shouldn't even have tried."

"God, Julia, why didn't you say what you were going through. I didn't realize. I thought you were getting over it all." Martie pulled her to him and held her too tightly.

"You couldn't do anything for me," she said. Her voice was muffled. She sighed deeply.

"I know. That's what makes it such hell." He pushed her back enough to see her face. "And you think it's over now? You're okay now?" She nodded. "I don't know what happened. I don't care. If you're okay, that's enough. Now let's put it behind us . . ."

"But it isn't over, Martie. It's just beginning. I know he's alive now. I have to find him."

"Can't get the tractor in the yard, Miss Sayre. Could of if you hadn't put them stones out there in the way." Mr. Stopes mopped his forehead with a red kerchief, although he certainly hadn't worked up a sweat, not seated on the compact red tractor, running it back and forth through the drive. Julia refilled his coffee cup and shrugged.

"All right. We'll get to it. The sun's warming it up so much. Maybe it'll just melt off."

"Nope. It'll melt some, then freeze. Be harder'n ever to get it out then."

Julia went to the door and called to Martie, "Honey, can you write Mr. Stopes a check for clearing the drive?"

Martie came in from the living room, taking his checkbook from his pocket. "Twenty?"

"Yep. Get yourself snowed in in town last night, Mr. Sayre?"

"Yep."

Mr. Stopes grinned and finished his coffee. "Some April's Fool Day, ain't it? Forsythia blooming in the snow. Don't know. Just don't know 'bout the weather anymore. Remember my dad used to plant his ground crops on April's Fool Day, without fail." He waved the check back and forth a minute, then stuffed it inside his sheepskin coat. "Well, thanks for the coffee, Miss Sayre. You take care now that you don't work too hard and come down with something. You don't want to get taken sick now that Doc Hendricks is gone."

"I thought that new doctor was working out fine," Martie said.

"Yep. For some people. You don't want him to put you in the hospital, though. The treatment's worse than the sickness anymore, it seems." He stood up and pulled on a flap-eared hat that matched his coat. "Not a gambling man myself, but even if I was, wouldn't want them odds. Half walks in gets taken out in a box. Not odds that I like at all."

Julia and Martie avoided looking at one another until he was gone. Then Julia said incredulously, "Half!"

"He must be jacking it way up."

"I don't think so. He exaggerates about some things, not things like that. That must be what they're saying."

"Have you met the doctor?"

"Yes, here and there. In the drugstore. At Dr. Saltzman's. He's young, but he seemed nice enough. Friendly. He asked me if we'd had our . . . flu shots." She finished very slowly, frowning slightly.

"And?"

"I don't know. I was just thinking that it was curious of him to ask. They were announcing at the time that there was such a shortage, that only vital people could get them. You know, teachers, doctors, hospital workers, that sort of thing. Why would he have asked if we'd had ours?"

"After the way they worked out, you should be glad that you didn't take him up on it."

"I know." She continued to look thoughtful, and puzzled. "Have you met an old doctor recently? Or even a middle-aged one?"

"Honey!"

"I'm serious. Dr. Saltzman is the only doctor I've seen in years who's over forty. And he doesn't count. He's a dentist."

"Oh, wow! Look, honey, I'm sorry I brought up any of this business with Boyle. I think something is going on, but not in such proportions, believe me. We're a community of what . . . seven hundred in good weather? I don't think we've been infiltrated."

She wasn't listening. "Of course, they couldn't have got rid of all the doctors, probably just the ones who were too honest to go along with it. Well, that probably wasn't many. Old and crooked. Young and . . . immortal. Boy!"

"Let's go shovel snow. You need to have your brain aired out."

While he cleared the path to the barn, Julia cleaned off the granite sculptures. She studied them. They were rough-quarried blocks, four feet high, almost as wide. The first one seemed untouched, until the light fell on it in a certain way, the rays low, casting long shadows. There were tracings of fossils, broken, fragmented. Nothing else. The second piece had a few things emerging from the surface, clawing their way up and out, none of them freed from it, though. A snail, a trilobite-like crustacean, a winged insect. What could have been a bird's head was picking its way out. The third one had defined animals, warm-blooded animals, and the suggestion of forests. Next came man and his works. Still rising from stone, too closely identified with the stone to say for certain where he started and the stone ended, if there was a beginning and an end at all. The whole work was to be called "The Wheel." These were the ends of the spokes, and at the hub of the wheel there was to be a solid granite seat, a pedestal-like seat. That would be the ideal place to sit and view the work, although she knew that few people would bother. But from the center, with the stones in a rough circle, the shadows should be right, the reliefs complementary to one another, suggesting heights that had been left out, suggesting depths that she hadn't shown. All suggestion. The wheel that would unlock the knowledge within the viewer, let him see what he usually was blind to . . .

"Honey, move!" Martie nudged her arm. He was panting hard.

"Oh, dear. Look at you. You've been moving mountains!" Half the path was cleared. "Let's make a snowman, right to the barn door."

The snow was wet, and they cleared the rest of the path by rolling snowballs, laughing, throwing snowballs at each other, slipping and falling. Afterward they had soup and sandwiches, both of them too beat to think seriously about cooking.

"Nice day," Julia said lazily, lying on the living room floor, her chin propped up by cupped hands, watching Martie work on the fire.

"Yeah. Tired?"

"Um. Martie, after you talked with Hilary, what did you do the rest of the night?"

"I looked up Smithers' work, what there was in the computer anyway. It's been a long time ago, I'd forgotten a lot of the arguments."

"And?"

"They refuted him thoroughly, with convincing data."

"Are you certain? Did you cross-check?"

"Honey, they were men like . . . like Whaite, and . . . Never mind. They're just names to you. They were the leaders at that time. Many of them are still the authorities. Men like that tried to replicate his experiments and failed. They looked for reasons for the failures and found methodological bungling on his part, erroneous conclusions, faulty data, mistakes in his formulae."

Julia rolled over, with her hands clasped under her head, and stared at the ceiling. "I half remember it all. Wasn't it almost a religious denunciation that took place? I don't remember the scientific details. I wasn't terribly interested in the background then, but I remember the hysteria."

"It got loud and nasty before it ended. Smithers was treated badly. Denounced from the pulpit, from the Vatican, from every scientific magazine . . . It got nasty. He died after a year of it, and they let the whole business die too. As they should have done."

"And his immortality serum will take its place along with the alchemist's stone, the universal solvent, a pinch of something in water to run the cars . . ."

" 'Fraid so. There'll always be those who will think it was suppressed." He turned to build up the fire that had died down completely.

"Martie, you know that room I told you about? The nursery? I would know it again if I saw it. How many nurseries do you suppose there are in the city?"

Martie stopped all motion, his back to her. "I don't know." His voice was too tight.

Julia laughed and tugged at his sweater. "Look at me, Martie. Do I look like a kook?"

He didn't turn around. He broke a stick and laid the pieces across each other. He topped them with another stick, slightly larger, then another.

"Martie, don't you think it's strange that suddenly you get the idea to look up these statistics, and Hilary approached you with different questions about the same thing? And at the same time I had this . . . this experience. Doesn't that strike you as too coincidental to dismiss? How many others do you suppose are asking questions too?"

"I had thought of it some, yes. But last night just seemed like a good time to get to things that have been bugging us. You know, for the first time in months no one was going anywhere in particular for hours."

She shook her head. "You can always rationalize coincidences if you are determined to. I was alone for the first time at night since I was in the hospital. I know. I've been over all that, too. But still . . ." She traced a geometrical pattern at the edge of the carpet. "Did you have a dream last night? Do you remember it?" Martie nodded.

"Okay. Let's test this coincidence that stretches on and on. I did too. Let's both write down our dreams and compare them. For laughs," she added hurriedly when he seemed to stiffen again. "Relax, Martie. So you think I've spun out. Don't be frightened by it. I'm not. When I thought that was the case, six months ago, or whenever it was, I was petrified. Remember? This isn't like that. This is kooky in a different way. I feel that a door that's always been there has opened a crack. Before, I didn't know it was there, or wouldn't admit that it was anyway. And now it's there, and open. I won't let it close again."

Martie laughed suddenly and stopped breaking sticks. He lighted the fire and then sat back with a notebook and pen. "Okay."

Martie wrote his dream simply with few descriptions. Alone, searching for her in an immense building. A hospital? An endless series of corridors and rooms. He had forgotten much of it, he realized, trying to fill in blanks. Finally he looked up to see Julia watching him with a faint smile. She handed him her pad and he stared at the line drawings that could have been made to order to illustrate his dream. Neither said anything for a long time.

"Martie, I want another baby. Now."

"God! Honey, are you sure? You're so worked up right now. Let's not decide . . ."

"But I have decided already. And it is in my hands, you know."

"So why tell me at all? Why not just toss the bottle out the window and be done with it?"

"Oh, Martie. Not like that. I want us to be deliberate about it, to think during coitus that we are really making a baby, to love it then . . ."

"Okay, honey. But why now? What made you say this now?"

"I don't know. Just a feeling."

"Dr. Wymann, is there anything I should do, or shouldn't do? I mean . . . I feel fine, but I felt fine the other times, too."

"Julia, you are in excellent health. There's no reason in the world for you not to have a fine baby. I'll make the reservation for you . . ."

"Not . . . I don't want to go back to that same hospital. Someplace else."

"But, it's–"

"I won't!"

"I see. Well, I suppose I can understand that. Okay. There's a very good, rather small hospital in Queens, fully equipped . . ."

"Dr. Wymann, this seems to be the only hangup I have. I have to see the hospital first, before you make a reservation. I can't explain it. . . ." Julia got up and walked to the window high over Fifth Avenue. "I blame the hospital, I guess. This time I want to pick it out myself. Can't you give me a list of the ones that you use, let me see them before I decide?" She laughed and shook her head. "I'm amazed at myself. What could I tell by looking? But there it is."

Dr. Wymann was watching her closely. "No, Julia. You'll have to trust me. It would be too tiring for you to run all over town to inspect hospitals . . ."

"No! I . . . I'll just have to get another doctor," she said miserably. "I can't go in blind this time. Don't you understand?"

"Have you discussed this with your husband?"

"No. I didn't even know that I felt this way until right now. But I do."

Dr. Wymann studied her for a minute or two. He glanced at her report spread out before him, and finally he shrugged. "You'll just wear yourself out for nothing. But, on the other hand, walking's good for you. I'll have my nurse give you the list." He spoke into the intercom briefly, then smiled again at Julia. "Now sit down and relax. The only thing I want you to concentrate on is relaxing, throughout the nine months. Every pregnancy is totally unlike every other one. . . ."

She listened to him dreamily. So young-looking, smooth-faced, tanned, if overworked certainly not showing it at all. She nodded when he said to return in a month.

"And I hope you'll have decided at that time about the hospital. We do have to make reservations far in advance, you know."

Again she nodded. "I'll know by then."

"Are you working now?"

"Yes. In fact I'm having a small showing in two weeks. Would you like to come?"

"Why don't you give me the date and I'll check with my wife and let you know."

Julia walked from the building a few minutes later feeling as though she would burst if she didn't find a private place where she could examine the list of hospitals the nurse had provided. She hailed a taxi and as soon as she was seated, she looked over the names of hospitals she never had heard of before.

Over lunch with Martie she said, "I'll be in town for the next few days, maybe we could come in together in the mornings and have lunch every day."

"What are you up to now?"

"Things I need. I'm looking into the use of plastics. I have an idea. . . ."

He grinned at her and squeezed her hand. "Okay, honey. I'm glad you went back to Wymann. I knew you were all right, but I'm glad you know it too."

She smiled back at him. If she found the nursery, or the nurse she had startled so, then she would tell him. Otherwise she wouldn't. She felt guilty about the smiles they exchanged, and she wished momentarily that he wouldn't make it so easy for her to lie to him.

"Where are you headed after lunch?" he asked.

"Oh, the library . . ." She ducked her head quickly and scraped her sherbet glass.

"Plastics?"

"Um." She smiled again, even more brightly. "And what about you? Tonight's show ready?"

"Yeah. This afternoon, in"–he glanced at his watch–"exactly one hour and fifteen minutes I'm to sit in on a little talk between Senator George Kern and Hilary. Kern's backing out of his weather control fight."

"You keep hitting blank walls, don't you?"

"Yes. Good and blank, and very solid. Well, we'd better finish up. I'll drop you at the library."

"Look at us," she said over the dinner table. "Two dismaler people you couldn't find. You first. And eat your hamburger. Awful, isn't it?"

"It's fine, honey." He cut a piece, speared it with his fork, then put it down. "Kern is out. Hilary thinks he got the treatment last month. And his wife too. They were both hospitalized for pneumonia at the same time."

"Do you know which hospital? In New York?"

"Hell, I don't know. What difference does . . . What are you getting at?"

"I . . . Was it one of these?" She got the list from her purse and handed it to him. "I got them from Dr. Wymann's nurse. I wouldn't go back to that one where . . . I made them give me a list so I could look them over first."

Martie reached for her hand and pressed it hard. "No plastics?"

She shook her head.

"Honey, it's going to be all right this time. You can go anyplace you want to. I'll look these over. You'll just be wearing . . ."

"It's all right, Martie. I already checked out three of them. Two in Manhattan, one in Yonkers. I . . . I'd rather do it myself. Did Senator Kern mention a hospital?"

"Someplace on Long Island. I don't remember . . ."

"There's a Brent Park Memorial Hospital on Long Island. Was that it?"

"Yes. No. Honey, I don't remember. If he did mention it, it passed right over my head. I don't know." He put the list down and took her other hand and pulled her down to his lap. "Now you give. Why do you want to know? What did you see in those hospitals that you visited? Why did you go to the library?"

"I went to three hospitals, all small, all private, all run by terribly young people. Young doctors, young nurses, young everybody. I didn't learn anything else about them. But in the library I tried to borrow a book on obstetrics, and there aren't any."

"What do you mean, there aren't any? None on open shelves? None in at the time?"

"None. They looked, and they're all out, lost, not returned, gone. All of them. I tried midwifery, and the same thing. I had a young boy who was terribly embarrassed by it all searching for me, and he kept coming back with the same story. Nothing in. So I went to the branch library in Yonkers, since I wanted to see the hospital there anyway, and it was the same thing. They have open shelves there, and I did my own looking. Nothing."

"What in God's name did you plan to do with a book on obstetrics?"

"Isn't that beside the point? Why aren't there any?"

"It is directly to the point. What's going through your mind, Julia? Exactly what are you thinking?"

"The baby is due the end of December. What if we have another blizzard? Or an ice storm? Do you know anything about delivering a baby? Oh, something, I grant you. Everyone knows something. But what about an emergency? Could you handle an emergency? I thought if we had a book . . ."

"I must have wandered into a nut ward. I'm surrounded by maniacs. Do you hear what you're saying? Listen to me, sweetheart, and don't say a word until I'm finished. When that baby is due, I'll get you to a hospital. I don't care which one you choose, or where it is. You'll be there. If we have to take an apartment next door to it for three months to make certain, we'll do it. You have to have some trust and faith in me, in the doctor, in yourself. And if it eases your mind, I'll get you a book on obstetrics, but by God, I don't plan to deliver a baby!"

Meekly she said, "You just get me a book, and I'll behave. I promise." She got up and began to gather up their dishes. "Maybe later on we'll want some scrambled eggs or something. Let's have coffee now."

They moved to the living room where she sat on the floor with her cup on the low table. "Is Kern satisfied that no BW agent got loose to start all this?"

Martie looked at her sharply. "You're a witch, aren't you? I never told you that's what I was afraid of."

She shrugged. "You must have."

"Kern's satisfied. I am, too. It isn't that. His committee decided to drop it, at his suggestion, because of the really dangerous condition of the world right now. It's like a powder keg, just waiting for the real statistics to be released. That would blow it. Everyone suspects that the death rate has risen fantastically, but without official figures, it remains speculation, and the fuse just sits there. He's right. If Hilary does go on, he's taking a terrible risk." He sighed. "It's a mutated virus that changes faster than the vaccines that we come up with. It won't be any better until it mutates into something that isn't viable, then it will vanish. Only then will the governments start opening books again, and hospitals give out figures for admittances and deaths. We know that the medical profession has been hit probably harder than any other. Overexposure. And the shortage of personnel makes everything that used to be minor very serious now."

Julia nodded, but her gaze didn't meet his. "Sooner or later," she said, "you'll have to turn that coin over to see what's on the other side. Soon now, I think."

Julia wore flowered pants and a short vest over a long-sleeved tailored blouse. With her pale hair about her shoulders, she looked like a very young girl, too young to be sipping champagne from the hollow-stemmed goblet that she held with both hands. Dwight Gregor was in the middle of the circle of stones, studying the effects from there. Gregor was the main critic, the one whose voice was heard if he whispered, although all others were shouting. Julia wished he'd come out of the circle and murmur something or other to her. She didn't expect him to let her off the hook that evening, but at least he could move, or something. She probably wouldn't know what his reactions had been until she read his column in the morning paper. She sipped again and turned despairingly to Martie. "I think he fell asleep out there."

"Honey, relax. He's trying to puzzle it out. He knows that you're cleverer than he is, and more talented, and that you worked with the dark materials of your unconscious. He feels it and can't grasp the meaning . . ."

"Who are you quoting?"

"Boyle. He's fascinated by the circle. He'll be in and out of it all evening. Watch and see. Haven't you caught him looking at you with awe all over his face?"

"Is that awe? I was going to suggest that you tell him I'm good and pregnant."

Martie laughed with her, and they separated to speak with the guests. It was a good show, impressive. The yard looked great, the lighting effects effective, the waterfall behind the basketweave fence just right, the pool at the bottom of the cascading water just dark and mysterious enough . . . Martie wandered about his yard proudly.

"Martie?" Boyle stopped by him. "Want to talk to you. Half an hour over by the fence. Okay?"

Gregor left the circle finally and went straight to Julia. He raised her hand to his lips and kissed it lightly, keeping his gaze on her face. "My dear. Very impressive. So nihilistic. Did you realize how nihilistic it is? But of course. And proud, also. Nihilistic but proud. Strange combination. You feel that man almost makes it, this time. Did you mean that? Only one toe restraining him. Sad. So sad."

"Or you can imagine that the circle starts with the devastation, the ruins, and the death of man. From that beginning to the final surge of life that lifts him from the origins in the dirt . . . Isn't that what you really meant to say, my dear?" Frances Lefever moved in too close to Julia, overwhelming her with the sweet, sickening scent of marijuana heavy on her breath. "If that's where the circle begins, then it is a message of nothing but hope. Isn't that right, my dear?"

Gregor moved back a step, waving his hand in the air. "Of course, one can always search out the most romantic explanation of anything . . ."

"Romantic? Realistic, my dear Dwight. Yours is the typical male reaction. Look what I've done. I've destroyed all mankind, right back down to the primordial ooze. Mine says, look, man is freeing himself, he is leaping from his feet-of-clay beginnings to achieve a higher existence. Did you really look at that one? There's no shadow, you know."

Dwight and Frances forgot about Julia. They argued their way back to the circle, and she leaned weakly against the redwood fence and drank deeply.

"Hey. Are you all right, Julia?"

"Dr. Wymann. Yes. Fine. Great."

"You looked as if you were ready to faint . . ."

"Only with relief. They like it. They are fascinated by it. It's enigmatic enough to make them argue about meanings, so they'll both write up their own versions, different from each other's, and that will make other people curious enough to want to see for themselves . . ."

Dr. Wymann laughed and watched the two critics as they moved about the large stones, pointing out to one another bits and pieces each was certain the other had missed.

"Congratulations, Julia."

"What did you think of it?"

"Oh, no. Not after real critics have expressed opinions."

"Really. I'd like to know."

Dr. Wymann looked again at the circle of stones and shrugged. "I'm a clod. An oaf. I had absolutely no art training whatever. I like things like Rodin. Things that are unequivocal. I guess I didn't know what you were up to with your work."

Julia nodded. "Fair enough."

"I'm revealed as an ass."

"Not at all, Dr. Wymann. I like Rodin too."

"One thing. I couldn't help overhearing what they were saying. Are you the optimist that the woman believes or the pessimist that Gregor assumes?"

Julia finished off her champagne, looking at the goblet instead of the doctor. She sighed when it was all gone. "I do love champagne." She smiled at him then. "The stones will give you the answer. But you'll have to find it yourself. I won't tell."

He laughed and they moved apart. Julia drifted back inside the house to check the buffet, and the bar. She spoke briefly with Margie Mellon who was taking care of the food and drinks. Everything was holding up well. A good party. Successful unveiling. A flashbulb went off outside, then another and another.

"Honey! It's really great, isn't it? They love it! And you! And me because I'm married to you!"

She never had seen Martie so pleased. He held her close for a minute, then kissed each eyelid. "Honey, I'm so proud of you I can't stand it. I want to strip you and take you to bed right now. That's how it's affected me."

"Me, too. I know."

"Let's drive them all off early . . ."

"We'll try, anyway."

She was called to pose by the circle, and she left him. Martie watched her. "She is so talented," a woman said, close to his ear. He turned. He didn't know her.

"I'm Esther Wymann," she said huskily. She was very drunk. "I almost envy her. Even if it is for a short time. To know that you have that much talent, a genius, creative genius. I think it would be worth having, even if you knew that tomorrow you'd be gone. To have that for a short time. So creative and so pretty too."

She drained a glass that smelled like straight scotch. She ran the tip of her tongue around the rim and turned vaguely toward the bar. "You too, sweetie? No drink? Where's our host? Why hasn't he taken care of you. That's all right. Esther will. Come on."

She tilted when she moved and he steadied her. "Thanks. Who're you, by the way?"

"I'm the host," he said coldly. "What did you mean by saying she has so little time? What's that supposed to mean?"

Esther staggered back from his hand. "Nothing. Didn't mean anything." She lurched away from him and almost ran the three steps that took her into a group of laughing guests. Martie saw Wymann put an arm about her to help hold her upright. She said something to him and the doctor looked up quickly to see Martie watching them. He turned around, still holding his wife, and they moved toward the door to the dining room. Martie started after them, but Boyle appeared at the doorway and motioned for him to go outside.

The doctor would keep, Martie decided. He couldn't talk to him with that drunken woman on his arm anyway. He looked once more toward the dining room doorway, then followed Boyle outside.

A picture or two, someone said. He stood by Julia, holding her hand, and the flashbulbs exploded. Someone opened a new bottle of champagne close by, and that exploded. Someone else began shrieking with laughter. He moved away from the center of the party again and sat down at a small table waiting for Boyle to join him.

"This is as safe as any place we're likely to find," Boyle said. He was drinking beer, carrying a quart bottle with him. "What have you dug out?"

The waterfall splashed noisily behind them, and the party played noisily before them. Martie watched the party. He said, "The death rate, extrapolated only, you understand. Nothing's available on paper anywhere. But the figures we've come up with are: from one million eight hundred thousand five years ago, up to fourteen and a quarter million this year." Boyle choked and covered his face with his handkerchief. He poured more beer and took a long swallow. Martie waited until he finished, then said, "Birth rate down from three and a half million to one million two hundred thousand. That's live births. At these rates, with the figures we could find, we come up with a loss per thousand of sixty-three. A death rate of sixty-three per thousand."

Boyle glared at him. He turned to watch the party again, saying nothing.

Martie watched Julia talking with guests. She never had looked more beautiful. Pregnancy had softened her thin face, had added a glow. What had that bitch meant by saying she had so little time? He could hear Julia's words inside his head: *You'll have to turn it over sooner or later.* She didn't understand. Boyle didn't understand. Men like Whaite wouldn't have repudiated a theory so thoroughly if there had been any merit whatsoever in it. It was myth only that said the science community was a real community. There were rivalries, but no corruption of that sort. The whole scientific world wouldn't unite behind a lie. He rubbed his eyes. But how many of the scientists knew enough about biochemistry to form independent judgments? They had to take the word of the men who were considered authorities, and if they, fewer than a dozen, passed judgment, then that judgment was what the rest of the community accepted as final. Only the amateurs on the outside would question them, no one on the inside would think of doing so. Martie tapped his fingers on the table impatiently. Fringe thinking. Nut thinking. They'd take away his badge and his white coat if he expressed such thoughts. But, damn it, they could! Six or eight, ten men could suppress a theory, for whatever reason they decided was valid, if only they all agreed. Over fourteen million deaths in the States in the past year. How many in the whole world? One hundred million, two hundred million? They'd probably never know.

"Hilary, I'm going up to Cambridge tomorrow, the next day, soon. I have to talk to Smithers' widow."

Hilary nodded. "At that death rate, how long to weed us out?"

"About twelve and a half years, starting two years ago." Martie spoke without stopping to consider his figures. He wasn't sure when he had done that figuring. He hadn't consciously thought of it.

He watched as Julia spoke with Dr. Wymann, holding his hand several seconds. She nodded, and the doctor turned and walked away. What had Wymann's wife meant? Why had she said what she had? If "they" existed, she was one of them. As Wymann was. As Senator Kern was. Who else?

"I don't believe it!"

"I know."

"They couldn't keep such figures quiet! What about France? England? Russia?"

"Nothing. No statistics for the last four years. Files burned, mislaid, not properly completed. Nothing."

"Christ!" Boyle said.

Julia smoked too much, and paced until the phone rang. She snatched it up. "Martie! Are you all right?"

"Sure. What's wrong, honey?" His voice sounded ragged; he was out of breath.

"Darling, I'm sorry. I didn't want to alarm you, but I didn't know how else to reach you. Don't say anything now. Just come home, Martie, straight home. Will you?"

"But . . . Okay, honey. My flight is in fifteen minutes. I'll be home in a couple of hours. Sit tight. Are you all right?"

"Yes. Fine. I'm fine." She listened to the click at the other end of the line, and felt very alone again. She picked up the brief note that she had written and looked at it again. "Lester B. Hayes Memorial Hospital, ask for Dr. Conant."

"It's one on my list," she said to Martie when he read it. "Hilary collapsed at his desk and they took him there. Martie, they'll kill him, won't they?"

Martie crumpled the note and let it drop. He realized that Julia was trembling and he held her for several minutes without speaking. "I have to make some calls, honey. Will you be all right?"

"Yes. I'm fine now. Martie, you won't go, will you? You won't go to that hospital."

"*Sh.* It's going to be all right, Julia. Sit down, honey. Try to relax."

Boyle's secretary knew only that she had found him sprawled across his desk and in the next few minutes, Kolchak, or someone, had called the ambulance, and he was taken away to the hospital. The report they had was that he was not in serious condition. It had happened before, no one was unduly alarmed, but it was awkward. It never had happened before a show. This time . . . Her voice drifted away. Martie slammed the receiver down.

"It really has happened before. The hospital could be a coincidence."

Julia shook her head. "I don't believe it." She looked at her hands. "How old is he?"

"Fifty, fifty-five. I don't know. Why?"

"He's too old for the treatment then. They'll kill him. He'll die of complications from flu, or a sudden heart attack. They'll say he had a heart attack at his desk. . . ."

"Maybe he did have a heart attack. He's been driving himself . . . Overweight, living too fast, too hard, too many women and too much booze . . ."

"What about Smithers? Did you see Mrs. Smithers?"

"Yes. I saw her. I was with her all morning . . ."

"And within an hour of your arrival there, Hilary collapses. You're getting too close, Martie. You're making them act now. Did you learn anything about Smithers, or his work?"

"It's a familiar kind of thing. He published prematurely, got clobbered, then tried to publish for over a year and had paper after paper returned. During that time he saw everything he'd done brought down around his ears. His wife believes he committed suicide, although she won't admit it even to herself. But it's there, in the way she talks about them, the ones who she says hounded him . . ."

"And his papers?"

"Gone. Everything was gone when she was able to try to

straighten things out. There wasn't anything left to straighten out. She thinks he destroyed them. I don't know. Maybe he did. Maybe they were stolen. It's too late now."

The phone shrilled, startling both of them. Martie answered. "Yes, speaking . . ." He looked at Julia, then turned his back. His hand whitened on the phone. "I see. Of course. An hour, maybe less."

Julia was very pale when Martie hung up and turned toward her. "I heard," she said. "The hospital . . . it's one of theirs. Dr. Conant must be one of them."

Martie sat down and said dully, "Hilary's on the critical list. I didn't think they'd touch him. I didn't believe it. Not him."

"You won't go, will you? You know it's a trap."

"Yes, but for what? They can get to me any time they want. They don't have to do it this way. There's no place to hide."

"I don't know for what. Please don't go."

"You know what this is? The battle of the Cro-Magnon and the Neanderthal all over again. One has to eliminate the other. We can't both exist in the same ecological niche."

"Why can't they just go on living as long as they want and leave us alone? Time is on their side."

"They know they can't hide it much longer. In ten years it would be obvious, and they're outnumbered. They're fighting for survival, too. Hitting back first, that's all. A good strategy."

He stood up. Julia caught his arm and tried to pull him to her. Martie was rigid and remote. "If you go, they'll win. I know it. You're the only one now who knows anything about what is going on. Don't you see? You're more valuable than Boyle was. All he had was his own intuition and what you gave him. He didn't understand most of it, even. But you . . . They must have a scheme that will eliminate you, or force you to help them. Something."

Martie kissed her. "I have to. If they just want to get rid of me, they wouldn't be this open. They want something else. Remember, I have a lot to come back for. You, the baby. I have a lot to hate them for, too. I'll be back."

Julia swayed and held onto the chair until he turned and left the house. She sat down slowly, staring straight ahead.

Martie looked at Dr. Wymann without surprise. "Hilary's dead?"

"Unfortunately. There was nothing that could be done. A fatal aneurism. . . ."

"How fortunate for you."

"A matter of opinion. Sit down, Dr. Sayre. We want to talk with you quite seriously. It might take a while." Wymann opened the door to an adjoining office and motioned. Two men in white coats entered, nodded at Martie and sat down. One carried a folder.

"Dr. Conant, and Dr. Fischer." Wymann closed the door and sat down in an easy chair. "Please do sit down, Sayre. You are free to leave at any time. Try the door if you doubt my word. You are not a prisoner."

Martie opened the door. The hallway was empty, gleaming black and white tiles in a zigzag pattern, distant noise of an elevator, sound of a door opening and closing. A nurse emerged from one of the rooms, went into another. Martie closed the door again.

"Okay, your show. I suppose you are in charge?"

"No. I'm not in charge. We thought that since you know me, and in light of certain circumstances, it might be easier if I talked to you. That's all. Either of these two . . . half a dozen others who are available. If you prefer, it doesn't have to be me."

Martie shook his head. "You wanted me. Now what?"

Wymann leaned forward. "We're not monsters, no more than any other human being, anyway. Smithers had exactly what he said he had. You know about that. He really died of a heart attack. So much for history. It works,

Sayre. For forty percent of the people. What would you do with it? Should we have made it public? Held a lottery? It would have gone underground even more than it has now, but it would be different. We don't want to kill anyone. The others, the ones who couldn't use it, would search us out and exterminate us like vermin. You know that. In the beginning we needed time. We were too accessible, too vulnerable. A handful of people knew what it was, how to prepare it, how to test for results, how to administer it, what to watch for, all the rest. It's very complicated. We had to protect them and we had to add numbers."

Martie watched him, thinking, Julia knew. The babies. Both of them. The new pregnancy. She was afraid time was running out. This man, or another like him. Had they done anything, or simply failed to do something for the first two? Was there any difference really? His skin felt clammy, and he opened his hands when he realized that his fingers were getting stiff.

"It's going on everywhere, more or less like here. Have you read . . . ? No, of course not . . . I'll be frank with you, Sayre. The world's on a powder keg, has been for over a year. Martial law in Spain, Portugal, Israel, most of the Mid-East. Nothing at all out of China. Japan ripped wide open by strikes and riots, tighter than a drum right now. Nothing's coming out of there. It's like that everywhere. Clampdown on all news. No travel that isn't high priority. France has been closed down for six months. More restrictions than when they were occupied. Same with England. Canada has closed her borders for the first time in history, as has Mexico. UNESCO recommended all this, in an effort to stop the epidemics, ostensibly. But really to maintain secrecy regarding the climbing death rate. And everyone's panic-stricken, terrified of being hit next. It must have been like this during the Plague outbreaks. Walled cities, fear. Your story coming now would ignite the whole world. There'd be no way to maintain any sort of order. You know I'm right. We couldn't let you and Boyle go on with it."

Martie stood up. "If you try to sell yourselves as humanitarians, I might kill you right now."

"It depends entirely on where you're standing. Most men with any kind of scientific training see almost immediately that what we've done, how we've done it was the only way this could have been handled. Out in the open, with more than half the people simply not genetically equipped to tolerate the RNA, there would have been a global catastrophe that would have destroyed all of mankind. Governments are made up of old men, Sayre. Old men can't use it. Can you imagine the uprising against all the world governments that would have taken place! It would have been a holocaust that would have left nothing. We've prevented that."

"You've set yourselves up as final judges, eliminating those who can't take it . . ."

"Eliminating? We upset the entire Darwinian framework for evolution by our introduction of drugs, our transplants, life-saving machines. We were perpetuating a planet of mental and physical degenerates, with each generation less prepared to live than the last. I know you think we're murderers, but is it murder to fail to prescribe insulin and let a diabetic die rather than pass on the genes to yet another generation?" Wymann started to pace, after glancing at his watch, checking it against the wall clock.

"There have been hard decisions; there'll be more even harder ones. Every one of us has lost someone he cared for. Every one! Conant lost his first wife. My sister . . . We aren't searching out people to kill, unless they threaten us. But if they come to us for treatment, and we know that they are terminal, we let them die."

Martie moistened his lips. "Terminal. You mean mortal, with a temporary sore throat, or a temporary appendix inflammation, things you could treat."

"They are terminal now, Sayre. Dying in stages. Dying

from the day they are born. We don't prolong their lives."

"Newborn infants? Terminal?"

"Would you demand that newborn idiots be preserved in institutions for fifty or sixty years? If they are dying, we let them die."

Martie looked at the other doctors who hadn't spoken. Neither of them had moved since arriving and sitting down. He turned again to Wymann. "You called me. What do you want?"

"Your help. We'll need people like you. Forty percent of the population, randomly chosen, means that there will be a shortage of qualified men to continue research, to translate that research into understandable language. The same sort of thing you're doing now. Or, if you prefer, a change of fields. But we will need you."

"You mean I won't suffer a thrombosis, or have a fatal wreck for the next twenty years if I play along?"

"More than that, Martie. Much more than that. During your last physical examination for insurance you were tested, a routine test by the way. Not conclusive, but indicative. You showed no gross reactions to the synthetic RNA. You would have to be tested more exhaustively, of course, but we are confident that you can tolerate the treatments . . ."

"What about Julia? What do you plan for her?"

"Martie, have you thought at all about what immortality means? Not just another ten years tacked on at the end, or a hundred, or a thousand. As far as we know now, from all the laboratory data, there is no end, unless through an accident. And with our transplant techniques even that is lessening every week. Forever, Martie. No, you can't imagine it. No one can. Maybe in a few hundred years, we'll begin to grasp what it means, but not yet . . ."

"What about Julia?"

"We won't harm her."

"You've tested her already. You know about her."

"Yes. She cannot tolerate the RNA."

"If anything goes wrong, you'll fold your hands and let her die. Won't you? *Won't you!"*

"Your wife is a terminal case! Can't you see that? If she were plugged into a kidney machine, a heart and lung machine, with brain damage, you'd want the plug pulled. You know you would. We could practice preventive medicine on her, others like her, for the next forty years or longer. But for what? For what, Dr. Sayre? As soon as they know, they'll turn on us. We can keep this secret only a few more years. We know we are pushing our luck even now. We took an oath that we would do nothing to prolong the lives of those who are dying. Do you think they would stop at that? If they knew today, we'd be hunted, killed, the process destroyed. Lepers would rather infect everyone with their disease than be eradicated. Your wife will be thirty-five when the child is born. A century ago she would have been doomed by such a late pregnancy. She would have been an old woman. Modern medicine has kept her youthful, but it's an artificial youthfulness. She is dying!"

Martie made a movement toward Wymann, who stepped behind his desk warily. Conant and Fischer were watching him very closely. He sank back down in the chair, covering his face. Later, he thought. Not now. Find out what you can now. Try to keep calm.

"Why did you tell me any of this?" he asked after a moment. "With Boyle gone my job is gone. I couldn't have hurt you."

"We don't want you to light that fuse. You're a scientist. You can divorce your emotions from your reason and grasp the implications. But aside from that, your baby, Martie. We want to save the baby. Julia has tried and tried to find a book on obstetrics, hasn't she? Has she been successful?"

He shook his head. The book. He had meant to ask about one at Harvard, and he'd forgotten. "The baby. You think it will be able to . . . The other two? Are they both . . . ?"

"The only concern we have now is for the successful delivery of the child that your wife is carrying. We suspect that it will be one of us. And we need it. That forty percent I mentioned runs through the population, young and old. Over forty, give or take a year or two, they can't stand the treatments. We don't know exactly why yet, but we will eventually. We just know that they die. So that brings us down to roughly twenty-five percent of the present population. We need the babies. We need a new generation of people who won't be afraid of death from the day they first grasp the meaning of the word. We don't know what they will be, how it will change them, but we need them."

"And if it isn't able to take the RNA?"

"Martie, we abort a pregnancy when it is known that the mother had German measles, or if there is a high probability of idiocy. You know that. Unfortunately, our technique for testing the fetus is too imperfect to be certain, and we have to permit the pregnancy to come to term. But that's the only difference. It would still be a therapeutic abortion."

Martie and Julia lay side by side, not touching, each wakeful, aware that the other was awake, pretending sleep. Julia had dried tears on her cheeks. Neither of them had moved for almost an hour.

"But goddamn it, which one is Cro-Magnon and which Neanderthal?" Martie said, and sat upright. Julia sat up, too.

"What?"

"Nothing. I'm sorry. Go back to sleep, honey. I'm getting up for a while."

Julia swung her legs off the bed. "Can we talk now, Martie? Will you talk to me about it now?"

Martie muttered a curse and left the room.

This was part of the plan, he knew. Drive them apart first, make it easier for him to join them later. He sat down in the kitchen with a glass half filled with bourbon and a dash of water.

"Martie? Are you all right?" Julia stood in the doorway. She was barely showing her pregnancy now, a small bulge was all. He turned away. She sat down opposite him. "Martie? Won't you tell me?"

"Christ, Julia, will you shove off! Get off my back for a while?"

She touched his arm. "Martie, they offered you the treatment, didn't they? They think you could take it. Are you going to?"

He jerked out of the chair, knocking it over, knocking his glass over. "What are you talking about?"

"That was the cruelest thing they could have done right now, wasn't it? After I'm gone, it would have been easier, but now . . ."

"Julia, cut it out. You're talking nonsense . . ."

"I'll die this time, won't I? Isn't that what they're planning? Did they tell you that you could have the babies if you want them? Was that part of it too?"

"Has someone been here?" Martie grabbed her arm and pulled her from the chair. She shook her head. He stared at her for a long time, and suddenly he yanked her against him hard.

"I must be out of my mind. I believed them. Julia, we're getting out of here, now. Tomorrow."

"Where?"

"I don't know. Somewhere. Anywhere. I don't know."

"Martie, we have to stop running. There are physical limits to how much I can run now. But besides that, there's really no place to run to. It's the same everywhere. You haven't found anyone who will listen to you. One check with your personal data file and that's it. We may never know what they put on your record, but it's enough to make every official pat you on the head and say, 'Don't worry, Dr. S. We'll take care of it.' We can't get out of the country, passport requests turned down for medical reasons. But even if we could . . . More of the same."

Julia was pale, with circles under her eyes. It was early in November, cold in Chicago where their apartment overlooked Lake Michigan. A flurry of powdery snow blew in a whirlwind across the street. Martie nodded. "They've covered everything, haven't they? Special maternity hospitals! For the safety and protection of the mother and child. To keep them from the filthy conditions that exist in most hospitals now. Keep them safe from pneumonia, flu, staph . . . Oh, Christ!" He leaned his head against the glass and watched the dry dustlike snow.

"Martie . . ."

"Damn. I'm out of cigarettes, honey. I'll just run out and get some."

"Okay. Fine."

"Want anything?"

"No. Nothing." She watched him pull on his coat and leave, then stood at the window and watched until he emerged from the building and started to walk down the street. The baby kicked and she put her hand over her stomach. "It's all right, little one. It's all right."

Martie was only a speck among specks standing at the corner, waiting for the light to turn. She could no longer pick out his figure from those around him. "Martie," she whispered. Then she turned away from the window and sat down. She closed her eyes for a moment. They wanted her baby, this baby, not just another child who would become immortal. They were too aware of the population curve that rises slowly, slowly, then with abandon becomes an exponential curve. No, not just a child, but her particular child. They wouldn't let it be harmed. But they wouldn't let her have it, and they knew that, this time, she wouldn't give it up. So she'd have to die. The child couldn't be tainted with her knowledge of death. Of course, if it too was unable to tolerate the RNA, there was no real problem. Mother and child. Too bad. No cures for . . .

whatever they'd say killed them. Or would they keep her, let her try again? She shook her head. They wouldn't. By then Martie would be one of them, or dead. This was the last child for her.

"So what can I do?" she asked.

Her hands opened and closed convulsively. She shut her eyes hard. "What?" she whispered desperately. *"What?"*

She worked on the red sandstone on the ground floor of the barn. It was too big to get up to her studio, so she'd had her tools, bench, table, everything brought down. It was drafty, but she wore heavy wool slacks and a tentlike top, and was warm.

She whistled tunelessly as she worked . . .

Julia stood up too fast, then clutched the chair for support. Have to remember, she told herself severely. Work. She had to go to work. She picked up her sketch pad, put it down again. Red sandstone, ten by ten by eight. And red quartzite, four by three by two. She called her supplier on Long Island.

"Funny, Mrs. Sayre. Just got some in," he said. "Haven't had sandstone for . . . oh, years, I guess."

"Can you have it delivered tomorrow?"

"Mrs. Sayre, everyone who's ever touched rock is working. Had to put on an extra man. Still can't keep up."

"I know. And the painters, and composers, and poets . . ." They settled for the day after her arrival home.

She reserved seats on the 6 p.m. flight to New York, asked for their hotel bill within the hour, and started to pack. She paused once, a puzzled frown on her forehead. Every one of her friends in the arts was working furiously. They either didn't know or didn't care about the disastrous epidemics, the travel bans, any of it.

Martie walked slowly, his head bowed. He kept thinking of the bridge that he had stood on for an hour, watching filthy water move sluggishly with bits and pieces of junk floating on the surface: a piece of orange, a plastic bag, a child's doll with both arms gone, one eye gone. The doll had swirled in a circle for several minutes, caught in a branch, then moved on out of sight. Of no use to anyone, unwanted, unloved now. Imperfect, cast away.

The wind blew, whipping his coat open, and he shivered. On trial, before his judges. Martin Sayre, do you dare risk your immortal soul for this momentary fling? Confess, go to the flame willingly, with confession on your lips, accept the flame, that too is momentary, and rejoice forever in Paradise.

"Dr. Sayre, you're a reasonable man. You know that we can't do anything for your wife. She will be allowed to bear her child here. No other hospital would admit her, none of the city hospitals would dare. We won't harm her, Dr. Sayre. We won't do anything that is not for her own good . . ."

Torquemada must have argued so.

And, somewhere else. He couldn't keep them apart, all the same, different faces, but the same. "Of course, the child will have to be taken from her, no matter what happens. The fear of death is a disease as dangerous almost as death itself. It drives man mad. These new children must not be infected with it. . . ."

And somewhere else. "Ah, yes, Dr. Sayre. Meant to call you back, but got tied up. Appropriations committee sessions, don't you know. Well now, Dr. Sayre, this little theory of yours about the serum. I've been doing some thinking on that, Dr. Sayre, and don't you know, I can't come up with anything to corroborate what you say. Now if you can furnish some hard proof, don't you know, well, now, that would make a difference. Yes, sir, make a big difference."

And again, "Hell, Martie, I just don't know. You may be absolutely right. But there's no way to get to anything to make sure. I can't risk everything here on a wild-goose chase. I checked your data file, as you suggested, and they have a diagnosis made by a Dr. Fischer of Lester B. Hayes Memorial Hospital, who examined you extensively in four examinations from March through August of this year. He recommended treatment for schizophrenia; you refused. Face it, Martie, I have to ask myself, isn't this just a schizophrenic construct?"

He should have jumped, he decided. He really should have jumped. He opened the door to the apartment to find Julia surrounded by their luggage, her coat over a chair, and sketch pads strewn about her on the floor.

"Honey, what's the matter?"

"I want to go home. Now. We have seats on the six o'clock plane . . ."

"But, Julia, you know . . ."

"Martie, with you, or without you, I'm going home."

"Are you giving up, then? Is that it? You go slinking back licked now, let them take away your baby, do whatever they mean to do to you . . ."

"Martie, I can't explain anything. I never can, you know. But I have to go back. I have work to do before the baby comes. I just have to. It's like this with every artist I know. Jacques Remy, Jean Vance, Porter, Dee Richardson . . . I've been in touch with different ones here and there, and they're all driven to work now. Some of my best friends simply didn't have time to see me. None of them can explain it. There's a creative explosion taking place, and we're helpless. Oh, if I could drink, I could probably resist it by getting dead drunk and staying that way . . ."

"What are you going to do?" He picked up several sheets of her drawing paper, but there were only meaningless scribbles on them.

"I don't know. I can't get it on paper. I need my tools, the sandstone. My hands know, will know when they start working . . ."

"Julia, you're feverish. Let me get you a sleeping pill. We'll go home in a day or two, if you still feel like this. Please . . ."

She grabbed up her coat and swung it about her shoulders, jerking her arms through the sleeves, paying no attention to him. "What time is it?"

"Four. Sit down, honey. You're as pale as a ghost . . ."

"We'll have to wait at the airport, but if we don't leave now, traffic will get so bad. Let's start now, Martie. We can have a sandwich and coffee while we wait."

At the airport she couldn't sit still. She walked the length of the corridors, rode the ramps to the upper levels, watched planes arriving and departing, walked to the lowest levels and prowled in and out of shops. Finally they boarded their plane and the strap forced her into a semblance of quietude.

"Martie, how do you explain dreams? The content of dreams? Wait, there's more. And the flashes of intuition that almost everyone experiences from time to time. The jumps into new fields that scientists make, proposing new theories explaining the universe in a way that no one had ever thought of before? *Déjà vu* feelings? Oh, what else? Flashes of what seems to be telepathy? Clairvoyance? Hilary's X factor? All those things that scientists don't usually want to talk about?"

"I don't. I don't try. I don't know the answer. And no one else does either." The engines roared and they were silent until the mammoth jet was above the clouds. Clouds covered the earth from Chicago to Kennedy Airport.

Julia looked down sometime later and said, "That's like it is with us. There are clouds hiding something from us, and once in a while a strong light probes through for a minute. The clouds thin out, or the light is strong for a short time, whatever. It doesn't last. The cloud layer thickens, or the power source can't keep up the strength of the beam, and there are only the clouds. No one who wasn't there or didn't see through them at that moment would believe they could be penetrated. And trying to make a whole out of such glimpses is a futile thing. Now a bit of blue sky, now a star, now pitch-black sky, now the lights of a passing plane . . ."

"So then we invent an infrared light that penetrates the clouds . . ."

"What if there were something on the other side of the layer that was trying to get through to us, just as much as we were trying to get through from this side, and with as little success . . ."

She hadn't even heard him. Martie took her hand and held it, letting her talk on. Her hand was warm and relaxed now that they were actually heading for home.

"Suppose that it, whatever it is, gets through only now and then, but when it does it is effective because it knows what it's looking for, and we never do. Not infrared . . ." She had heard. "But the other direction. Inward. We send other kinds of probes. Psychoanalysis, EEG, drugs, hypnosis, dream analysis . . . We are trying to get through, but we don't know how, or what we're trying to reach, or how to know when we have reached it."

"God?" Martie turned to look at her. "You're talking about reaching God?"

"No. I think that man has always thought of it as God, or some such thing, but only because man has always sensed its presence and didn't know what it was or how it worked, but he knew that it was more powerful than anything else when it did work. So he called it God."

"Honey, we've always been afraid of what we didn't understand. Magic, God, devils . . ."

"Martie, until you can explain why it is that more comes out of some minds than goes in, you haven't a leg to stand on, and you know it."

Like the new geometries, he thought. The sum can be greater than its parts. Or parallel lines might meet in some remote distance. He was silent, considering it, and Julia dozed. "But, dammit," he breathed a few minutes later . . .

"You're a Hull, Watson, Skinner man," Julia finished, not rousing from her light sleep. He stared at her. She hadn't studied psychology in her life. She didn't know Hull from Freud from Jung.

The polishing wheel screamed for hours each day as the carborundum paste cut into the quartzite. Martie dragged Julia from it for her meals, when it was time to rest, at bedtime.

"Honey, you'll hurt yourself. It might be hard on the baby . . ."

She laughed. "Have I ever looked better or healthier?"

Thin, pale, but with a fiery intensity that made her more beautiful than he had seen her in their lives together. Her eyes were luminous. The tension that had wracked her for months was gone. She carried the baby as if unaware of the extra burden, and when she slept, it was deep untroubled sleep that refreshed her wholly.

"You're the one who is suffering, darling," she said softly, fairy-touching his cheek. Her hands were very rough now, fingernails split and broken jaggedly. He caught her rough hand and pressed it hard against his cheek.

"Wymann has been calling, hasn't he?" Julia asked after a moment. She didn't pull her hand from his face. He turned it over and kissed the palm. "It's all right to talk about it, Martie. I know he's been calling. They want to see me as soon as possible, to make sure of the baby, to see if the delivery will be normal, or if a section is called for. It's all right."

"Have you talked to him?"

"No. No. But I know what they're thinking now. They're afraid of me, of people like me. You see, people who have high creativity don't usually have the right sort of genes to take their RNA. A few, but not enough. It worries them."

"Who've you been talking to?"

"Martie, you know where I've been spending my time." She laughed. "It is nice to be home, isn't it?" The fireplace half of the living room was cheerful and glowing, while shadows filled the rest of the long room. "Of course, when you consider that only about twenty-five percent of the people are getting the RNA, it isn't surprising that there aren't many with creative abilities that have been developed to any extent. But what is sad is that those few who were writers or painters, or whatever, don't seem to continue their work once they know they are immortal. Will women want to continue bearing children, if they know they're immortal already?"

"I don't know. You think that the maternal instinct is just a drive to achieve immortality, although vicariously?"

"Why not? Is a true instinct stilled with one or two satisfying meals, or sex acts, or whatever? Women seem to be satisfied as soon as they have a child or two."

"If that's so, then whatever happens, the race will be finished. If women don't want children, don't have to satisfy this drive, I should say, it's a matter of time. We have the means to prevent pregnancy, why would they keep on getting knocked up?"

"Because something else needs the children, the constantly shifting, renewing vision that is provided by children. Not us, not me. It. Something else. That thing that is behind us pushing, learning through us. You have the books. You've been reading everything you can find on psychology. The nearest we have been able to describe that something is by calling it the collective unconscious, I think."

"Jung's collective unconscious," Martie muttered. "You know, some scientists, philosophers, artists work right down the middle of a brightly illuminated strip, never go off it. Darwin for instance. Skinner. Others work so close to the edge that half the time they are in the grey areas where the light doesn't follow, where you never know if madness guided the pen or genius. Jung spent most of his time on the border, sometimes in the light, sometimes in the shadows. His collective unconscious, the fantasy of a man who couldn't stand mysteries not solved during his own lifetime."

Julia stood up and stretched. "God, I'm tired. Bath time." Martie wouldn't let her get into and out of the bathtub alone now. "Martie, if there is such a thing, and there is. There is. It's been threatened. It has to have the constantly shifting viewpoint of mankind in order to learn the universe. A billion experiences, a trillion, who knows how many it will need before it is finished. It was born with mankind, it has grown with mankind, as it matures so does man, and if mankind dies now, so will it. We are its sensory receptors. And what Wymann and the others propose is death to it, death to them eventually. It feeds the unconscious, nourishes it, gives it its dreams and its flashes of genius. Without it, man is just another animal, clever with his hands perhaps, but without the dream to work toward. All our probes into space, into the oceans, so few inward. We are so niggardly in exploring the greatest mystery of all, potentially the most rewarding of all."

She had her bath, and he helped her from the tub and dried her back and smoothed lotion over it. He tucked her into bed, and she smiled at him. "Come to bed, Martie. Please."

"Soon, honey. I'm . . . restless right now."

A few minutes later when he looked in on her, she was sound asleep. He smoked and drank and paced, as he did night after night. Julia was like one possessed. He grimaced at the choice of words. She worked from dawn until night, when he forced her to stop. He made their meals, or she wouldn't have eaten. He had to touch her before she knew he was there to collect her for a meal. He stood sometimes and watched her from the doorway, and he was frightened of her at those times. She was a stranger to him, her eyes almost closed, sometimes, he thought, and discarded the thought immediately, her eyes were all the way closed. Her hands held life of their own, strong, thin hands grasping mallet and chisel with whitened knuckles. She couldn't wear gloves while she worked. She dressed in heavy wool pants, and a heavy sweater, covered by a tentlike poncho that she had made from an army blanket. She wore fleece-lined boots, but her hands had to be bare. He would touch her arm, shake her, and slowly recognition would return to her eyes, she would smile at him and put down her tools; without looking at the thing she was making, she would go with him. He would rub her freezing hands for her, help her out of the heavy garments that were much too warm for the house.

Sometimes after she had gone to bed, usually by nine, he would turn on the barn lights and stand and stare at her work. He wanted, at those times, to pull it down and smash it to a million pieces. He hated it for possessing her when he would have her sit on a velvet cushion and spend her last months and weeks with . . .

He threw his glass into the fireplace, then started to pick up the pieces and put them in an ashtray. Something wet sparkled on his hand, and he stared at it for a moment. Suddenly he put his head down on the floor and sobbed for her, for himself, for their child.

"Sayre, why haven't you brought her in for an examination?"

Martie watched Wymann prowl the living room. Wymann looked haggard, he thought suddenly. He laughed. Everyone was looking haggard except Julia. Wymann turned toward him with a scowl.

"I'm warning you, Sayre. If the child is orphaned at birth, the state won't quibble a bit about our taking it. With you or without you . . ."

Martie nodded. "I've considered that." He rubbed his hand over his face. A four- or five-day beard was heavy on his cheeks and chin. His hand was unsteady. "I've thought of everything," he said deliberately. "All of it. I lose if I take you up, lose if I don't."

"You won't lose with us. One woman. There are other women. If she died in childbirth, in an accident, you'd be married again in less than five years . . ."

Martie nodded. "I've been through all that, too. No such thing as the perfect love, lasting love. Why'd you come out here, Wymann? I thought you were too busy for just one patient to monopolize your time. Farthest damn house call I've ever heard of. And not even called." He laughed again. "You're scared. What's going wrong?"

"Where's Julia?"

"Working. Out in the barn."

"Are you both insane? Working now? She's due in two weeks at the most!"

"She seems to think this is important. Something she has to finish before she becomes a mother and stops for a year or two."

Wymann looked at him sharply. "Is she taking that attitude?"

"You first. Why are you out here? What's wrong with the master plan for the emerging superman?"

"He's here because people aren't dying anymore. Are they, Dr. Wymann?"

Julia stood in the doorway in her stocking feet, stripping off the poncho. "You have to do things now, don't you, Doctor? Really do things, not just sit back and watch."

"There is some sort of underground then, isn't there? That's why you two made the grand tour, organizing an underground."

Julia laughed and pulled off her sweater. "I'll make us all some coffee."

Martie watched her. "A final solution, Doctor. You have to come up with a new final solution, don't you? And you find it difficult."

"Difficult, yes. But not impossible."

Martie laughed. "Excuse me while I shave. Make yourself comfortable. Won't take five minutes."

He went through the kitchen and caught Julia from behind, holding her hard. "They'll have to change everything if that's true. They won't all go along with murder, wholesale murder. This will bring it out into the open where we can decide . . ."

Julia pulled away and turned to look at him squarely.

"This isn't the end. Not yet. There's something else to come . . ."

"What?"

"I don't know. I just know that this isn't the end, not yet. Not like this. Martie, have you decided? It's killing you. You have to decide."

He shrugged. "Maybe it will be decided for me. I'm going up to shave now."

She shook her head. "You'll have to make the decision. Within a week, I think."

"Dr. Wymann, why is it that proportionately more doctors than laymen are suicides?" Julia poured coffee and passed the sugar as she spoke. "And why are there more alcoholics and drug users among the medical profession?"

Wymann shrugged. "I give, why?"

"Oh, because doctors as a group are so much more afraid of death than anyone else. Don't you think?"

"Rather simplistic, isn't it?"

"Yes. Often the most unrelenting drives are very simplistic."

"Julia, you have to come in to be examined. You know that. There could be unsuspected complications that might endanger the baby."

"I'll come in, as soon as I finish what I'm doing. A few more days. I'll check in then if you like. But first, I have to finish. It's Martie's Christmas present."

Martie stared at her. Christmas. He'd forgotten. She smiled. "It's all right. The baby is my present. The sculpture is yours."

"What are you doing? Can I see?" Wymann asked. "Although, remember, I like understandable things. Nothing esoteric or ambiguous."

"This one is as simple . . . as a sunset. I'll go get my boots."

As soon as she had left them, Wymann stood up and paced back and forth in quick nervous strides. "I bet it reeks of death. They're all doing it. A worldwide cultural explosion, that's what the Sunday *Times* called it. All reeking of death."

"Ready? You'll need warm clothes, Doctor."

Muffled in warm garments, they walked together to the barn. The work was ten feet high, in places. The quartzite was gone, out of sight. Martie didn't know what she had done with it. What remained was rough sandstone, dull red, with yellow streaks. It looked very soft. She had chiseled and cut into it what looked like random lines. At first glance it seemed to be a medieval city, with steeples, flattened places, roofs. The illusion of a city faded, and it became a rough mountainous landscape, with stiletto-like peaks, unknowable chasms. Underwater mountains, maybe. Martie walked around it. He didn't know what it was supposed to be. He couldn't stop looking, and strangely, there was a yearning deep within him. Dr. Wymann stood staring at it with a puzzled expression. He seemed to be asking silently, "This is it? Why bother?"

"Martie, hold my hand. Let me explain . . ." Her hand, cold and rough in his. She led him around it and stopped at the side that the west light hit. "It has to be displayed outside. It should rest on a smooth black basalt base, gently curved, not polished, but naturally smooth. I know that they can be found like that, but I haven't been able to yet. And it should weather slowly. Rain, snow, sun, wind. It shouldn't be protected from anything. If people want to, they should be able to touch it. Sculpture should be touched, you know. It's a tactile art. Here, feel . . ." Martie put his hand where she directed and ran his fingers up one of the sharply rising peaks. "Close your eyes a minute," she said. "Just feel it." She reached out for Wymann's hand. He was standing a foot or slightly more to her left. He resisted momentarily, but she smiled and guided his hand to the work.

"You can see that there's order," she said, "even if you can't quite grasp it. Order covering something else . . ."

Martie didn't know when she stopped talking. He knew, his hand knew what she meant. Order over something wild and unordered, ungraspable. Something unpredictable. Something that began to emerge, that overcame the order with disorder, distorting the lines. The feeling was not visual. His hand seemed to feel the subliminally skewed order. Rain. Snow. Wind. The imperfections became greater, a deliberate deterioration of order, exposing the inexplicable, almost fearful inside. A nightmare quality now, changing always changing, faster now. Grosser changes. A peak too thin to support itself, falling sideways, striking another lesser peak, cracking off the needle end of it. Lying at the base, weathering into sand, running away in a stream of red-yellow water, leaving a clean basalt base. Deeper channels being cut into the thing, halving it, dividing it into smaller and smaller bits, each isolated from the rest, each yielding to the elements, faster, faster. A glimpse of something hard and smooth, a gleam of the same red and yellow, but firm, not giving, not yielding. A section exposed, the quartzite, polished and gleaming. Larger segments of it now, a corner, squared, perfect, sharp. Even more unknowable than the shifting sandstone, untouched by the erosion.

But it would go, too. Eventually. Slowly, imperceptibly, it would give. And ultimately there would be only the basalt, until in some distant future it would be gone too.

Martie opened his eyes, feeling as if he had been standing there for a very long time. Julia was watching him serenely. He blinked at her. "It's good," he said. Not enough, but he couldn't say anything more then.

Wymann pulled his hand from the stone and thrust it deep inside his pocket. "Why build something that you know will erode away? Isn't it like ice sculpture, only slower?"

"Exactly like it. But we will have a chance to look at it before it is gone. And feel it." She turned toward the door and waited for them to finish looking. "Next year, if you look at it, it will be different, and ten years from now, and twenty years from now. Each change means something, you know. Each change will tell you something about yourself, and your world, that you didn't know before." She laughed. "At least, I hope so."

They were silent as they returned to the house and the dancing fire. Martie made drinks for Wymann and himself, and Julia had a glass of milk. Wymann drank his scotch quickly. He had opened his coat but hadn't taken it off. "It reeks of death," he said suddenly. "Death and decay and dissolution. All the things we are dedicated to eradicating."

"And mystery and wonder and awe," Martie said. "If you also kill those things, what's left? Will man be an animal again, clever with his hands and the tools he's made, but an animal without a dream? Inward, that's what it means. Isn't that right, Julia? Inward is the only direction that matters."

"It itself is what it means," she said, helplessly almost. "I tried to explain what it means, but if I could say it, I wouldn't have had to do it. Inward. Yes. A particular way of looking, of experiencing the world, my life in it. When it doesn't apply any longer, it should be gone. Others will reinterpret the world, their lives. Always new interpretations, new ways of seeing. Letting new sensations pass into the unconscious, into the larger thing that uses these impressions and also learns." She drained her glass. "I'll see you in a week at the latest, Doctor. I promise. You personally will deliver my baby."

Why? Why? Why? Martie paced and watched the fire burn itself out and paced some more in the darkened, cooling room. Snow was falling softly, lazily, turning the backyard into an alien world. Why did she promise to go to them? Why to Wymann? What had he felt out there in the barn? Martie flung himself down in an easy chair, and eventually, toward dawn, fell asleep.

The hospital. The same dream, over and over, the same dream. He tried to wake up from it, but while he was aware of himself dreaming, he couldn't alter anything, could only wander through corridors, searching for her. Calling her. Endless corridors, strange rooms, an eternity of rooms to search . . .

"Julia is in good condition. Dilating already. Three or four days probably, but she could go into labor any time. I recommend that she stay here, Sayre. She is leaving it up to you."

Martie nodded. "I want to see her before we decide." He pulled a folded section of newspaper from his pocket and tossed it down on Wymann's desk. "Now you tell me something. Why did Dr. Fischer jump out of his window?"

"I don't know. There wasn't a note."

"Fischer was the doctor who, quote, examined me, unquote, wasn't he? The one who added that charming little note to my personal data record, that I'm schizophrenic? A psychiatrist."

"Yes. You met him here."

"I remember, Wymann. And you can't tell me why he jumped. Maybe I can tell you. He dried up, didn't he? A psychiatrist without intuition, without dreams, without an unconscious working for and with him. When he reached in, he closed on emptiness, didn't he? Don't all of you!"

"I don't know what you're talking about. Conant has scheduled you for testing starting tomorrow morning. If positive . . ."

"Go to hell, Wymann. You, Conant, the rest of you. Go to hell!"

"All right. Maybe that's rushing it. We'll wait until Julia has delivered. You'll want to be with your child. We'll wait. Julia's in room four nineteen. You can go up whenever you want."

He tapped lightly on the door. Julia pulled it open,

laughing, with tears on her cheeks. "I know. I know. You're going to be all right," she cried.

"Me? I came to tell you that you'd be all right."

"I've known that for a long time now. Martie, are you sure? Of course, you are. You've seen. He, Wymann doesn't realize yet. I don't think many of them do . . ."

"Honey, stop. You're six jumps ahead of me. What are you talking about?"

"You'll catch up. It, the thing, the collective unconscious, whatever it is, has withdrawn from them. They're pariahs to it. Empty. They think that it's a reaction to the RNA, but it isn't. They want babies desperately, but already the reason for wanting the babies is getting dimmer . . ." She stopped suddenly and pressed her hand against her stomach. A startled look crossed her face. "You'd better see if he's still in the building."

"She'll be all right. A few hours more." Dr. Wymann sat down in the waiting room with Martie. "Tell me something, Sayre. Why did she make that stone thing? Why do any of them make the things they do, write poetry, plays, paint? Why?"

Martie laughed.

"Funny," Wymann said, rubbing his eyes, "I feel that I should know. Maybe that I did know, once. Well, I should look in on her now and then." He stood up. "By the way, I found a memo on my desk, telling me to remind you of your appointment with Dr. Conant in the morning. Are you sick or something?"

"I'm fine, Doctor. Just fine."

"Good. Good. See you in a little while."

He walked down the hallways, glancing into rooms here and there, all equally strange. "Martie, down here. I'm down here." He turned toward the sound of her voice and followed it. "It's a boy, darling. Big, husky boy." He bowed his head and felt tears warm on his cheeks. When

Wymann came out to tell him about his son, he found Martie sound asleep, smiling.

He stood over him for a minute, frowning. There was something else that he had to do. Something else. He couldn't remember what it was. Perfect delivery. No complications. Good baby. Good mother. No trouble at all. He shrugged and tiptoed from the room and went home, leaving Martie sleeping. The nurse would wake him as soon as Julia was ready to see him.

"Darling, you're beautiful. Very, very beautiful. I brought you a Christmas present after all." He held it out for her to take. A stuffed dog, one eye closed in a wink, a ridiculous grin on its face. "You knew how it would be just like I knew about our son, didn't you?"

"I just knew. It was threatened. Any other way of countering the threat would have endangered it even more. We have all those terrible things that we would have used on each other. No one would have survived the war that would have come. It left them. That awful vacuum in Wymann, in Conant, all of them. They do what they are trained to do, no more. They do it very well." She patted her newly flat stomach.

"You did it. You, others like you. The ones who could open to it, accept, and be possessed wholly. A two-way communication must take place during such times. That cultural explosion, all over the world. You at the one end of the spectrum, Wymann, them, at the other, from total possession to total absence."

"It will take some time to search the records, find our babies . . ."

"They'll help us now. They need guidance. They'll have to be protected . . ."

"Forever and ever."

Eyebem

by Gene Wolfe

I am lying, I say again, in the dark; in the dark in the hut Mark has built of frozen earth and pounded snow. My pack transformer ratio .06 and I am dying. My identity, I say again, is 887332 and my friends call me Eyebem.

Inside me, I know, my words are going around and around in slow circles as they have all my life; I never thought it would matter—when you are young you think you will live forever. I remember very clearly old Ceedeesy describing this interior looped tape all of us contain. (I think setting my pack transformer ratio so low has called all these memories forth, though why it should I can't comprehend; memory chips burning bright as the spark dies.) A tape going around and around, Ceedeesy said, recording the last half hour of our talk, and then when end meets beginning writing over it so that only the last half hour remains. It was an idea, he told us, more than a hundred years old, having been originally used to record the last transmissions of those picturesque air-burning rockets called jets.

Ceedeesy was my group's principal instructor at the creche and I looked up to him. Now I want to talk about him, and though since it doesn't pertain to the cause of my death you won't like it, what can you do about it? I will be beyond the reach of your vindictive reprogramming, voltage gone, mind and memory zeroed.

To tell the truth I have said a great many things you would not like during the past eighteen or twenty hours as I lay here talking to myself in the dark. Yes, talking, even though the voltage in my speaker is so low that Mark, lying a few feet away, cannot hear me. He cannot hear me, but I know he is awake, lying there eating and thinking. I cannot see his eyes, but how they burn in the dark!

Ceedeesy, as I said, was old. So old that he could no longer be repaired sufficiently for active service, which was why we youngsters received the benefit of the deep wisdom he had won during his decades in the wild parts of the world. I recall his saying, "How many times, Eyebem, I've seen the trumpeter swans black against the morning sun!" then the little pause as he searched–the pause that told of hysteresis gathering on his aging mind like cobwebs. "A hundred and twenty-three times, Eyebem. That's an average of 3.8622 times a year, but the hundred and twenty-fourth time will never come for me."

No. Nor will the first for me.

Ceedeesy's skin had yellowed. They said at the creche that it was an older type of vinyl and that they had since improved the color stability so that our own will be virtually unaffected by the ultraviolet in sunlight, but I suspect that when my creche-mates are as old as Ceedeesy, their skin too will be yellowed at the back of the neck and the back of the hands, where the harsh noon light will have seen it too often.

It was because his skin was yellowed–or so I used to think–that Ceedeesy never left the compound. I was too young then to know that humans could always identify one of us in a second or two in spite of new skin and different face patterns with each creche-cycle. Once I persuaded him to go with me to a little store my creche-mates and I had found scarcely more than a block from the compound gate. It was run by a plump woman who, in order to get our custom, pretended to be too simple to recognize us. I think, too, that having us there attracted tourists for her. At least several times when I was there people–humans, I mean–entered the store and stared, only buying something when the plump woman pressed it into their hands. As young as I was I understood that she was exerting some form of psychological pressure on them.

Since our faces within the creche-cycle were all the same, this woman pretended to think we were all the same human person, a young man who was her best customer, coming ten or twenty times a day into her little shop. Pretending, as I said, to think we were all the same person, she called us all Mark; one of my creche-mates had told her to, no doubt; it's the name stupid youngsters always give when they want to pass, useful because it's a human name as well as being one of ours. How ironic that seems now.

We would wander about the store one at a time looking at the trusses and contraceptives we had no use for, and pretending to drink a carbonated liquid until the woman, with what I realize now was the most elephantine tact, contrived to turn her back so that we could pour it into a conveniently placed spittoon.

On the one occasion that Ceedeesy accompanied me we sat on high, swiveling stools, sloshing the sweet drinks in our cups and occasionally putting the straws to our mouths. Ceedeesy, I am certain, was only doing it to please me. He must have known I was the only one being deceived, but at the time I believe he felt I was weak in marine biology, and he was ready to take any opportunity to tutor me before the junior examination. The store faced west, and as we talked I watched a spot of sunlight creep along the floor to his feet, then up his faded denim trousers, then past the moose-hide belt he had made himself and over his patched hunting shirt until his face and throat, and the hand that held his cup, were all brightly illuminated. I looked at them then, cracked with minute cracks and discolored, and it was as though Ceedeesy were an old piece of furniture covered with stiff, peeling plastic; it was terrible. I thought then that the woman *must* know (being too innocent to realize that she had known when the first of us walked in), but she was puttering in the back of the store–waiting, no doubt, for the display at her soda fountain to attract tourists.

To keep myself from staring at Ceedeesy I began watching the crowds on the street outside. In the space of a few minutes a thousand human beings must have passed the store. It made me interrupt Ceedeesy's lecture to ask, "When it's so beautiful out there—as the training tapes show and you and the other old ones say—why don't some of them"—I waved a hand at the window—"go out and look at it? Why send us?"

Ceedeesy laughed. "When I was a youngster, the explanation given was always blackflies."

"Blackflies?"

"A stinging insect. That explanation's just a put-off, of course. There are repellents to take care of them."

"Then—"

"A few of them do go out," Ceedeesy said. He went on to tell me about a man he had once rescued in the gorge of the Colorado. The man had been a fanatic Ecumenical Neo-Catholic, and had wanted to shoot the river on an air mattress because St. Kennedy the Less was reputed to have done something of the kind. "He was so naïve," Ceedeesy said, "that he called me Ranger the whole time he was with me. Or perhaps he was just afraid of me, out there away from the cities, and thought that was safest. I doubt if there are ten human rangers left in the world now." A pot-bellied man leading two children came into the store then, pointing at Ceedeesy and me and whispering; we left.

I think that was the only time Ceedeesy went out of the compound. Last month (it seems so much longer) when we graduated he saw us off as we climbed into the trucks that would take us to the launch area. I was on the last truck, and I can still picture him waving as we went through the compound gate. At the time I was eager to leave.

The launch area was a new world to all of us, a huge building filled with bustling humans and machines, with the ships rising outside on columns of fire. I wasn't thinking about it then, but I suppose it's having these ships, as well as being able to synthesize food, that have caused human beings to concentrate more and more in the cities. In the old days they had to go out to get from one to another, or at least fly low enough that treetops and lakes became familiar. Now—well, my own experience was typical, I suppose. We were issued tickets, and after several hours (we sat around and compared tickets—the North for me) my ship was called. An enclosed traveling walk put me into it. That was the last I saw of my creche-mates.

After a few minutes more a human girl with inquisitive fingers came and strapped me to my couch, giving herself a lesson on how our anatomy differs from theirs. Another wait, a recorded announcement, and the ship was rising under me, slowly at first, then faster and faster until the acceleration drove me down against the upholstery so hard I could sense there wasn't enough strength in my servos to move my arms.

And then nothing. The acceleration faded and I was disoriented, feeling sure that something had gone wrong. After a short time the disoriented feeling changed to one of descending in an elevator. The couch was beneath me again and we were going down. Slowly. There was no sensation of speed.

This time instead of the enclosed walk there was an aluminum ramp; the building was older and the concrete pad small enough for its edges to be visible, but there was no more feeling of having traveled or having been out of the city than I would have gotten from going to the top of the central shop complex in our compound.

For me there was, however, at least one valid difference in emotional quality. I was alone, and as I carried my one small bag into the old and rather grimy port building, I came to realize what that meant. There were several machines moving smoothly over the terrazzo floor, but to these machines I was a man. There were a number of humans waiting for their ships to leave or greeting arriving relatives, but to them I was a machine in spite of my pointed, broad-brimmed field hat and high-laced boots, and they stared.

My orders had stated that I would be met here by someone from my assigned station, but for over an hour I was by myself in the middle of that crowd. In retrospect I think the experience was good for me, and perhaps it was planned that way. I had been anticipating the loneliness of duty in some remote part of the wilderness outside of the cities, and I had been trained for that. But this was different. It taught me that I was vulnerable after all, and I think it made me accept Mark, when he came, more than I would have otherwise.

I still remember how glad I was when I saw a hat like mine over the heads of that surging mass of people. I took off my own and waved it over my head to let him know where I was, and grasped his hand eagerly when he extended it. Half shouting to make myself heard, I said, "Identity 887332. Call me Eyebem."

He said, "Call me Mark."

I still don't know whether "Mark" is really Mark's name or merely one he has assumed to put us at our ease. I could ask him now, turning up my speaker until he heard me over the whistling wind, but he is thinking. All our own names, of course, derive from the dawn age of cybernetics: Ceedeesy's from the old Control Data Corporation computers, and "Mark" from the famous series which included the Mark VII and Mark VIII. At any rate I had been expecting one of us, and the name postponed for half a minute at least my discovery that Mark was human. To be truthful, I don't believe I was really sure of it until we were alone in the cab of the copter. Then, sitting next to him as he started the engine, I could study the skin of his neck. After that it seemed best to say something so he wouldn't realize I was staring, so I asked where we were going.

"Main station," he said. "About thirty miles up the Kobuk River." I could tell that he wasn't accustomed to talking a great deal, but he was perfectly friendly. I asked if it were far, and he said two hundred and fifty miles farther north. We had lifted off by then and I was too busy looking at the country to want to ask more questions. It was rocky, with conifers on the higher ground and alders following the watercourses. In places they had already shed their leaves, and I knew this must be one of the last good days we would have before the short Arctic summer ended and winter closed in.

At the main station I was reassured to find that Mark was the only human. The station boss was one of us, very imposing in a huge old grey cabinet with sensors scattered all over the station, but he made me welcome in a hearty, pleasant voice that made me feel right at home. There was another fellow too, from the creche-cycle two years ahead of mine as it turned out, who had come in from a tour to report and rest up.

With my own anxiety gone I began to feel sorry for Mark. He had to prepare food when the rest of us were sitting around recharging our power packs, and a lot of the little jokes and things that were said pretty well left him out—not intentionally but just by the nature of things. Since I had the least seniority I had to cut wood for the fireplace and do the odd jobs the station boss couldn't be bothered with around the low-yield pile that kept our generator running, but I didn't mind and I felt sure Mark would have traded places with me gladly if he could.

Then the pleasant time at the station was over and Mark and I left for our tour. By then I had learned that Mark, who was nearly thirty, would be retiring the next year, and I was to work with him until then, learning the territory and getting the specialized knowledge that can only be acquired in the field. We could have flown since the first big storm of the winter hadn't come yet, but Mark was afraid that if we did we wouldn't be able to get the copter back out when it turned nasty, so we took a snow jeep instead.

The first night that we camped I knew that I had reached the life in which I could fulfill myself, the thing I had been made and trained for. Without his asking I carried water up from the creek for Mark so that he could wash and make coffee. After he had gone to bed I sat up half the night staring at the polestar–so bright and so high here–and listening to the sounds the wind made in the little spruce trees around us.

The next day Mark showed me the tracks of a bear overlapping my own beside the creek. "He came before the frost got to the mud," Mark said, "so it must have been pretty early in the evening. Did you see him?"

I shook my head. "He's not dangerous, is he?"

"I wouldn't want to blunder into him in the dark, and he might go after the grub I've got locked in the jeep."

I hadn't thought of that. The bear couldn't eat amperes out of my power pack, but if it got to Mark's food–not here where we could easily get back to the station, but when we were farther out–Mark might starve. That knowledge hung like a dark cloud at the back of my mind while we broke camp and loaded the snow jeep. I hadn't realized I was allowing the worry to show on my face, but when we were under way Mark asked, "What's the matter, Eyebem?"

I told him what was troubling me and he laughed. "I'm an old hand. Funny, but while you were worrying about me I was fretting about you and the boss and the rest of you; wondering if you'll be all right when I leave."

"About us?" Frankly I was shocked.

"Uh-huh." He swung the snow jeep around a fallen tree. "I know there are a lot of these completely automated stations operating successfully, but I still worry."

Completely automated? I suppose in a sense Mark was right, but I hadn't thought of it that way. I said as gently as I could, "We're designed for it, Mark. This is our home out here. If anyone's out of place it's you, and I'm sure the station boss and all of us will feel a lot less concern when you go to one of the cities."

Mark didn't say anything to that, but I could see he

didn't really agree. To change the subject I said, "The bears will be going into hibernation soon, I suppose. Then we won't have to worry about them."

"Most of them are in already." Mark sounded like a bear himself. "The one we had around camp was probably an old male; some of them don't go until the last bit of food's gone, and they'll stick their heads out any time during the winter when there's a little stretch of better than average weather."

I know all that, of course. I had asked the question to give him something to talk about that wouldn't hurt his pride. It worked, too. Bears around camp are always a problem, and he told bear stories for the rest of that day as we picked our way north.

The storm came on our fifth day out, but we were expecting it and had made ourselves as secure as possible, pitching our tent in a sheltered spot and weighing down the edges with rocks until it looked almost like a stone house. The storm kept us there for three days, but when it was over we could put the skis on the snow jeep and skim along where we had had to pick our way before. We looked in on the sea otter rookeries north of the abandoned city of Kivalina, then followed the coast north toward Point Hope. We were still about two days' travel south of it when the second storm came.

That one held us five days, and when it was over Mark decided we'd better cut our tour short and head back toward the station. We dug the snow jeep out of the drifts and got ready to leave, but when Mark engaged the transmission the engine died and would not restart.

I know very little about turbines–I've only so much program capacity after all–but Mark seemed to be quite familiar with them, so while I built a snow wall to give him some shelter from the wind, he tore the engine down.

A drive shaft bearing race had shattered. It was broken so badly it wouldn't even keep the shaft in place, much less allow it to turn. It had jammed the turbine, and the overtorque breaker was what had actually shut down the engine; the trouble with the bearing had probably been due to cold-shortness, the weakness that will make an ax head fly into a thousand pieces sometimes when it's been left outside all night in sub-zero cold and you slam it into a frozen knot. All our equipment is supposed to be tested against it, but apparently this slipped through, or more likely, as Mark says, some mechanic doing an overhaul made an unauthorized substitution.

For as long as the battery lasted we tried to raise the station boss on the radio, but the cold reduced its efficiency so badly that we were forced to disconnect it from time to time so that we could carry it into the tent to warm up. For a while we considered tearing the entire radio out of the jeep so that we could take it inside, but we were afraid we'd damage something in the process (neither of us were too clear on how closely its wiring was integrated with the jeep's), and by the time we had about made up our minds to do it, the battery failed completely.

After that we had to reassess our position pretty thoroughly and we did, sitting by our little stove in the tent that night. Mark had food for at least ten days more, twenty with rationing, but it was too heavy to carry with us together with our other gear, and the loss of the snow jeep's engine meant no more power-pack recharges for me. We decided the smart thing to do was to stay with the jeep and our equipment, making what we had last as long as possible. We could burn the jeep's fuel in our stove, and if we kept the snow off it, just having it near us would make us a lot more visible to a search party than we would be otherwise. When we failed to return from our tour on schedule the station boss would send someone after us, and if we conserved what we had we thought he ought to find us in pretty good shape.

At first everything went quite well. I cut my pack transformer ratio: first to .5, then as the days went by to .3 without seeming to lose too much. I wasn't strong, of course, but as I told Mark it kept my monitor on, kept me going, and I didn't feel too bad. If you're not familiar with us, you who are hearing this tape, you may wonder why I didn't simply turn myself off altogether and instruct Mark to reactivate me when rescue came. The reason is that my memory is dependent on subminiature semiconductor chips which make up bistable circuits. When there is no electromotive force on them, the semiconductors "forget" their position, and that would mean wiping out every memory I possess—the total erasure of my personality as well as the loss of all my training.

Two days ago Mark built this hut of earth and snow for us with the tent as a liner, but I was too weak to help him much. The truth is that for the past week I have been simply lying here conserving as much energy as I can. Yesterday Mark went out and was able to shoot a seal on the beach, and when he dragged it inside I know he thought I was dead. He knelt beside me and passed his hand in front of my eyes, then slipped it inside my parka to feel the place in my chest above the heaters that prevent my hydraulic pump's freezing. There was so little current that he felt nothing, and I could see him shake his head as he drew his hand out.

I should not have done it, but for some reason that made me angry, and I turned up the power to my speaker until I could make myself heard and said, "I'm alive, Mark. Don't junk me yet."

He said, "I wouldn't junk you, Eyebem."

Then it all burst out of me, all the horror and frustration of these past days. I shouldn't have talked to Mark that way, he has never done me any harm and in fact has done whatever he could to help me, but I lost control of myself. Perhaps the long period at reduced voltage had something to do with it. Perhaps I am going mad, but I told him over and over how unjust it was: "We are the advance of the future, not you men. All your stupid human history has been just your own replacement by us, and there's nothing, not one thing, that you can do that we can't do better. Why don't you help me?" I suppose I was raving.

He only took my hand and said, "I'll think of something, Eyebem; turn down your power before you exhaust yourself."

And now another storm has come up, which means that whoever has been sent out to look for me, if anyone has, is pinned down just as we are; sitting in his tent while my power drains ampere by ampere, electron by electron on the way to nothing while Mark lies across from me in the dark eating his filthy seal blubber. Has the half-hour loop completed its cycle yet? Have I already erased the last beginning I made? I have no way of knowing.

I am lying, I say again, in the dark. . . .

Continued on Next Rock

by R. A. Lafferty

Up in the Big Lime country there is an upthrust, a chimney rock that is half fallen against a newer hill. It is formed of what is sometimes called Dawson Sandstone and is interlaced with tough shell. It was formed during the glacial and recent ages in the bottomlands of Crow Creek and Green River when these streams (at least five times) were mighty rivers.

The chimney rock is only a little older than mankind, only a little younger than grass. Its formation had been upthrust and then eroded away again, all but such harder parts as itself and other chimneys and blocks.

A party of five persons came to this place where the chimney rock had fallen against a newer hill. The people of the party did not care about the deep limestone below: they were not geologists. They *did* care about the newer hill (it was man-made) and they did care a little about the rock chimney; they were archeologists.

Here was time heaped up, bulging out in casing and accumulation, and not in line sequence. And here also was striated and banded time, grown tall, and then shattered and broken.

The five party members came to the site early in the afternoon, bringing the working trailer down a dry creek bed. They unloaded many things and made a camp there. It wasn't really necessary to make a camp on the ground. There was a good motel two miles away on the highway; there was a road along the ridge above. They could have lived in comfort and made the trip to the site in five minutes every morning. Terrence Burdock, however, believed that one could not get the feel of a digging unless he lived on the ground with it day and night.

The five persons were Terrence Burdock, his wife Ethyl, Robert Derby, and Howard Steinleser: four beautiful and balanced people. And Magdalen Mobley who was neither beautiful nor balanced. But she was electric; she was special. They rouched around in the formations a little after they had made camp and while there was still light. All of them had seen the formations before and had guessed that there was promise in them.

"That peculiar fluting in the broken chimney is almost like a core sample," Terrence said, "and it differs from the rest of it. It's like a lightning bolt through the whole length. It's already exposed for us. I believe we will remove the chimney entirely. It covers the perfect access for the slash in the mound, and it is the mound in which we are really interested. But we'll study the chimney first. It is so available for study."

"Oh, I can tell you everything that's in the chimney," Magdalen said crossly. "I can tell you everything that's in the mound too."

"I wonder why we take the trouble to dig if you already know what we will find," Ethyl sounded archly.

"I wonder too," Magdalen grumbled. "But we will need the evidence and the artifacts to show. You can't get appropriations without evidence and artifacts. Robert, go kill that deer in the brush about forty yards northeast of the chimney. We may as well have deer meat if we're living primitive."

"This isn't deer season," Robert Derby objected. "And there isn't any deer there. Or, if there is, it's down in the draw where you couldn't see it. And if there's one there, it's probably a doe."

"No, Robert, it is a two-year-old buck and a very big one. Of course it's in the draw where I can't see it. Forty yards northeast of the chimney would have to be in the draw. If I could see it, the rest of you could see it too. Now go kill it! Are you a man or a *mus microtus*? Howard, cut poles and set up a tripod to string and dress the deer on."

"You had better try the thing, Robert," Ethyl Burdock said, "or we'll have no peace this evening."

Robert Derby took a carbine and went northeastward of the chimney, descending into the draw at forty yards. There was the high ping of the carbine shot. And after some moments, Robert returned with a curious grin.

"You didn't miss him, Robert, you killed him," Magdalen called loudly. "You got him with a good shot through the throat and up into the brain when he tossed his head high like they do. Why didn't you bring him? Go back and get him!"

"Get him? I couldn't even lift the thing. Terrence and Howard, come with me and we'll lash it to a pole and get it here somehow."

"Oh Robert, you're out of your beautiful mind," Magdalen chided. "It only weighs a hundred and ninety pounds. Oh, I'll get it."

Magdalen Mobley went and got the big buck. She brought it back, carrying it listlessly across her shoulders and getting herself bloodied, stopping sometimes to examine rocks and kick them with her foot, coming on easily with her load. It looked as if it might weigh two hundred and fifty pounds; but if Magdalen said it weighed a hundred and ninety, that is what it weighed.

Howard Steinleser had cut poles and made a tripod. He knew better than not to. They strung the buck up, skinned it off, ripped up its belly, drew it, and worked it over in an almost professional manner.

"Cook it, Ethyl," Magdalen said.

Later, as they sat on the ground around the fire and it had turned dark, Ethyl brought the buck's brains to Magdalen, messy and not half cooked, believing that she was playing an evil trick. And Magdalen ate them avidly. They were her due. She had discovered the buck.

If you wonder how Magdalen knew what invisible things were where, so did the other members of the party always wonder.

"It bedevils me sometimes why I am the only one to notice the analogy between historical geology and depth psychology," Terrence Burdock mused as they grew lightly profound around the campfire. "The isostatic principle applies to the mind and the under-mind as well as it does to the surface and undersurface of the earth. The mind has its erosions and weatherings going on along with its deposits and accumulations. It also has its upthrusts and its stresses. It floats on a similar magma. In extreme cases it has its volcanic eruptions and its mountain building."

"And it has its glaciations," Ethyl Burdock said, and perhaps she was looking at her husband in the dark.

"The mind has its hard sandstone, sometimes transmuted to quartz, or half transmuted into flint, from the drifting and floating sand of daily events. It has its shale from the old mud of daily ineptitudes and inertias. It has limestone out of its more vivid experiences, for lime is the remnant of what was once animate: and this limestone may be true marble if it is the deposit of rich enough emotion, or even travertine if it has bubbled sufficiently through agonized and evocative rivers of the under-mind. The mind has its sulphur and its gemstones–" Terrence bubbled on sufficiently, and Magdalen cut him off.

"Say simply that we have rocks in our heads," she said. "But they're random rocks, I tell you, and the same ones keep coming back. It *isn't* the same with us as it is with the earth. The world gets new rocks all the time. But it's the same people who keep turning up, and the same minds. Damn, one of the samest of them just turned up again! I wish he'd leave me alone. The answer is still no."

Very often Magdalen said things that made no sense. Ethyl Burdock assured herself that neither her husband, nor Robert, nor Howard, had slipped over to Magdalen in the dark. Ethyl was jealous of the chunky and surly girl.

"I am hoping that this will be as rich as Spiro Mound," Howard Steinleser hoped. "It could be, you know. I'm told that there was never a less prepossessing site than that, or a trickier one. I wish we had someone who had dug at Spire."

"Oh, he dug at Spire," Magdalen said with contempt.

"He? Who?" Terrence Burdock asked. "No one of us was at Spiro. Magdalen, you weren't even born yet when that mound was opened. What could you know about it?"

"Yeah, I remember him at Spiro," Magdalen said, "always turning up his own things and pointing them out."

"*Were* you at Spiro?" Terrence suddenly asked a piece of the darkness. For some time, they had all been vaguely aware that there were six, and not five, persons around the fire.

"Yeah, I was at Spiro," the man said. "I dig there. I dig at a lot of the digs. I dig real well, and I always know when we come to something that will be important. You give me a job."

"Who are you?" Terrence asked him. The man was pretty visible now. The flame of the fire seemed to lean toward him as if he compelled it.

"Oh, I'm just a rich old poor man who keeps following and hoping and asking. There is *one* who is worth it all forever, so I solicit that one forever. And sometimes I am other things. Two hours ago I was the deer in the draw. It is an odd thing to munch one's own flesh." And the man was munching a joint of the deer, unasked.

"Him and his damn cheap poetry!" Magdalen cried angrily.

"What's your name?" Terrence asked him.

"Manypenny. Anteros Manypenny is my name forever."

"What are you?"

"Oh, just Indian. Shawnee. Choc, Creek, Anadarko, Caddo and pre-Caddo. Lots of things."

"How could anyone be pre-Caddo?"

"Like me. I am."

"Is Anteros a Creek name?"

"No. Greek. Man, I am a going Jessie, I am one digging man! I show you tomorrow."

Man, he was one digging man! He showed them tomorrow. With a short-handled rose hoe he began the gash in the bottom of the mound, working too swiftly to be believed.

"He will smash anything that is there. He will not know what he comes to," Ethyl Burdock complained.

"Woman, I will *not* smash whatever is there," Anteros said. "You can hide a wren's egg in one cubic meter of sand. I will move all the sand in one minute. I will uncover the egg wherever it is. And I will not crack the egg. I sense these things. I come now to a small pot of the proto-Plano period. It is broken, of course, but I do not break it. It is in six pieces and they will fit together perfectly. I tell you this beforehand. Now I reveal it."

And Anteros revealed it. There was something wrong about it even before he uncovered it. But it was surely a find, and perhaps it *was* of the proto-Plano period. The six shards came out. They were roughly cleaned and set. It was apparent that they would fit wonderfully.

"Why, it is perfect!" Ethyl exclaimed.

"It is too perfect," Howard Steinleser protested. "It was a turned pot, and who had turned pots in America without the potter's wheel? But the glyphs pressed into it do correspond to proto-Plano glyphs. It is fishy." Steinleser was in a twitchy humor today and his face was livid.

"Yes, it is the ripple and the spinosity, the fish-glyph," Anteros pointed out. "And the sun-sign is riding upon it. It is fish-god."

"It's fishy in another way," Steinleser insisted. "Nobody finds a thing like that in the first sixty seconds of a dig. And there *could not be* such a pot. I wouldn't believe it was proto-Plano unless points were found in the exact site with it."

"Oh here," Anteros said. "One can smell the very shape

of the flint points already. Two large points, one small one. Surely you get the whiff of them already? Four more hoe cuts and I come to them."

Four more hoe cuts, and Anteros *did* come to them. He uncovered two large points and one small one, spearheads and arrowhead. Lanceolate they were, with ribbon flaking. They were late Folsom, or they were proto-Plano; they were what you will.

"This cannot be," Steinleser groaned. "They're the missing chips, the transition pieces. They fill the missing place too well. I won't believe it. I'd hardly believe it if mastodon bones were found on the same level here."

"In a moment," said Anteros, beginning to use the hoe again. "Hey, those old beasts *did smell funny*! An elephant isn't in it with them. And a lot of it still clings to their bones. Will a sixth thoracic bone do? I'm pretty sure that's what it is. I don't know where the rest of the animal is. Probably somebody gnawed the thoracic here. Nine hoe cuts, and then very careful."

Nine hoe cuts—and then Anteros, using a mason's trowel, unearthed the old gnawed bone very carefully. Yes, Howard said almost angrily, it was a sixth thoracic of a mastodon. Robert Derby said it was a fifth or a sixth; it is not easy to tell.

"Leave the digging for a while, Anteros," Steinleser said. "I want to record and photograph and take a few measurements here."

Terrence Burdock and Magdalen Mobley were working at the bottom of the chimney rock, at the bottom of the fluting that ran the whole height of it like a core sample.

"Get Anteros over here and see what he can uncover in sixty seconds," Terrence offered.

"Oh him! He'll just uncover some of his own things."

"What do you mean, his own things? Nobody could have made an intrusion here. It's hard sandstone."

"And harder flint here," Magdalen said. "I might have

known it. Pass the damned thing up. I know just about what it says anyhow."

"What it says? What do you mean? But it is marked! And it's large and dressed rough. Who'd carve in flint?"

"Somebody real stubborn, just like flint," Magdalen said. "All right then, let's have it out. Anteros! Get this out in one piece. And do it without shattering it or tumbling the whole thing down on us. He can do it, you know, Terrence. He can do things like that."

"What do you know about his doings, Magdalen? You never saw or heard about the poor man till last night."

"Oh well, I know that it'll turn out to be the same damned stuff."

Anteros did get it out without shattering it or bringing down the chimney column. A cleft with a digging bar, three sticks of the stuff and a cap, and he touched the leads to the battery when he was almost on top of the charge. The blast, it sounded as if the whole sky were falling down on them, and some of those sky-blocks were quite large stones. The ancients wondered why fallen pieces of the sky should always be dark rock-stuff and never sky-blue clear stuff. The answer is that it is only pieces of the night sky that ever fall, even though they may sometimes be most of the daytime in falling, such is the distance. And the blast that Anteros set off did bring down rocky hunks of the night sky even though it was broad daylight. They brought down darker rocks than any of which the chimney was composed.

Still, it was a small blast. The chimney tottered but did not collapse. It settled back uneasily on its base. And the flint block was out in the clear.

"A thousand spearheads and arrowheads could be shattered and chipped out of that hunk," Terrence marveled. "That flint block would have been a primitive fortune for a primitive man."

"I had several such fortunes," Anteros said dully, "and this one I preserved and dedicated."

They had all gathered around it.

"Oh the poor man!" Ethyl suddenly exclaimed. But she was not looking at any of the men. She was looking at the stone.

"I wish he'd get off that kick," Magdalen sputtered angrily. "I don't care *how* rich he is. I can pick up better stuff than him in the alleys."

"What are the women chirping about?" Terrence asked. "But those do look like true glyphs. Almost like Aztec, are they not, Steinleser?"

"Nahuat-Tanoan, cousins-german to the Aztec, or should I say cousins-yaqui?"

"Call it anything, but can you read it?"

"Probably. Give me eight or ten hours on it and I should come up with a contingent reading of many of the glyphs. We can hardly expect a rational rendering of the message, however. All Nahuat-Tanoan translations so far have been gibberish."

"And remember, Terrence, that Steinleser is a slow reader," Magdalen said spitefully. "And he isn't very good at interpreting *other* signs either."

Steinleser was sullen and silent. How had his face come to bear those deep livid claw-marks today?

They moved a lot of rock and rubble that morning, took quite a few pictures, wrote up bulky notes. There were constant finds as the divided party worked up the shag-slash in the mound and the core-flute of the chimney. There were no more really startling discoveries; no more turned pots of the proto-Plano period; how could there be? There were no more predicted and perfect points of the late Folsom, but there were broken and unpredictable points. No other mastodon thoracic was found, but bones were uncovered of *bison latifrons,* of dire wolf, of coyote, of man. There were some anomalies in the relationships of the things discovered, but it was not as fishy as it had been in the early morning, not as fishy as when Anteros had announced and then dug out the shards of the pot, the three points, the mastodon bone. The things now were as authentic as they were expected, and yet their very profusion had still the smell of a small fish.

And that Anteros was one digging man. He moved the sand, he moved the stone, he missed nothing. And at noon he disappeared.

An hour later he reappeared in a glossy station wagon, coming out of a thicketed ravine where no one would have expected a way. He had been to town. He brought a variety of cold cuts, cheeses, relishes, and pastries, a couple cases of cold beer, and some V.O.

"I thought you were a poor man, Anteros," Terrence chided.

"I told you that I was a rich old poor man. I have nine thousand acres of grassland, I have three thousand head of cattle, I have alfalfa land and clover land and corn land and hay-grazer land–"

"Oh, knock it off!" Magdalen snapped.

"I have other things," Anteros finished sullenly.

They ate, they rested, they worked the afternoon. Magdalen worked as swiftly and solidly as did Anteros. She was young, she was stocky, she was light-burned-dark. She was not at all beautiful. (Ethyl was.) She could have any man there any time she wanted to. (Ethyl couldn't.) She was Magdalen, the often unpleasant, the mostly casual, the suddenly intense one. She was the tension of the party, the string of the bow.

"Anteros!" she called sharply just at sundown.

"The turtle?" he asked. "The turtle that is under the ledge out of the current where the backwater curls in reverse? But he is fat and happy and he has never harmed anything except for food or fun. I know you do not want me to get that turtle."

"I do! There's eighteen pounds of him. He's fat. He'll be good. Only eighty yards, where the bank crumbles down to Green River, under the lower ledge that's shale that looks like slate, two feet deep—"

"I know where he is. I will go get the fat turtle," Anteros said. "I myself am the fat turtle. I am the Green River." He went to get it.

"Oh that damned poetry of his!" Magdalen spat when he was gone.

Anteros brought back the fat turtle. He looked as if he'd weigh twenty-five pounds; but if Magdalen said he weighed eighteen pounds, then it was eighteen.

"Start cooking, Ethyl," Magdalen said. Magdalen was a mere undergraduate girl permitted on the digging by sheer good fortune. The others of the party were all archeologists of moment. Magdalen had no right to give orders to anyone, except her born right.

"I don't know how to cook a turtle," Ethyl complained.

"Anteros will show you how."

"The late evening smell of newly exposed excavation!" Terrence Burdock burbled as they lounged around the campfire a little later, full of turtle and V.O. and feeling rakishly wise. "The exposed age can be guessed by the very timbre of the smell, I believe."

"Timbre of the smell! What is your nose wired up to?" from Magdalen.

And, indeed, there was something time-evocative about the smell of the diggings: cool, at the same time musty and musky, ripe with old stratified water and compressed death. Stratified time.

"It helps if you already know what the exposed age is," said Howard Steinleser. "Here there is an anomaly. The chimney sometimes acts as if it were younger than the mound. The chimney cannot be young enough to include written rock, but it is."

"Archeology is made up entirely of anomalies," said Terrence, "rearranged to make them fit in a fluky pattern. There'd be no system to it otherwise."

"Every science is made up entirely of anomalies rearranged to fit," said Robert Derby. "Have you unriddled the glyph-stone, Howard?"

"Yes, pretty well. Better than I expected. Charles August can verify it, of course, when we get it back to the university. It is a non-royal, non-tribal, non-warfare, non-hunt declaration. It does not come under any of the usual radical signs, any of the categories. It can only be categorized as uncategoried or personal. The translation will be rough."

"Rocky is the word," said Magdalen.

"On with it, Howard," Ethyl cried.

" 'You are the freedom of wild pigs in the sour-grass, and the nobility of badgers. You are the brightness of serpents and the soaring of vultures. You are passion of mesquite bushes on fire with lightning. You are serenity of toads.' "

"You've got to admit he's got a different line," said Ethyl. "Your own love notes were less acrid, Terrence."

"What kind of thing is it, Steinleser?" Terrence questioned. "It must have a category."

"I believe Ethyl is right. It's a love poem. 'You are the water in rock cisterns and the secret spiders in that water. You are the dead coyote lying half in the stream, and you are the old entrapped dreams of the coyote's brains oozing liquid through the broken eyesocket. You are the happy ravening flies about that broken socket.' "

"Oh, hold it, Steinleser," Robert Derby cried. "You can't have gotten all that from scratches on flint. What is 'entrapped dreams' in Nahuat-Tanoan glyph-writing?"

"The solid-person sign next to the hollow-person sign, both enclosed in the night sign—that has always been interpreted as the dream glyph. And here the dream glyph is enclosed in the glyph of the deadfall trap. Yes, I believe it means entrapped dreams. To continue: 'You are the corn-worm in the dark heart of the corn, the naked small bird in the nest. You are the pustules on the sick rabbit, devouring life and flesh and turning it into your own serum. You are stars compressed into charcoal. But you cannot give, you cannot take. Once again you will be broken at the foot of the cliff, and the word will remain unsaid in your swollen and purpled tongue.' "

"A love poem, perhaps, but with a difference," said Robert Derby.

"I never was able to go his stuff, and I tried, I really tried," Magdalen moaned.

"Here is the change of person-subject shown by the canted-eye glyph linked with the self-glyph," Steinleser explained. "It is now a first-person talk. 'I own ten thousand back-loads of corn. I own gold and beans and nine buffalo horns full of watermelon seeds. I own the loincloth that the sun wore on his fourth journey across the sky. Only three loincloths in the world are older and more valued than this. I cry out to you in a big voice like the hammering of herons' (that sound-verb-particle is badly translated, the hammer being not a modern pounding hammer but a rock angling, chipping hammer) 'and the belching of buffalos. My love is sinewy as entwined snakes, it is steadfast as the sloth, it is like a feathered arrow shot into your abdomen–such is my love. Why is my love unrequited?' "

"I challenge you, Steinleser," Terrance Burdock cut in. "What is the glyph for 'unrequited'?"

"The glyph of the extended hand–with all the fingers bent backwards. It goes on, 'I roar to you. Do not throw yourself down. You believe you are on the hanging sky bridge, but you are on the terminal cliff. I grovel before you. I am no more than dog-droppings.' "

"You'll notice he said that and not me," Magdalen burst out. There was always a fundamental incoherence about Magdalen.

"Ah–continue, Steinleser," said Terrence. "The girl is daft, or she dreams out loud."

"That is all of the inscription, Terrence, except for a final glyph which I don't understand. Glyph writing takes a lot of room. That's all the stone would hold."

"What is the glyph that you don't understand, Howard?"

"It's the spear-thrower glyph entwined with the time glyph. It sometimes means 'flung forward or beyond.' But what does it mean here?"

"It means 'continued,' dummy, 'continued,' " Magdalen said. "Do not fear. There'll be more stones."

"I think it's beautiful," said Ethyl Burdock, "in its own context, of course."

"Then why don't you take him on, Ethyl, in his own context, of course?" Magdalen asked. "Myself, I don't care how many back-loads of corn he owns. I've had it."

"Take whom on, dear?" Ethyl asked. "Howard Steinleser can interpret the stones, but who can interpret our Magdalen?"

"Oh, I can read her like a rock," Terrence Burdock smiled. But he couldn't.

But it had fastened on them. It was all about them and through them: the brightness of serpents and the serenity of toads, the secret spiders in the water, the entrapped dreams oozing through the broken eyesocket, the pustules of the sick rabbit, the belching of buffalo, and the arrow shot into the abdomen. And around it all was the night smell of flint and turned earth and chuckling streams, the mustiness, and the special muskiness which bears the name Nobility of Badgers.

They talked archeology and myth talk. Then it was steep night, and the morning of the third day.

Oh, the sample digging went well. This was already a richer mound than Spiro, though the gash in it was but a small promise of things to come. And the curious twin of the mound, the broken chimney, confirmed and confounded and contradicted. There was time gone wrong in the chimney, or at least in the curious fluted core of it; the rest of it was normal enough, and sterile enough.

Anteros worked that day with a soft sullenness, and Magdalen brooded with a sort of lightning about her.

"Beads, glass beads!" Terrence Burdock exploded angrily. "All right! Who is the hoaxer in our midst? I will not tolerate this at all." Terrence had been angry of face all day. He was clawed deeply, as Steinleser had been the day before, and he was sour on the world.

"There have been glass-bead caches before, Terrence, hundreds of them," Robert Derby said softly.

"There have been hoaxers before, hundreds of them," Terrence howled. "These have 'Hong Kong Contemporary' written all over them, damned cheap glass beads sold by the pound. They have no business in a stratum of around the year seven hundred. All right, who is guilty?"

"I don't believe that any one of us is guilty, Terrence," Ethyl put in mildly. "They are found four feet in from the slant surface of the mound. Why, we've cut through three hundred years of vegetable loam to get to them, and certainly the surface was eroded beyond that."

"We are scientists," said Steinleser. "We find these. Others have found such. Let us consider the improbabilities of it."

It was noon, so they ate and rested and considered the improbabilities. Anteros had brought them a great joint of white pork, and they made sandwiches and drank beer and ate pickles.

"You know," said Robert Derby, "that beyond the rank impossibility of glass beads found so many times where they *could not be found,* there is a real mystery about *all* early Indian beads, whether of bone, stone, or antler. There are millions and millions of these fine beads with pierced holes finer than any piercer ever found. There are residues, there are centers of every other Indian industry, and there is evolution of every other tool. Why have there been these millions of pierced beads, and never one piercer? There was no technique to make so fine a piercer. How were they done?"

Magdalen giggled. "Bead-spitter," she said.

"Bead-spitter! You're out of your fuzzy mind," Terrence erupted. "That's the silliest and least sophisticated of all Indian legends."

"But it *is* the legend," said Robert Derby, "the legend of more than thirty separate tribes. The Carib Indians of Cuba said that they got their beads from Bead-spitters. The Indians of Panama told Balboa the same thing. The Indians of the pueblos told the same story to Coronado. Every Indian community had an Indian who was its Bead-spitter. There are Creek and Alabama and Koasati stories of Bead-spitter; see Swanton's collections. And his stories were taken down within living memory.

"More than that, when European trade-beads were first introduced, there is one account of an Indian receiving some and saying, 'I will take some to Bead-spitter. If he sees them, he can spit them too.' And that Bead-spitter did then spit them by the bushel. There was never any other Indian account of the origin of their beads. *All* were spit by a Bead-spitter."

"Really, this is very unreal," Ethyl said. Really it was.

"Hog hokey! A Bead-spitter of around the year seven hundred could not spit future beads, he could not spit cheap Hong Kong glass beads of the present time!" Terrence was very angry.

"Pardon me, yes sir, he could," said Anteros. "A Bead-spitter can spit future beads, if he faces North when he spits. That has always been known."

Terrence was angry, he fumed and poisoned the day for them, and the claw marks on his face stood out livid purple. He was angrier yet when he said that the curious dark capping rock on top of the chimney was dangerous, that it would fall and kill someone; and Anteros said that there was no such capping rock on the chimney, that

Terrence's eyes were deceiving him, that Terrence should go sit in the shade and rest.

And Terrence became excessively angry when he discovered that Magdalen was trying to hide something that she had discovered in the fluted core of the chimney. It was a large and heavy shale-stone, too heavy even for Magdalen's puzzling strength. She had dragged it out of the chimney flute, tumbled it down to the bottom, and was trying to cover it with rocks and scarp.

"Robert, mark the extraction point!" Terrence called loudly. "It's quite plain yet. Magdalen, stop that! Whatever it is, it must be examined now."

"Oh, it's just more of the damned same thing! I wish he'd let me alone. With his kind of money he can get plenty girls. Besides, it's private, Terrence. You don't have any business reading it."

"You are hysterical, Magdalen, and you may have to leave the digging site."

"I wish I could leave. I can't. I wish I could love. I can't. Why isn't it enough that I die?"

"Howard, spend the afternoon on this," Terrence ordered. "It has writing of a sort on it. If it's what I think it is, it scares me. It's too recent to be in any eroded chimney rock formation, Howard, and it comes from far below the top. Read it."

"A few hours on it and I may come up with something. I never saw anything like it either. What did you think it was, Terrence?"

"What do you think I think it is? It's much later than the other, and that one was impossible. I'll not be the one to confess myself crazy first."

Howard Steinleser went to work on the incised stone; and two hours before sundown they brought him another one, a gray soapstone block from higher up. Whatever this was covered with, it was not at all the same thing that covered the shale-stone.

And elsewhere things went well, too well. The old fishiness was back on it. No series of finds could be so perfect, no petrification could be so well ordered.

"Robert," Magdalen called down to Robert Derby just at sunset, "in the high meadow above the shore, about four hundred yards down, just past the old fence line–"

"–there is a badger hole, Magdalen. Now you have me doing it, seeing invisible things at a distance. And if I take a carbine and stroll down there quietly, the badger will stick his head out just as I get there (I being strongly downwind of him), and I'll blam him between the eyes. He'll be a big one, fifty pounds."

"Thirty. Bring him, Robert. You're showing a little understanding at last."

"But, Magdalen, badger is rampant meat. It's seldom eaten."

"May not the condemned girl have what she wishes for her last meal? Go get it, Robert."

Robert went. The voice of the little carbine was barely heard at that distance. Soon, Robert brought back the dead badger.

"Cook it, Ethyl," Magdalen ordered.

"Yes, I know. And if I don't know how, Anteros will show me." But Anteros was gone. Robert found him on a sundown knoll with his shoulders hunched. The odd man was sobbing silently and his face seemed to be made out of dull pumice stone. But he came back to aid Ethyl in preparing the badger.

"If the first of today's stones scared you, the second should have lifted the hair right off your head, Terrence," Howard Steinleser said.

"It does, it does. All the stones are too recent to be in a chimney formation, but this last one is an insult. It isn't two hundred years old, but there's a thousand years of strata above it. What time is deposited there?"

They had eaten rampant badger meat and drunk inferior whisky (which Anteros, who had given it to them, didn't know was inferior), and the muskiness was both inside them and around them. The campfire sometimes spit angrily with small explosions, and its glare reached high when it did so. By one such leaping glare, Terrence Burdock saw that the curious dark capping rock was once more on the top of the chimney. He thought he had seen it there in the daytime; but it had not been there after he had sat in the shade and rested, and it had absolutely not been there when he climbed the chimney itself to be sure.

"Let's have the second chapter and then the third, Howard," Ethyl said. "It's neater that way."

"Yes. Well, the second chapter (the first and lowest and apparently the earliest rock we came on today) is written in a language that no one ever saw written before; and yet it's no great trouble to read it. Even Terrence guessed what it was and it scared him. It is Anadarko-Caddo hand-talk graven in stone. It is what is called the sign language of the Plains Indians copied down in formalized pictograms. And it *has* to be very recent, within the last three hundred years. Hand-talk was fragmentary at the first coming of the Spanish, and well developed at the first coming of the French. It was an explosive development, as such things go, worked out within a hundred years. This rock has to be younger than its *situs,* but it was absolutely found in place."

"Read it, Howard, read it," Robert Derby called. Robert was feeling fine and the rest of them were gloomy tonight.

" 'I own three hundred ponies,' Steinleser read the rock out of his memory. 'I own two days' ride north and east and south, and one day's ride west. I give you all. I blast out with a big voice like fire in tall trees, like the explosion of crowning pine trees. I cry like closing-in wolves, like the high voice of the lion, like the hoarse scream of torn calves. Do you not destroy yourself again! You are the dew on crazy-weed in the morning. You are the swift crooked wings of the night-hawk, the dainty feet of the skunk, you are the juice of the sour squash. Why can you not take or give? I am the humpbacked bull of the high plains, I am the river itself and the stagnant pools left by the river, I am the raw earth and the rocks. Come to me, but do not come so violently as to destroy yourself.'

"Ah, that was the text of the first rock of the day, the Anadarko-Caddo hand-talk graven in stone. And final pictograms which I don't understand: a shot-arrow sign, and a boulder beyond."

" 'Continued on next rock,' of course," said Robert Derby. "Well, why *wasn't* hand-talk ever written down? The signs are simple and easily stylized and they were understood by many different tribes. It would have been natural to write it."

"Alphabetical writing was in the region *before* hand-talk was well developed," Terrence Burdock said. "In fact, it was the coming of the Spanish that gave the impetus to hand-talk. It was really developed for communication between Spanish and Indian, not between Indian and Indian. And yet, I believe, hand-talk *was* written down once; it was the beginning of the Chinese pictographs. And there also it had its beginning as communication between differing peoples. Depend on it, if all mankind had always been of a single language, there would never have been any written language developed at all. Writing always began as a bridge, and there had to be some chasm for it to bridge."

"We have one to bridge here," said Steinleser. "That whole chimney is full of rotten smoke. The highest part of it should be older than the lowest part of the mound, since the mound was built on a base eroded away from the chimney formation. But in many ways they seem to be contemporary. We must all be under a spell here. We've worked two days on this, parts of three days, and the total impossibility of the situation hasn't struck us yet.

"The old Nahuatlan glyphs for Time are the chimney glyphs. Present time is a lower part of a chimney and fire burning at the base. Past time is black smoke from a chimney, and future time is white smoke from a chimney. There was a signature glyph running through our yesterday's stone which I didn't and don't understand. It seemed to indicate something coming down out of the chimney rather than going up it."

"It really doesn't look much like a chimney," Magdalen said.

"And a maiden doesn't look much like dew on crazyweed in the morning, Magdalen," Robert Derby said, "but we recognize these identities."

They talked a while about the impossibility of the whole business.

"There are scales on our eyes," Steinleser said. "The fluted core of the chimney is wrong. I'm not even sure the rest of the chimney is right."

"No, it isn't," said Robert Derby. "We can identify most of the strata of the chimney with known periods of the river and stream. I was above and below today. There is one stretch where the sandstone was not eroded at all, where it stands three hundred yards back from the shifted river and is overlaid with a hundred years of loam and sod. There are other sections where the stone is cut away variously. We can tell when most of the chimney was laid down, we can find its correspondences up to a few hundred years ago. But when were the top ten feet of it laid down? There were no correspondences anywhere to that. The centuries represented by the strata of the top of the chimney, people, those centuries haven't happened yet."

"And when was the dark capping rock on top of it all formed—?" Terrence began. "Ah, I'm out of my mind. It isn't there. I'm demented."

"No more than the rest of us," said Steinleser. "I saw it too, I thought, today. And then I didn't see it again."

"The rock-writing, it's like an old novel that I only half remember," said Ethyl.

"Oh, that's what it is, yes," Magdalen murmured.

"But I don't remember what happened to the girl in it."

"*I* remember what happened to her, Ethyl," Magdalen said.

"Give us the third chapter, Howard," Ethyl asked. "I want to see how it comes out."

"First you should all have whisky for those colds," Anteros suggested humbly.

"But none of us have colds," Ethyl objected.

"You take your own medical advice, Ethyl, and I'll take mine," Terrence said. "I will have whisky. My cold is not rheum but fear-chill."

They all had whisky. They talked a while, and some of them dozed.

"It's late, Howard," Ethyl said after a while. "Let's have the next chapter. Is it the last chapter? Then we'll sleep. We have honest digging to do tomorrow."

"Our third stone, our second stone of the day just past, is another and even later form of writing, and it has never been seen in stone before. It is Kiowa picture writing. The Kiowas did their out-turning spiral writing on buffalo skins dressed almost as fine as vellum. In its more sophisticated form (and this is a copy of that) it is quite late. The Kiowa picture writing probably did not arrive at its excellence until influenced by white artists."

"How late, Steinleser?" Robert Derby asked.

"Not more than a hundred and fifty years old. But I have never seen it copied in stone before. It simply isn't stone-styled. There's a lot of things around here lately that I haven't seen before.

"Well then, to the text, or should I say the pictography? 'You fear the earth, you fear rough ground and rocks, you fear moister earth and rotting flesh, you fear the flesh itself, all flesh is rotting flesh. If you love not rotting flesh, you love not at all. You believe the bridge hanging in the sky, the bridge hung by tendrils and woody vines that diminish as they go up and up till they are no thicker than hairs. There is no sky-bridge, you cannot go upon it. Did you believe that the roots of love grow upside down? They come out of deep earth that is old flesh and brains and hearts and entrails, that is old buffalo bowels and snakes' pizzles, that is black blood and rot and moaning underground. This is old and worn-out and bloody time, and the roots of love grow out of its gore.' "

"You seem to give remarkable detailed translations of the simple spiral pictures, Steinleser, but I begin to get in the mood of it," Terrence said.

"Ah, perhaps I cheat a little," said Steinleser.

"You lie a lot," Magdalen challenged.

"No I do not. There is some basis for every phrase I've used. It goes on: 'I own twenty-two trade rifles. I own ponies. I own Mexico silver, eight-bit pieces. I am rich in all ways. I give all to you. I cry out with big voice like a bear full of mad-weed, like a bullfrog in love, like a stallion rearing against a puma. It is the earth that calls you. I am the earth, woollier than wolves and rougher than rocks. I am the bog earth that sucks you in. You cannot give, you cannot take, you cannot love, you think there is something else, you think there is a sky-bridge you may loiter on without crashing down. I am bristled-boar earth, there is no other. You will come to me in the morning. You will come to me easy and with grace. Or you will come to me reluctant and you be shattered in every bone and member of you. You be broken by our encounter. You be shattered as by a lightning bolt striking up from the earth. I am the red calf which is in the writings. I am the rotting red earth. Live in the morning or die in the morning, but remember that love in death is better than no love at all.' "

"Oh brother! Nobody gets that stuff from such kid pictures, Steinleser," Robert Derby moaned.

"Ah well, that's the end of the spiral picture. And a Kiowa spiral pictograph ends with either an in-sweep or an out-sweep line. This ends with an out-sweep, which means—"

" 'Continued on next rock,' that's what it means," Terrence cried roughly.

"You won't find the next rocks," Magdalen said. "They're hidden, and most of the time they're not there yet, but they will go on and on. But for all that, you'll read it in the rocks tomorrow morning. I want it to be over with. Oh, I don't know what I want!"

"I believe I know what you want tonight, Magdalen," Robert Derby said.

But he didn't.

The talk trailed off, the fire burned down, they went to their sleeping sacks.

Then it was long jagged night, and the morning of the fourth day. But wait! In Nahuat-Tanoan legend, the world ends on the fourth morning. All the lives we lived or thought we lived had been but dreams of third night. The loincloth that the sun wore on the fourth day's journey was not so valuable as one has made out. It was worn for no more than an hour or so.

And, in fact, there was something terminal about fourth morning. Anteros had disappeared. Magdalen had disappeared. The chimney rock looked greatly diminished in its bulk (something had gone out of it) and much crazier in its broken height. The sun had come up a garish gray-orange color through fog. The signature-glyph of the first stone dominated the ambient. It was as if something were coming down from the chimney, a horrifying smoke; but it was only noisome morning fog.

No it wasn't. There was something else coming down from the chimney, or from the hidden sky: pebbles, stones, indescribable bits of foul oozings, the less fastidious pieces of the sky; a light nightmare rain had begun to fall there; the chimney was apparently beginning to crumble.

"It's the damnedest thing I ever heard about," Robert

Derby growled. "Do you think that Magdalen really went off with Anteros?" Derby was bitter and fumatory this morning and his face was badly clawed.

"Who is Magdalen? Who is Anteros?" Ethyl Burdock asked.

Terrence Burdock was hooting from high on the mound. "All come up," he called. "Here is a find that will make it all worthwhile. We'll have to photo and sketch and measure and record and witness. It's the finest basalt head I've ever seen, man-sized, and I suspect that there's a man-sized body attached to it. We'll soon clean it and clear it. Gah! What a weird fellow he was!"

But Howard Steinleser was studying a brightly colored something that he held in his two hands.

"What is it, Howard? What are you doing?" Derby demanded.

"Ah, I believe this is the next stone in the sequence. The writing is alphabetical but deformed, there is an element missing. I believe it is in modern English, and I will solve the deformity and see it true in a minute. The text of it seems to be–"

Rocks and stones were coming down from the chimney, and fog, amnesic and wit-stealing fog.

"Steinleser, are you all right?" Robert Derby asked with compassion. "That isn't a stone that you hold in your hand."

"It isn't a stone. I thought it was. What is it then?"

"It is the fruit of the Osage orange tree, the American Meraceous. It isn't a stone, Howard." And the thing was a tough, woody, wrinkled mock-orange, as big as a small melon.

"You have to admit that the wrinkles look a little bit like writing, Robert."

"Yes, they look a little like writing, Howard. Let us go up where Terrence is bawling for us. You've read too many stones. And it isn't safe here."

"Why go up, Howard? The other thing is coming down."

It was the bristled-boar earth reaching up with a rumble. It was a lightning bolt struck upward out of the earth, and it got its prey. There was explosion and roar. The dark capping rock was jerked from the top of the chimney and slammed with terrible force to the earth, shattering with a great shock. And something else that had been on that capping rock. And the whole chimney collapsed about them.

She was broken by the encounter. She was shattered in every bone and member of her. And she was dead.

"Who—who is she?" Howard Steinleser stuttered.

"Oh God! Magdalen, of course!" Robert Derby cried.

"I remember her a little bit. Didn't understand her. She put out like an evoking moth but she wouldn't be had. Near clawed the face off me the other night when I misunderstood the signals. She believed there was a sky-bridge. It's in a lot of the mythologies. But there isn't one, you know. Oh well."

"The girl is dead! Damnation! What are you doing grubbing in those stones?"

"Maybe she isn't dead in them yet, Robert. I'm going to read what's here before something happens to them. This capping rock that fell and broke, it's impossible, of course. It's a stratum that hasn't been laid down yet. I always did want to read the future and I may never get another chance."

"You fool! The girl's dead! Does nobody care? Terrence, stop bellowing about your find. Come down. The girl's dead."

"Come up, Robert and Howard," Terrence insisted. "Leave that broken stuff down there. It's worthless. But nobody ever saw anything like this."

"Do come up, men," Ethyl sang. "Oh, it's a wonderful piece! I never saw anything like it in my life."

"Ethyl, is the whole morning mad?" Robert Derby demanded as he came up to her. "She's dead. Don't you really remember her? Don't you remember Magdalen?"

"I'm not sure. Is she the girl down there? Isn't she the same girl who's been hanging around here a couple days? She shouldn't have been playing on that high rock. I'm sorry she's dead. But just look what we're uncovering here!"

"Terrence. Don't *you* remember Magdalen?"

"The girl down there? She's a little bit like the girl that clawed the hell out of me the other night. Next time someone goes to town they might mention to the sheriff that there's a dead girl here. Robert, did you ever see a face like this one? And it digs away to reveal the shoulders. I believe there's a whole man-sized figure here. Wonderful, wonderful!"

"Terrence, you're off your head. Well, do you remember Anteros?"

"Certainly, the twin of Eros, but nobody ever made much of the symbol of unsuccessful love. Thunder! That's the name for him! It fits him perfectly. We'll call him Anteros."

Well, it *was* Anteros, lifelike in basalt stone. His face was contorted. He was sobbing soundlessly and frozenly and his shoulders were hunched with emotion. The carving was fascinating in its miserable passion, his stony love unrequited. Perhaps he was more impressive now than he would be when he was cleaned. He was earth, he was earth itself. Whatever period the carving belonged to, it was outstanding in its power.

"The live Anteros, Terrence. Don't you remember our digging man, Anteros Manypenny?"

"Sure. He didn't show up for work this morning, did he? Tell him he's fired."

"Magdalen is dead! She was one of us! Dammit, she was the main one of us!" Robert Derby cried. Terrence and

Ethyl Burdock were earless to his outburst. They were busy uncovering the rest of the carving.

And down below, Howard Steinleser was studying dark broken rocks before they would disappear, studying a stratum that hadn't been laid down yet, reading a foggy future.

To Sport with Amaryllis

by Richard Hill

The neon lights of *Fuzzy Lipschits' Tit City Topless Taco Parlor and Ye Olde Donut Shoppe* blinked expensively and seductively through the smog. A neon girl's breasts became donuts, then tacos, then donuts again, as Harley Mode tooled his 74 dress bike smoothly into the parking lot, pleasantly aware of the soft pressure of his wife, Amaryllis, on the seat behind him. He found a space and cut the engine, set the stand and turned to her. "Honey, we're here."

She was beautiful like this, he thought, her eyes closed in pleasure and her plump, dungaree-encased thighs unaware that the vibration had stopped. God, she loved to ride that bike. He kissed her on an eyelid, darkened either by cosmetics or soot, and hefted a soft breast under her T-shirt. "Amaryllis, this is it. We're here. Remember Andy Warhol, maybe Andy Warhol will be here tonight."

Amaryllis moved slowly on the seat and opened her eyes. "Jesus, Harley, that was a good ride. That was a gooood ride."

"I know," said Harley fondly, helping her off the bike. Amaryllis was still walking tenderly when the doorman smiled and admitted them.

It was clear immediately that Andy Warhol was not there, at least not yet, though there was a gigantic photograph of him hanging from the ceiling, in which he appeared to be accepting a taco and a Margarita from one of Fuzzy's topless waitresses. The photo nagged at Harley. He didn't like to think about it but he had the suspicion it might be doctored; it looked too much like an *Esquire* cover. But he put that from his mind, as a waitress showed them to a booth. After all, there was the Early American furniture, a nice eclectic touch, he thought, and the

Visi-Box which showed underground movies, and the Chem-Sac sound system, and, of course, the waitresses, not a minus 37 in the lot. He noticed a pudgy man in a sharkskin suit and wondered if it might be Lipschits himself. The man was standing in a corner, looking worried, and that did not improve Harley's mood.

Amaryllis and Harley had really wanted to see Andy Warhol, especially Amaryllis, who had visions of herself as a star, but this hardly seemed the right crowd for it. Tourists occupied a few booths, blushing and elbowing one another when a waitress walked by. A dark man in a turban sat alone near the bar and shot frame after frame with his 35-millimeter camera. Some high-school kids were getting juiced on $2.50 Margaritas near the front door. And a very obviously stoned Negro hummed "Bernie's Tune" in a booth behind them. Altogether a drag.

Harley tried to soften the blow. "Hey, dig, they've got Chem-Sac here," he said with false enthusiasm. Amaryllis was unmoved. But Harley read from the sampler on the wall anyway, hoping something would cheer her: *Chem-Sac is a dramatic innovation in the world of popular as well as serious music. The sound you hear comes from strings of various lengths and tensions being parted by the action of a powerful space-age acid. The musician pours from a vial in each hand on the string or strings of his choice, and the sound of the string parting is amplified by the most sophisticated equipment money can buy. The music is taped and played continuously for your listening pleasure.*

"Bullshit," said Amaryllis, and they sat silently for a while as the various sized and tensioned strings made a variety of boings and pyoings and pings. "The squares are here and you know it," she said finally. "He's not coming."

"Maybe not," Harley said softly. "You wanta split?"

"I'm too uptight. Let's have a drink first. Get me a Margarita . . . and a donut."

Harley sensed the order was a form of protest and signaled quickly for a waitress. The one who came was Wanda, whom they knew from the days when she and Amaryllis had worked together in the Lace Spittoon as Israeli belly dancers. When the topless craze came, Amaryllis, who had beautiful but almost nippleless breasts, had bitterly gone back to work as a masseuse while Wanda, amply nippled, went topless. They realized with some surprise that she was also bottomless.

"Wanda, what's happening?" asked Amaryllis, brightening at the prospect of a raid.

"Fuzzy just gave the word to go bottomless," said Wanda, nervously shielding herself with her order book. "Figures a raid will hypo business until he thinks of something else. It was either that or let some of us go."

So that was Lipschits he saw, thought Harley with some excitement. It was a name of some consequence in the avant-garde. At least they had seen him.

"But what's the shyness routine?" asked Amaryllis, who opposed any form of repression.

"This damn appendix scar," said Wanda. "Fuzzy almost didn't let me come on with the others, until I convinced him the leather crowd might dig it. I gotta keep it covered from the straights."

"Like us?" asked Amaryllis, delighted with the irony. They all laughed at this, and Harley flushed with pleasure at seeing his wife happy again.

Wanda brought their order and hurried off to serve a growing crowd. It was amazing how quickly word spread along the freeways. Harley entertained briefly the idea of Warhol coming after all, but didn't want to raise Amaryllis' hopes. There were still a lot of tourists around, and another crowd of teenies from the Strip. The turbaned man had a movie camera now and was zooming madly over his untouched tequila. The stoned spade was still behind them, still humming softly to himself Cannonball's solo on "Milestones" or an occasional June Christy tune. But there was still hope. They ordered again, and again, until Harley began to get jumpy from caffeine and switched to tequila and Amaryllis began to get drunk and switched to coffee. (Wouldn't do to be gassed if he did come.)

But as the evening wore on, the crowd thinned and hope began to wane. Harley had been afraid to speak for over an hour, not wanting to give Amaryllis a focus for her despair. But when a cop walked in, had a cup of coffee, and walked out, he knew it was over.

"Harley," she said, "we've got to talk about our life."

"Sure, baby, anything you want."

"Harley, I've been thinking a lot about it, and I think I know what's wrong. You may not understand it at first, but I think I'm right."

"What is it, sweetheart?"

"Harley, you're square."

He could tell she was serious, and he didn't know what to say.

"Harley, who did you vote for for governor?"

"Honey, you *know*–"

"No bullshit now, Harley, did you vote for Reagan?"

"Amaryllis! How could you–"

"Harley, you voted for him. I knew it at the time. When you came out of the booth I could feel–"

"But it was a protest vote," offered Harley lamely.

"Against who, Harley?"

"Against Jane Wyman. Did you see her in *Johnny Belinda*? It was–"

"Very funny, Harley, but it won't work . . . Harley, something drastic has to happen."

"Christ, baby, how *un*square can I be? I mean I slipped that once, but how about the other things? We've swapped with half the kinky couples in L.A. county. I even joined that computerized swap club and got you a coded bumper sticker for the bike so the guys who liked what they saw could get in touch. I've put up with some weird chicks for your sake, sweetheart."

"Hugh Hefner says–"

"I know what he says. I read his advice to you along with the other millions of people. And you couldn't even use *initials,* for Christ sake. I almost lost my job over that little caper. Really, baby, what else can I *do*?"

While Harley's question hung in the air over the booth, the stoned spade, whose name was really Lamont Cranston, turned slowly in his booth, rose to peer over Harley's shoulder, and said, "Split."

Lamont's mother had been greatly impressed with the powers of her son's radio namesake, and had been in those days unaware of any pejorative connotations attached to Cranston's alias. Lamont Cranston the younger, seated behind the Modes, rarely used the other name anyway, though he was, as they would learn, a shadowy character.

"What did you say?" asked Amaryllis, somewhat recovered from the shock.

"I said split," said Cranston. "Cut. Make it."

"We haven't met," said Harley, trying to twist his neck in order to see Cranston.

"Your wife is right. You are a square," said Lamont, moving slowly around into their booth. "But I feel sorry for you both and so I am going to lay the word on you in the following manner: Frisco."

"Frisco?" said Harley and Amaryllis together.

"San Francisco to you, my man," said Lamont. "It is the only place where you are going to lose those bourgeois hangups which so obviously are contributing toward putting you down. I must go now."

"Wait," said Amaryllis, sensing Cranston had something for them. "How will that change anything?"

"You will have split this scene of crassness for a life of grooving, growing your own, and like that," said Cranston with an edge of impatience.

"But why are *you* here?" asked Amaryllis, smelling a contradiction.

"My mission is a secret. You might say I am a kind of

wigging travel agent. Or you might say I am something else. Who knows what evil lurks, man. Dig?"

"But we heard you humming 'Bernie's Tune.' I mean how square is that?" said Amaryllis.

"Which is only toward indicating that my disguise is a success, my dear. Besides which you are not ready to hear the real music I could lay on you humming or otherwise, making this acid string shit sound like Strauss waltzes. I have told you what you must do and I must cut." And Lamont left, humming "Work Song" and making weird faces at the turbaned cameraman.

"Well, what do you make of that?" asked Harley.

"We're packing tonight," said Amaryllis, with a dreamy look as though she too heard a different kind of music now.

Harley knew he couldn't fight it. He resigned his position in the Median Strip Division of the Highway Maintenance Department and turned in his keys to the lawnmower barn. Amaryllis told Igor at Rub-a-Rama to stick the massage business. They called a realtor at nine a.m. and sold their split level with pool at ten for five grand more than they paid for it. They decided, for Amaryllis' sake, to take the bike to Frisco, then get a car more suitable to their new way of life. Amaryllis called and canceled at the Swap Agency, and by noon they were on the road.

The long trip was uneventful for Harley (except for losing the way to San Jose), ecstatic for Amaryllis. Harley began to hope that the ten or more orgasms she had on the way up would take the edge off her San Francisco obsession. But she was just as firm when they arrived as when they left.

Things moved quickly as they settled into the Hashbury groove. They rented the former prep room of the now defunct Dimlawn Funeral Home, Amaryllis taking great pride in adapting the various prep tables and gurnies to their more homely uses. Other couples and groups occupied other rooms in the same building and there was a great camaraderie among the Dimlawn Group, as they called themselves. To celebrate the Modes' arrival, a hashish punch was made in a left-behind embalming pump, and the party later delighted a busload of conventioning Seventh Day Adventists by weaving down the street wearing decayed wreaths and crying "We are ready."

There was no longer any need for the Swap Club, although it took the Modes some time to adjust to the different hygienic habits of the Dimlawners. Amaryllis, in fact, came down with a good case, and gave it to Harley so he could go for penicillin, an act which some of the Dimlawners considered a cop-out.

They bought a more appropriate wardrobe, Harley finally finding a use for some of the junk he'd bought on a family vacation to Cherokee, and a new car. It was a beauty, an authentic 1948 Citroën Saloon Car, used by the Vichy High Command and still showing bullet holes inflicted by the Free French. Or so the topless Indian maiden salesgirl at *Honest Fuzzy Lipschits' Old West Auto Mart and Art Gallery* told them. Fuzzy, it seemed, had seen the handwriting on the wall for tacos and had bought this agency. Then he had moved on, selling his name to a smaller entrepreneur named Albert Schweitzer (no relation), who now owned the business. Anyway, it was a beautiful car and life among the Dimlawners was, for a while, sweet.

Then, slowly, something began to grow between them again. Somehow, despite all their efforts, they could not quite fit into the Dimlawn world. For one thing, everyone knew the Modes had money. The profit on the house, plus a sizeable pension refund from the Highway Maintenance Department, made quite a bundle. And since there was little to spend it on that would not appear middle class to the Dimlawners, it sat in the Hashbury National Bank drawing five percent. Then, at the worst possible time,

Amaryllis discovered, hidden in the coffin crate that was Harley's armoire, his stash of Max Rafferty campaign literature.

He knew he should have destroyed it, but somehow he couldn't bring himself to do it. A woman had given it to him on the street, and he had carelessly stuffed it into his serape. Once, while Amaryllis was attending her night course in the *Kama Sutra,* he had taken it out and read it with the same guilty thrill he used to get from the nude primitives in *National Geographic.* But then he had put it back and forgotten about it until the terrible discovery.

They both recognized it as a crisis. But it wouldn't do to have it out where the Dimlawners would hear. So they went to *Fuzzy's Nitty Gritty City, Soul Food Restaurant and Rare Chinchilla Ranch,* the town's latest rage. From a waitress, nude except for body paint and graffiti, they ordered Chitterlings Amandine, Grits with Garlic Butter, and Ripple Wine. Amaryllis seemed willing to set the crisis aside until they had eaten. Finally, moving a watermelon seed pensively on her plate, she spoke:

"Harley, what are we going to do? It's all wrong."

"I won't do it again, baby, I promise I won't."

"But you know you will, Harley. We both know you will. And you know why you will, Harley, my love, you know why? Because *you're still square as a fucking brick.*"

Harley sat shattered as the accusation rang in his ears.

"Still square," echoed a voice nearby, not Amaryllis', and slowly Lamont Cranston materialized. He was shaking his head like a patient mother. "I can see," he said in an injured tone, "that getting you people with it is going to be in the nature of a fantastic hassle. But I am willing to do so by laying this on you: that your hangup is that you are married to each other and liberation depends on your like getting a divorce."

"A divorce," said Harley, half rising. "Now just a minute you goddamn creep. If you—"

"Harley," said Amaryllis softly, with that mystical look again, "he's right."

"Oh, God," said Harley, and took a belt of Ripple.

"You see, baby," she went on, "it's been our problem all along really. Do you remember how our neighbors were shocked when we introduced ourselves as Mr. and Mrs.? How do you think I've felt all these times, at all those parties with people eyeballing us like some freaks?"

"But I've let you do anything–"

"It's not what you *do,* it's how you *feel* when you do it. Don't you see we can't be *really* free until we've shaken this? Can't you see that Cranston here is right?"

But Cranston was not there. He had disappeared, along with Harley's last hope. The next morning they were on the road for Las Vegas.

The place to go, Amaryllis learned, was *Lipschits' Hitch and Ditch, Mud Wedding and Divorce Parlor and Jai Alai Fronton.* Rumor was that Warhol himself had married or divorced there only last week, using Fuzzy's specialty, Marriage à la Mud. The Modes, of course, would have the special too.

Fuzzy's famous Mud Wedding required the couples being joined or parted to roll nude in a gigantic mud bath before the ceremony, thereby adding a sense of mystery to the personality of one's partner. It was remarkable how many divorced couples immediately remarried and vice versa, a trend of which Fuzzy heartily approved. Harley, of course, was more than willing to pay for two ceremonies to have his Amaryllis. He loved her, muddy or no, and wanted to be married to her, even if it was a hangup. But she was adamant, and when they walked away from Fuzzy's that day, still muddy in a place or two, they were just plain Harley and Amaryllis.

Harley had to admit it had done something good for them. Amaryllis was as amorous as he had ever seen her. She could hardly wait until he found a half-hour parking space and joined her in the back seat, that beautiful back seat which still seemed to echo the "Marseillaise." Afterwards, they wandered in a daze, until they had lost all the money they brought from the Hashbury National in slot machines, and until the old dissatisfaction had come to live with them again.

They found themselves driving the Citroën aimlessly through the back streets of Vegas, until finally they came to a lot full of motorcycles. Even at three in the morning, the neon flashed above it, identifying it as *L & C's Machine Scene, Exclusive Agents for the Libidomobile.* The Libidomobile, it turned out, was a bike which was not only tuned for performance, but for satisfying sexual vibrations. They traded the Citroën even.

By the time Harley hit the first red light, he knew Amaryllis had finally found her thing. He looked back at her, bouncing there, with mixed feelings. She had found her thing, and that was fine, but now what about him? What was he supposed to do?

"Honey," he said softly, "where should we go now?"

"I don't care, Harley, Mexico, Alaska, Tibet, Sweden, just *get this mother moving!"*

And so they rode, neither sure where the desert road would take them. He could feel her arms tighten around him now and then with amazing strength, but otherwise he was alone. Left to himself, something inside Harley snapped. The mind he had disciplined so long now fantasized out of control. He dreamed of addressing the Republican Convention. "My friends," he would say, "I give you a man . . ." He saw himself aboard a slim white yacht, drinking all the martinis he had ever wanted. He played golf with Paul Harvey, corresponded with William F. Buckley, Jr., mowed his own yard with a riding mower. He read the *Wall Street Journal* and called his broker. He wandered deliciously through a country club of the mind. As he dreamed, the tears drained from the sides of his goggles and were whipped away by the wind.

Neither of them saw the black limousine pass them in the night. Nor, of course, were they aware of the conversation taking place within, between Mr. Fenton (Fuzzy) Lipschits and his partner. "Tell me, sweetheart," said Fuzzy as he handed the man a drink from the custom bar, "what do the Shadow know new?"

In the Queue

by Keith Laumer

The old man fell just as Farn Hestler's power wheel was passing his place in line, on his way back from the comfort station. Hestler, braking, stared down at the twisted face, a mask of soft, pale leather in which the mouth writhed as if trying to tear itself free of the dying body. Then he jumped from the wheel, bent over the victim. Quick as he was, a lean woman with fingers like gnarled roots was before him, clutching at the old man's fleshless shoulders.

"Tell them *me,* Millicent Dredgewicke Crump," she was shrilling into the vacant face. "Oh, if you only knew what I've been through, how I *deserve* the help–"

Hestler sent her reeling with a deft shove of his foot. He knelt beside the old man, lifted his head.

"Vultures," he said. "Greedy, snapping at a man. Now, I *care.* And you were getting so close to the head of the line. The tales you could tell, I'll bet. An old-timer. Not like these line, er, jumpers," he diverted the obscenity. "I say a man deserves a little dignity at a moment like this–"

"Wasting your time, Jack," a meaty voice said. Hestler glanced up into the hippopotamine features of the man he always thought of as Twentieth Back. "The old coot's dead."

Hestler shook the corpse. "Tell them Argall Y. Hestler!" he yelled into the dead ear. "Argall, that's A-R-G-A-L-L–"

"Break it up," the brassy voice of a line policeman sliced through the babble. "You, get back." A sharp prod lent urgency to the command. Hestler rose reluctantly, his eyes on the waxy face slackening into an expression of horrified astonishment.

"Ghoul," the lean woman snarled. "Line––!" She mouthed the unmentionable word.

"I wasn't thinking of myself," Hestler countered hotly. "But my boy Argall, through no fault of his own—"

"All right, quiet!" the cop snarled. He jerked a thumb at the dead man. "This guy make any disposition?"

"Yes!" the lean woman cried. "He said, to Millicent Dredgewicke Crump, that's M, I, L—"

"She's lying," Hestler cut in. "I happened to catch the name Argall Hestler—right, sir?" He looked brightly at a slack-jawed lad who was staring down at the corpse.

The boy swallowed and looked Hestler in the face.

"Hell, he never said a word," he said, and spat, just missing Hestler's shoe.

"Died intestate," the cop intoned, and wrote a note in his book. He gestured and a cleanup squad moved in, lifted the corpse onto a cart, covered it, trundled it away.

"Close it up," the cop ordered.

"Intestate," somebody grumbled. "Crap!"

"A rotten shame. The slot goes back to the government. Nobody profits. Goddam!" The fat man who had spoken looked around at the others. "In a case like this we ought to get together, have some equitable plan worked out and agreed to in advance—"

"Hey," the slack-jawed boy said. "That's conspiracy!"

"I meant to suggest nothing illegal." The fat man faded back to his place in line. As if by common consent, the small crowd dissipated, sliding into their places with deft footwork. Hestler shrugged and remounted his wheel, putt-putted forward, aware of the envious eyes that followed him. He passed the same backs he always passed, some standing, some sitting on canvas camp stools under sun-faded umbrellas, here and there a nylon queuebana, high and square, some shabby, some, owned by the more fortunate, ornate. He was a lucky man; he had never been a standee, sweating the line exposed to the sun and prying eyes.

It was a bright afternoon. The sun shone down on the vast concrete ramp across which the line snaked from a point lost in distance across the plain. Ahead–not far ahead now, and getting closer every day–was the blank white wall perforated only by the window, the terminal point of the line. Hestler slowed as he approached the Hestler queuebana; his mouth went dry as he saw how close it was to the head of the line now. One, two, three, four slots back! Ye Gods, that meant six people had been processed in the past twelve hours–an unprecedented number. And it meant–Hestler caught his breath–he might reach the window himself, this shift. For a moment, he felt a panicky urge to flee, to trade places with First Back, and then with Second, work his way back to a safe distance again, give himself a chance to think about it, get ready . . .

"Say, Farn." The head of his Cousin Galpert poked from the curtains of the nylon-walled queuebana. "Guess what? I moved up a spot while you were gone."

Hestler folded the wheel and leaned it against the weathered cloth. He waited until Galpert had emerged, then surreptitiously twitched the curtains wide open. The place always smelled fudgy and stale after his cousin had spent half an hour in it while he was away for his comfort break.

"We're getting close to the head," Galpert said excitedly, handing over the lockbox that contained the papers. "I have a feeling–" He broke off as sharp voices were suddenly raised a few spaces behind. A small, pale-haired man with bulging blue eyes was attempting to force himself into line between Third Back and Fifth Back.

"Say, isn't that Four Back?" Hestler asked.

"You don't understand," the little man was whimpering. "I had to go answer an unscheduled call of nature . . ." His weak eyes fixed on Fifth Back, a large, coarse-featured man in a loud shirt and sunglasses. "You said you'd watch my place . . . !"

"So whatta ya think ya got a comfort break for, ya bum? Beat it!"

Lots of people were shouting at the little man now:

"Line-ine-ucker-bucker-line bucker, line bucker . . ."

The little man fell back, covering his ears. The obscene chant gained in volume as other voices took it up.

"But it's my *place,*" the evictee wailed. "Father left it to me when he died, you all remember him . . ." His voice was drowned in the uproar.

"Serves him right," Galpert said, embarrassed by the chant. "A man with no more regard for his inheritance than to walk off and leave it . . ."

They watched the former Fourth Back turn and flee, his hands still over his ears.

After Galpert left on the wheel, Hestler aired the queuebana for another ten minutes, standing stony-faced, arms folded, staring at the back of One Up. His father had told him some stories about One Up, back in the old days, when they'd both been young fellows, near the end of the line. Seemed he'd been quite a cut-up in those days, always joking around with the women close to him in line, offering to trade places for a certain consideration. You didn't see many signs of that now: just a dumpy old man in burst-out shoe-leather, sweating out the line. But he himself was lucky, Hestler reflected. He'd taken over from Father when the latter had had his stroke, a twenty-one thousand two hundred and ninety-four slot jump. Not many young fellows did that well. Not that he was all that young, he'd put in his time in the line; it wasn't as if he didn't deserve the break.

And now, in a few hours maybe, he'd hit the head of the line. He touched the lockbox that contained the old man's papers—and of course his own, and Cluster's and the kids'—everything. In a few hours, if the line kept moving, he could relax, retire, let the kids, with their own places in line, carry on. Let them do as well as their dad had done, making head of the line at under forty-five!

Inside the queuebana it was hot, airless. Hestler pulled off his coat and squatted in the crouch-hammock—not the most comfortable position in the world, maybe, but in full compliance with the Q-law requirement that at least one foot be on the ground at all times, and the head higher than the waist. Hestler remembered an incident years before, when some poor devil without a queuebana had gone to sleep standing up. He'd stood with his eyes closed and his knees bent, and slowly sunk down to a squat; then bobbed slowly up and blinked and gone back to sleep. Up and down, they'd watched him for an hour before he finally let his head drop lower than his belt. They'd pitched him out of line then, and closed ranks. Ah, there'd been some wild times in the queue in the old days, not like now. There was too much at stake now, this near the head. No time for horseplay.

Just before dusk, the line moved up. Three to go! Hestler's heart thumped.

It was dark when he heard the voice whisper: "*Four Up!*"

Hestler jerked wide awake. He blinked, wondering if he'd dreamed the urgent tone.

"Four Up!" the voice hissed again. Hestler twitched the curtain open, saw nothing, pulled his head back in. Then he saw the pale, pinched face, the bulging eyes of Four Back, peering through the vent slot at the rear of the tent.

"You have to help me," the little man said. "You saw what happened; you can make a deposition that I was cheated, that–"

"Look here, what are you doing out of line?" Hestler cut in. "I know you're on-shift, why aren't you holding down a new slot?"

"I . . . I couldn't face it," Four Back said brokenly. "My wife, my children–they're all counting on me."

"You should have thought of that sooner."

"I swear I couldn't help it. It just hit me so suddenly. And–"

"You lost your place. There's nothing I can do."

"If I have to start over now—I'll be seventy when I get to the window!"

"That's not my lookout—"

". . . but if you'll just tell the line police what happened, explain about my special case—"

"You're crazy, I can't do that!"

"But you . . . I always thought you looked like a decent sort—"

"You'd better go. Suppose someone sees me talking to you?"

"I had to speak to you here, I don't know your name, but after all we've been four spaces apart in line for nine years—"

"Go away! Before I call a line cop!"

Hestler had a hard time getting comfortable again after Four Back left. There was a fly inside the queuebana. It was a hot night. The line moved up again, and Hestler had to emerge and roll the queuebana forward. Two spaces to go! The feeling of excitement was so intense that it made Hestler feel a little sick. Two more moves up, and he'd be at the window. He'd open the lockbox, and present the papers, taking his time, getting it all correct, all in order. With a sudden pang he wondered if anyone had goofed, anywhere back along the line, failed to sign anything, missed a notary's seal, or a witness's signature. But they couldn't have. Nothing as dumb as that. For that you could get bounced out of line, lose your place, have to go all the way back—

Hestler shook off the morbid fancies. He was just nervous, that was all. Well, who wouldn't be? After tonight, his whole life would be different; his days of standing in line would be over. He'd have time—all the time in the world to do all the things he hadn't been able to think about all these years . . .

Someone shouted, near at hand. Hestler stumbled out of the queuebana to see Two Up—at the head of the line now—raise his fist and shake it under the nose of the small, black-mustached face in the green eyeshade framed in the window, bathed in harsh white light.

"Idiot! Dumbbell! Jackass!" Two Up yelled. "What do you mean take it back home and have my wife spell out her middle name!"

Two burly line police appeared, shone lights in Two Up's wild face, grabbed his arms, took him away. Hestler trembled as he pushed the queuebana forward a space on its roller-skate wheels. Only one man ahead of him now. He'd be next. But no reason to get all upset; the line had been moving like greased lightning, but it would take a few hours to process the man ahead. He had time to relax, get his nerves soothed down, get ready to answer questions . . .

"I don't understand, sir," the reedy voice of One Up was saying to the small black mustache behind the window. "My papers are all in order, I swear it—"

"You said yourself your father is dead," the small, dry voice of Black Mustache said. "That means you'll have to reexecute Form 56839847565342-B in sextuplicate, with an endorsement from the medical doctor, the residential police, and waivers from Department A, B, C, and so on. You'll find it all, right in the regulations."

"But—but he only died two hours ago: I just received word—"

"Two hours, two years—he's just as dead."

"But—I'll lose my place! If I hadn't mentioned it to you—"

"Then I wouldn't have known about it. But you *did* mention it, quite right, too."

"Couldn't you just pretend I didn't say anything? That the messenger never reached me?"

"Are you suggesting I commit fraud?"

"No . . . no . . ." One Up turned and tottered away, his invalidated papers clutched in his hand. Hestler swallowed hard.

"Next," Black Mustache said.

Hestler's fingers shook visibly as he opened the box. He laid out the salmon-colored papers (twelve copies), the puce papers (nine copies), the lemon-yellow papers (fourteen copies), the lime papers (five copies . . . only five? Could that be right? Had he lost one?). Panic clutched at his chest.

"Salmon-colored: twelve copies." The clerk was frowning ominously.

"Y-yes. Isn't that right?" Hestler stammered.

"Of course." The clerk went on counting papers, making obscure notations in the corners.

It was almost dawn six hours later when the clerk stamped the last paper, licked the last stamp, thrust the stack of processed documents into a slot and looked past Hestler at the next man in line.

Hestler hesitated, holding the empty lockbox in nerveless fingers. It felt abnormally light.

"That's all," the clerk said. "Next."

One Down jostled Hestler getting to the window. He was a small, bandy-legged standee with large, loose lips and long ears. Hestler had never really looked at him before. He felt an urge to tell him all about how it had been, give him a few friendly tips, as an old window veteran to a newcomer. But the man didn't give him a glance.

Moving off, Hestler noticed the queuebana. It looked abandoned, functionless. He thought of all the hours, the days, the years he had spent in it, crouched in the sling . . .

"You can have it," he said on impulse to Two Down, a woman, dumpy, slack-jowled. He gestured toward the queuebana. She made a snorting sound and ignored him. He wandered off down the line, staring curiously at the people in it, at the varied faces and figures, tall, wide, narrow, old, young—not so many of those—dressed in used clothing, with hair combed or uncombed, some with facial hair, some with paint on their lips, all unattractive in their own individual ways.

He encountered Galpert whizzing toward him on the

power wheel. Galpert slowed, gaping, came to a halt. Hestler noticed that his cousin had thin, bony ankles in maroon socks, one of which suffered from perished elastic so that the sock drooped, exposing clay-white skin.

"Farn–what . . . ?"

"All done." Hestler held up the empty lockbox.

"All done . . . ?" Galpert looked across toward the distant window in a bewildered way.

"All done. Not much to it, really."

"Then . . . I . . . I guess I don't need to . . ." Galpert's voice died away.

"No, no need, never again, Galpert."

"Yes, but what . . . ?" Galpert looked at Hestler, looked at the line, back at Hestler. "You coming, Farn?"

"I . . . I think I'll just take a walk for a while. Savor it, you know."

"Well," Galpert said. He started up the wheel and rode slowly off across the ramp.

Suddenly, Hestler was thinking about time–all that time stretching ahead, like an abyss. What would he do with it? He almost called after Galpert, but instead turned and continued his walk along the line. Faces stared past him, over him, through him.

Noon came and went. Hestler obtained a dry hot dog and a paper cup of warm milk from a vendor on a three-wheeler with a big umbrella and a pet chicken perched on the back. He walked on, searching the faces. They were all so ugly. He pitied them, so far from the window. Once he saw Argall and waved; but Argall was looking the other way. He looked back; the window was barely visible, a tiny dark point toward which the line dwindled. What did they think about, standing in line? How they must envy him!

But no one seemed to notice him. Toward sunset he began to feel lonely. He wanted to talk to someone; but none of the faces he passed seemed sympathetic.

It was almost dark when he reached the end of the line.

Beyond, the empty plain stretched toward the dark horizon. It looked cold out there, lonely.

"It looks cold out there," he heard himself say to the oatmeal-faced lad who huddled at the tail of the line, hands in pockets. "And lonely."

"You in line, or what?" the boy asked.

Hestler looked again at the bleak horizon. He came over and stood behind the youth.

"Certainly," he said.

The Living End

by Sonya Dorman

It wasn't easy to get up the long, shallow flight of steps to the big hospital complex, with my belly so big and heavy, but I made it by going very slowly. Went through the mesh helix of the entrance, down a broad corridor to the rear, and entered the Department of Checks and Balances.

I spent several minutes hunting for the Admitting Office, and then was waved to a chair by the lady at the desk. So I sat, waiting; the daily hospital activities went on around me as if I weren't there. They brought in a leg. A yellow ticket was attached with the donor's name and a code number on it. As if in response, the baby gave me a kick, and my knees jerked sympathetically.

A half hour had gone by, and I was bored, in spite of the exhibits. The main one, of course, was the heart in its wired box; pump-pump, fluids ran through from wall-tubes. A printed card explained that it was the only heart ever rejected by thirty-seven recipients in a row. In the center of the dark, pulsing mass, *Mother* was tattooed in a semicircle.

"Miss?" I said to the lady at the desk, but she shook her head brusquely at me. I had to wait some more, which didn't seem right. Not even the holographs could attract my attention anymore. I'd already looked round and round the room staring at the sequence: the Marrow Fungus spores taking hold, little roots probing into the porous bone, extending, being nourished, the pale shelf extruding from a tibia.

The final holograph in the series showed the man, alive and well, with various bulges at brow, elbow, and knee, all of him well-kept with daily injections.

After the leg's number was filed by the lady behind the

desk, who had continued to ignore me in spite of the fact that she knew I was in labor, an attendant came and removed the leg with speed and delicacy.

They brought in a pair of crossed fingers, ticketed. Entered, filed, catalogued, and removed.

"Be with you in a moment," the lady said, flicking me a glance. Her contacts must be old ones, for her lids were pink and her eyes bloodshot. Wouldn't you think she'd take better care of herself? With such excellent care available.

"Name? Address?" she asked me, running a new card into the machine which put it on a spindle and creased the pattern in. We went on through my references and code number. Tick tick, the machine made its record. The baby gave a final heave before another contraction squeezed it into temporary submission. A moment later I spread my knees a little and the child gave its unborn cry.

"Oh, shut him up," the lady said, pulling levers and punching buttons. "How can I be expected to work in such a racket? I don't know what they want; they could at least give me an office aide."

While she was carrying on like this, and I increasingly dilated, and the baby continuing to squall and gulp, unceremoniously helping himself to oxygen, two men came in carrying a head. It had no ticket, but the donor's name had been stamped in government purple across the forehead. The lids were shut, but the lips fluttered, and now and then it sounded as if a croak came out of them. At the first of these, the lady glanced suspiciously at me.

I said, "I never did that."

The head was catalogued, and removed.

"Listen," I said to the lady. "I really think I'm going to have the baby almost immediately, right here."

"Well of course you are, why else would you have come?" she replied crossly, triple-indexing my code number, not to mention my blood count, though they hadn't taken a blood sample.

"Doesn't it happen in another room?" I asked. I was finally getting nervous about it. It was my first baby, and after all the tales I'd heard, I didn't know for sure what to expect. They'd only warned me to look out for interns.

She rose from her chair, went to the blank-faced box on the wall directly in front of where I sat. She pressed its button, and the front lit up with a moving picture. A table. A huge central light like a sun. Around the table, an assortment of figures, male and female, dressed in pale green, and well masked. I lay on the table with my legs upheld.

"There you are," the lady said, and added ungraciously, "Now that we've got that settled, would you like a cup of tea?"

Although my mouth felt dry, I didn't think I could swallow a thing, so I replied, "No, thank you very much, though."

I watched the screen, sliding down a bit more comfortably in the chair where I sat, my knees spread awkwardly apart. The baby gave a rip-snorting screech, the figures on the screen reached down between my legs and lifted up a dripping baby boy.

I said, "Ooof," and pressed my hands against my belly. I took several deep breaths, still watching the screen where a female figure tied off the cord, cleaned the boy, and wrapped it in a cocoon of nylon.

The lady was back at her machine, one eye on the moving picture, her lips moving. I could hear her whisper, "One boy, normal, delivered in eight minutes," as the machine tick-ticked the information into creased cards on the spindle.

Slowly, I began to draw myself up in the chair until I was sitting up straight. I felt breathless, but relieved, after carrying that burden all week. After a moment, I asked the lady, "Is that all now?"

"That's it," she said. "Except for our usual advice: don't return before the end of next month. You must not use up all your privileges at once, no matter how many maternity pills you're tempted to gobble. After all, you've got five years of childbearing ahead of you. If that's what you want," she added the last with a certain sneer which I knew had been practiced on many others.

She got up from her chair to file the cards. I got up, pressing my skirt down over my flat stomach. "Look," I said, angered by her attitude, "as far as the law goes, I could come in here and have a baby every single week for a year. So don't threaten me."

She disdained to answer. I was on my way to the door when another woman came in, rushing, and plunged past me to the lady's desk. She said, "I'm in labor!"

"Do sit down, you'll have to wait until they clear the spools," the lady said.

I looked back as the woman sat down, balancing her belly in her lap, and she caught my eye. "Did you have one yet?" she asked.

"Yes, a lovely boy. Good luck with yours."

She said, "Thanks, I'll need it. I'm having twins again."

"Greedy, greedy," said the lady disapprovingly to her, as I went out.

A Dream at Noonday

by Gardner R. Dozois

I remember the sky, and the sun burning in the sky like a golden penny flicked into a deep blue pool, and the scuttling white clouds that changed into magic ships and whales and turreted castles as they drifted up across that bottomless ocean and swam the equally bottomless sea of my mind's eye. I remember the winds that skimmed the clouds, smoothing and rippling them into serene grandeur or boiling them into froth. I remember the same wind dipping low to caress the grass, making it sway and tremble, or whipping through the branches of the trees and making them sing with a wild, keening organ note. I remember the silence that was like a bronzen shout echoing among the hills.

–It is raining. The sky is slate-grey and grittily churning. It looks like a soggy dishrag being squeezed dry, and the moisture is dirty rain that falls in pounding sheets, pressing down the tall grass. The rain pocks the ground, and the loosely-packed soil is slowly turning into mud and the rain spatters the mud, making it shimmer–

And I remember the trains. I remember lying in bed as a child, swathed in warm blankets, sniffing suspiciously and eagerly at the embryonic darkness of my room, and listening to the big trains wail and murmur in the freight yard beyond. I remember lying awake night after night, frightened and darkly fascinated, keeping very still so that the darkness wouldn't see me, and listening to the hollow booms and metallic moans as the trains coupled and linked below my window. I remember that I thought the trains were alive, big dark beasts who came to dance and to hunt each other through the dappled moonlight of the world outside my room, and when I would listen to the whispering clatter of their passing and feel the room quiver ever so slightly in shy response, I would get a crawly feeling in my chest and a prickling along the back of my neck, and I would wish that I could watch them dance, although I knew that I never would. And I remember that it was different when I watched the trains during the daytime, for then even though I clung tight to my mother's hand and stared wide-eyed at their steam-belching and spark-spitting they were just big iron beasts putting on a show for me; they weren't magic then, they were hiding the magic inside them and pretending to be iron beasts and waiting for the darkness. I remember that I knew even then that trains are only magic in the night and only dance when no one can see them. And I remember that I couldn't go to sleep at night until I was soothed by the muttering lullaby of steel and the soft, rhythmical hiss-clatter of a train booming over a switch. And I remember that some nights the bellowing of a fast freight or the cruel, whistling shriek of a train's whistle would make me tremble and feel cold suddenly, even under my safe blanket-mountain, and I would find myself thinking about rain-soaked ground and blood and black cloth and half-understood references to my grandfather going away, and the darkness would suddenly seem to curl in upon itself and become diamond-hard and press down upon my straining eyes, and I would whimper and the fading whistle would snatch the sound from my mouth and trail it away into the night. And I remember that at times like that I would pretend that I had tiptoed to the window to watch the trains dance, which I never really dared to do because I knew I would die if I did, and then I would close my eyes and pretend that I was a train, and in my mind's eye I would be hanging disembodied in the darkness a few inches above the shining tracks, and then the track would begin to slip along under me, slowly at first then fast and smooth like flowing syrup, and then the darkness would be flashing by and then I would be moving out and away, surrounded by the wailing roar and evil steel chuckling of a fast freight slashing through the night, hearing my whistle scream with the majestic cruelty of a stooping eagle and feeling the switches boom and clatter hollowly under me, and I would fall asleep still moving out and away, away and out.

–The rain is stopping slowly, trailing away across the field, brushing the ground like long, dangling grey fingers. The tall grass creeps erect again, bobbing drunkenly, shedding its burden of water as a dog shakes himself dry after a swim. There are vicious little crosswinds in the wake of the storm, and they make the grass whip even more violently than the departing caress of the rain. The sky is splitting open above, black rain clouds pivoting sharply on a central point, allowing a sudden wide wedge of blue to appear. The overcast churns and tumbles and clots like wet heavy earth turned by a spade. The sky is now a crazy mosaic of mingled blue and grey. The wind picks up, chews at the edge of the tumbling wrack, spinning it to the fineness of cotton candy and then lashing it away. A broad shaft of sunlight falls from the dark undersides of the clouds, thrusting at the ground and drenching it in a golden cathedral glow, filled with shimmering green highlights. The effect is like that of light through a stained-glass window, and objects bathed in the light seem to glow very faintly from within, seem to be suddenly translated into dappled molten bronze. There is a gnarled, shaggy tree in the center of the pool of sunlight, and it is filled with wet, disgruntled birds, and the birds are hesitantly, cautiously, beginning to sing again–

And I remember wandering around in the woods as a boy and looking for nothing and finding everything and that clump of woods was magic and those rocks were a rustlers' fort and there were dinosaurs crashing through the brush just out of sight and everybody knew that there were dragons swimming in the sea just below the waves and an old glittery piece of coke bottle was a magic jewel that could let you fly or make you invisible and everybody knew that you whistled twice and crossed your fingers when you walked by that deserted old house or something shuddery and scaly would get you and you argued about bang you're dead no I'm not and you had a keen gun that could endlessly dispatch all the icky monsters who hung out near the swing set in your backyard without ever running out of ammunition. And I remember that as a kid I was nuts about finding a magic cave and I used to think that there was a cave under every rock, and I would get a long stick to use as a lever and I would sweat and strain until I had managed to turn the rock over, and then when I didn't find any tunnel under the rock I would think that the tunnel was there but it was just filled in with dirt, and I would get a shovel and I would dig three or four feet down looking for the tunnel and the magic cave and then I would give up and go home for a dinner of beans and franks and brown bread. And I remember that once I did find a little cave hidden under a big rock and I couldn't believe it and I was scared and shocked and angry and I didn't want it to be there but it was and so I stuck my head inside it to look around because something wouldn't let me leave until I did and it was dark in there and hot and very still and the darkness seemed to be blinking at me and I thought I heard something rustling and moving and I got scared and I started to cry and I ran away and then I got a big stick and came back, still crying, and pushed and heaved at that rock until it thudded back over the cave and hid it forever. And I remember that the next day I went out again to hunt for a magic cave.

–The rain has stopped. A bird flaps wetly away from the tree and then settles back down onto an outside branch. The branch dips and sways with the bird's weight, its leaves heavy with rain. The tree steams in the sun, and a million raindrops become tiny jewels, microscopic prisms, gleaming and winking, loving and transfiguring the light even as it destroys them and they dissolve into invisible vapor puffs to be swirled into the air and absorbed by the waiting clouds above. The air is wet and clean and fresh; it seems to squeak as the tall grass saws through it and the wind runs its fingernails lightly along its surface. The day is squally and gusty after the storm, high shining overcast split by jagged ribbons of blue that look like aerial fjords. The bird preens and fluffs its feathers disgustedly, chattering and scolding at the rain, but keeping a tiny bright eye carefully cocked in case the storm should take offense at the liquid stream of insults and come roaring back. Between the tufts of grass the ground has turned to black mud, soggy as a sponge, puddled by tiny pools of steaming rainwater. There is an arm and a hand lying in the mud, close enough to make out the texture of the tattered fabric clothing the arm, so close that the upper arm fades up and past the viewpoint and into a huge featureless blur in the extreme corner of the field of vision. The arm is bent back at an unnatural angle and the stiff fingers are hooked into talons that seem to claw toward the grey sky—

And I remember a day in the sixth grade when we were struggling in the cloakroom with our coats and snow-encrusted overshoes and I couldn't get mine off because one of the snaps had frozen shut and Denny was talking about how his father was a jet pilot and he sure hoped the war wasn't over before he grew up because he wanted to kill some Gooks like his daddy was doing and then later in the boy's room everybody was arguing about who had the biggest one and showing them and Denny could piss further than anybody else. I remember that noon at recess we were playing kick the can and the can rolled down the side of the hill and we all went down after it and somebody said hey look and we found a place inside a bunch of bushes where the grass was all flattened down and broken and there were pages of a magazine scattered all over and Denny picked one up and spread it out and it was a picture of a girl with only a pair of pants on and everybody got real quiet and I could hear the girls chanting in the schoolyard as they jumped rope and kids yelling and everybody was scared and her eyes seemed to be looking back right out of the picture and somebody finally licked his lips and said what're those things stickin' out of her, ah, and he didn't know the word and one of the bigger kids said tits and he said yeah what're those things stickin' outta her tits and I couldn't say anything because I was so surprised to find out that girls had those little round brown things like we did except that hers were pointy and hard and made me tremble and Denny said hell I knew about that I've had hundreds of girls but he was licking nervously at his lips as he said it and he was breathing funny too. And I remember that afternoon I was sitting at my desk near the window and the sun was hot and I was being bathed in the rolling drone of our math class and I wasn't understanding any of it and listening to less. I remember that I knew I had to go to the bathroom but I didn't want to raise my hand because our math teacher was a girl with brown hair and eyeglasses and I was staring at the place where I knew her pointy brown things must be under her blouse and I was thinking about touching them to see what they felt like and that made me feel funny somehow and I thought that if I raised my hand she would be able to see into my head and she'd know and she'd tell everybody what I was thinking and then she'd get mad and punish me for thinking bad things and so I didn't say anything but I had to go real bad and if I looked real close I thought that I could see two extra little bulges in her blouse where her pointy things were pushing against the cloth and I started thinking about what it would feel like if she pushed them up against me and that made me feel even more funny and sort of hollow and sick inside and I couldn't wait any longer and I raised my hand and left the room but it was too late and I wet myself when I was still on the way to the boy's room and I didn't know what to do so I went back to the classroom with my pants all wet and smelly and the math teacher looked at me and said what did you do and I was scared and Denny yelled he pissed in his pants he pissed in his pants and I said I did not the water bubbler squirted me but Denny yelled he pissed in his pants he pissed in his pants and the math teacher got very mad and everybody was laughing and suddenly the kids in my class didn't have any faces but only laughing mouths and I wanted to curl up into a ball where nobody could get me and once I had seen my mother digging with a garden spade and turning over the wet dark earth and there was half of a worm mixed in with the dirt and it writhed and squirmed until the next shovelful covered it up.

–Most of the rain has boiled away, leaving only a few of the larger puddles that have gathered in the shallow depressions between grass clumps. The mud is slowly solidifying under the hot sun, hardening into ruts, miniature ridges and mountains and valleys. An ant appears at the edge of the field of vision, emerging warily from the roots of the tall grass, pushing its way free of the tangled jungle. The tall blades of grass tower over it, forming a tightly interwoven web and filtering the hot yellow sunlight into a dusky green half-light. The ant pauses at the edge of the muddy open space, reluctant to exchange the cool tunnel of the grass for the dangers of level ground. Slowly, the ant picks its way across the sticky mud, skirting a pebble half again as big as it is. The pebble is streaked with veins of darker rock and has a tiny flake of quartz embedded in it near the top. The elements have rounded it into a smooth oval, except for a dent on the far side that exposes its porous core. The ant finishes its cautious circumnavigation of the pebble and scurries slowly toward the arm, which lies across its path. With infinite patience, the ant begins to climb up the arm, slipping on the slick, mud-spattered fabric. The ant works its way down the arm to the wrist and stops, sampling the air. The ant stands among the bristly black hairs on the wrist, antennae vibrating. The big blue vein in the wrist can be seen under its tiny feet. The ant continues to walk up the wrist, pushing its way through the bristly hair, climbing onto the hand and walking purposefully through the hollow of the thumb. Slowly, it disappears around the knuckle of the first finger–

And I remember a day when I was in the first year of high school and my voice was changing and I was starting to grow hair in unusual places and I was sitting in English class and I wasn't paying too much attention even though I'm usually pretty good in English because I was in love with the girl who sat in front of me. I remember that she had long legs and soft brown hair and a laugh like a bell and the sun was coming in the window behind her and the sunlight made the downy hair on the back of her neck glow very faintly and I wanted to touch it with my fingertips and I wanted to undo the knot that held her hair to the top of her head and I wanted her hair to cascade down over my face soft against my skin and cover me and with the sunlight I could see the strap of her bra underneath her thin dress and I wanted to slide my fingers underneath it and unhook it and stroke her velvety skin. I remember that I could feel my body stirring and my mouth was dry and painful and the zipper of her dress was open a tiny bit at the top and I could see the tanned texture of her skin and see that she had a brown mole on her shoulder and my hand trembled with the urge to touch it and something about Shakespeare and when she turned her head to whisper to Denny across the row her eyes were deep and beautiful and I wanted to kiss them softly brush them lightly as a bird's wing and Hamlet was something or other and I caught a glimpse of her tongue darting wetly from between her lips and pressing against her white teeth and that was almost too much to bear and I wanted to kiss her lips very softly and then I wanted to crush them flat and then I wanted to bite them and sting them until she cried and I could comfort and soothe her and that frightened me because I didn't understand it and my thighs were tight and prickly and the blood pounded at the base of my throat and Elsinore something and the bell rang shrilly and I couldn't get up because all I could see was the fabric of her dress stretched taut over her hips as she stood up and I stared at her hips and her belly and her thighs as she walked away and wondered what her thing would look like and I was scared. I remember that I finally got up enough nerve to ask her for a date during recess and she looked at me incredulously for a second and then laughed, just laughed contemptuously and walked away without saying a word. I remember her laughter. And I remember wandering around town late that night heading aimlessly into nowhere trying to escape from the pressure and the emptiness and passing a car parked on a dark street corner just as the moon swung out from behind a cloud and there was light that danced and I could hear the freight trains booming far away and she was in the back seat with Denny and they were locked together and her skirt was hiked up and I could see the white flash of flesh all the way up her leg and he had his hand under her blouse on her breast and I could see his knuckles moving under the fabric and the freight train roared and clattered as it hit the switch and he was kissing her and biting her and she was kissing him back with her lips pressed tight against her teeth and her hair floating all around them like a cloud and the train was whispering away from town and then he was on top of her pressing her down and I felt like I was going to be sick and I started to vomit but stopped because I was afraid of the noise and she was moaning and making small low whimpering noises I'd never heard anyone make before and I had to run before the darkness crushed me and I didn't want to do that when I got home because I'd feel ashamed and disgusted afterward but I knew that I was going to have to because my stomach was heaving and my skin was on fire and I thought that my heart was going to explode. And I remember that I eventually got a date for the dance with

Judy from my history class who was a nice girl although plain but all night long as I danced with her I could only see my first love moaning and writhing under Denny just as the worm had writhed under the thrust of the garden spade into the wet dark earth long ago and as I ran toward home that night I heard the train vanish into the night trailing a cruelly arrogant whistle behind it until it faded to a memory and there was nothing left.

–The ant reappears on the underside of the index finger, pauses, antennae flickering inquisitively, and then begins to walk back down the palm, following the deep groove known as the life line until it reaches the wrist. For a moment, it appears as if the ant will vanish into the space between the wrist and the frayed, bloodstained cuff of the shirt, but it changes its mind and slides back down the wrist to the ground on the far side. The ant struggles for a moment in the sticky mud, and then crawls determinedly off across the crusted ground. At the extreme edge of the field of vision, just before the blur that is the upper arm, there is the jagged, pebbly edge of a shellhole. Half over the lip of the shellhole, grossly out of proportion at this distance, is half of a large earthworm, partially buried by the freshly turned earth thrown up by an explosion. The ant pokes suspiciously at the worm–

And I remember the waiting room at the train station and the weight of my suitcase in my hand and the way the big iron voice rolled unintelligibly around the high ceiling as the stationmaster announced the incoming trains and cigar and cigarette smoke was thick in the air and the massive air-conditioning fan was laboring in vain to clear some of the choking fog away and the place reeked of urine and age and an old dog twitched and moaned in his ancient sleep as he curled close against an equally ancient radiator that hissed and panted and belched white jets of steam and I stood by the door and looked up and watched a blanket of heavy new snow settle down over the sleeping town with the ponderous invulnerability of a pregnant woman. I remember looking down into the train tunnel and out along the track to where the shining steel disappeared into darkness and I suddenly thought that it looked like a magic cave and then I wondered if I had thought that was supposed to be funny and I wanted to laugh only I wanted to cry too and so I could do neither and instead I tightened my arm around Judy's waist and pulled her closer against me and kissed the silken hollow of her throat and I could feel the sharp bone in her hip jabbing against mine and I didn't care because that was pain that was pleasure and I felt the gentle resilience of her breast suddenly against my rib-cage and felt her arm tighten protectively around me and her fingernails bite sharply into my arm and I knew that she was trying not to cry and that if I said anything at all it would make her cry and there would be that sloppy scene we'd been trying to avoid and so I said nothing but only held her and kissed her lightly on the eyes and I knew that people were looking at us and snickering and I didn't give a damn and I knew that she wanted me and wanted me to stay and we both knew that I couldn't and all around us about ten other young men were going through similar tableaux with their girlfriends or folks and everybody was stern and pale and worried and trying to look unconcerned and casual and so many women were trying not to cry that the humidity in the station was trembling at the saturation point. I remember Denny standing near the door with a foot propped on his suitcase and he was flashing his too-white teeth and his too-wide smile and he reeked of cheap cologne as he told his small knot of admirers in an overly loud voice that he didn't give a damn if he went or not because he'd knocked up a broad and her old man was tryin to put the screws on him and this was a good way to get outta town anyway and the government would protect him from the old man and he'd come back in a year or so on top of the world and the heat would be off and he could start collectin female scalps again and besides his father had been in and been a hero and he could do anything better than that old bastard and besides he hated those goddamned Gooks and he was gonna get him a Commie see if he didn't. I remember that the train came quietly in then and that it still looked like a big iron beast although now it was a silent beast with no smoke or sparks but with magic still hidden inside it although I knew now that it might be a dark magic and then we had to climb inside and I was kissing Judy goodbye and telling her I loved her and she was kissing me and telling me she would wait for me and I don't know if we were telling the truth or even if we knew ourselves what the truth was and then Judy was crying openly and I was swallowed by the iron beast and we were roaring away from the town and snickering across the web of tracks and booming over the switches and I saw my old house flash by and I could see my old window and I almost imagined that I could see myself as a kid with my nose pressed against the window looking out and watching my older self roar by and neither of us suspecting that the other was there and neither ever working up enough nerve to watch the trains dance. And I remember that all during that long train ride I could hear Denny's raucous voice somewhere in the distance talking about how he couldn't wait to get to Gookland and he'd heard that Gook snatch was even better than nigger snatch and free too and he was gonna get him a Commie he couldn't wait to get him a goddamned Commie and as the train slashed across the wide fertile farmlands of the Midwest the last thing I knew before sleep that night was the wet smell of freshly turned earth.

—The ant noses the worm disdainfully and then passes out of the field of vision. The only movement now is the ripple of the tall grass and the flash of birds in the shaggy tree. The sky is clouding up again, thunderheads rumbling up over the horizon and rolling across the sky. Two large forms appear near the shaggy tree at the other extreme of the field of vision. The singing of the birds stops as if turned off by a switch. The two forms move about vaguely near the shaggy tree, rustling the grass. The angle of the field of vision gives a foreshortening effect, and it is difficult to make out just what the figures are. There is a sharp command, the human voice sounding strangely thin under the sighing of the wind. The two figures move away from the shaggy tree, pushing through the grass. They are medics; haggard, dirty soldiers with big red crosses painted on their helmets and armbands and several days' growth on their chins. They look tired, harried, scared and determined, and they are moving rapidly, half-crouching, searching for something on the ground and darting frequent wary glances back over their shoulders. As they approach they seem to grow larger and larger, elongating toward the sky as their movement shifts the perspective. They stop a few feet away and reach down, lifting up a body that has been hidden by the tall grass. It is Denny, the back of his head blown away, his eyes bulging horribly open. The medics lower Denny's body back into the sheltering grass and bend over it, fumbling with something. They finally straighten, glance hurriedly about and move forward. The two grimy figures swell until they fill practically the entire field of vision, only random patches of sky and the ground underfoot visible around their bulk. The medics come to a stop about a foot away. The scarred, battered, mud-caked combat boot of the medic now dominates the scene, looking big as a mountain. From the combat boot, the medic's leg seems to stretch incredibly toward the sky, like a fatigue-swathed beanstalk, with just a suggestion of a head and a helmet floating somewhere at the top. The other medic cannot be seen at all now, having stepped over and out of the field of vision. His shallow breathing and occasional muttered obscenities can be heard. The first medic bends over, his huge hand seeming to leap down from the sky, and touches the arm, lifting the wrist and feeling for a pulse. The medic holds the wrist for a while and then sighs and lets it go. The wrist plops limply back into the cold sucking mud, splattering it. The medic's hand swells in the direction of the upper arm, and then fades momentarily out of the field of vision, although his wrist remains blurrily visible and his arm seems to stretch back like a highway into the middle distance. The medic tugs, and his hand comes back clutching a tarnished dog tag. Both of the medic's hands disappear forward out of the field of vision. Hands prying the jaw open, jamming the dog tag into the teeth, the metal cold and slimy against the tongue and gums, pressing the jaws firmly closed again, the dog tag feeling huge and immovable inside the mouth. The world is the medic's face now, looming like a scarred cliff inches away, his bloodshot twitching eyes as huge as moons, his mouth, hanging slackly open with exhaustion, as cavernous and bottomless as a magic cave to a little boy. The medic has halitosis, his breath filled with the richly corrupt smell of freshly turned earth. The medic stretches out two fingers which completely occupy the field of vision, blocking out even the sky. The medic's fingertips are the only things in the world now. They are stained and dirty and one has a white scar across the whorls. The medic's fingertips touch the eyelids and gently press down. And now there is nothing but darkness–

And I remember the way dawn would crack the eastern sky, the rosy blush slowly spreading and staining the black of night, chasing away the darkness, driving away the stars. And I remember the way a woman looks at you when she loves you, and the sound that a kitten makes when it is happy, and the way that snowflakes blur and melt against a warm windowpane in winter. I remember. I remember.

Woman Waiting

by Carol Emshwiller

There goes the plane for Chicago. They're up safely. In here you can't hear any of their racket.

There they go, climbing in a trail of black smoke, engines screaming, but we can't hear it.

For us, they're silent as birds.

For them, we here below are diminishing in size. We are becoming doll-like and soon we will be like ants, soon no more than scurrying gnats and, later still, bacteria perhaps and fungi, I, too, nothing but a microbic creature. I might be the size of a camel or a mouse, it's all the same to them up there. Even if I were to stand in the center of the landing field (as camel *or* mouse) they couldn't see me at all.

There they go, swelling towards the sun. Only the sky will have room enough for them now. This landing field will seem infinitesimal. There will be no place on this whole planet, not a bit of land anywhere, unless some gigantic desert, that will seem to them large enough to land on. There, they have already swelled themselves up out of sight.

But now I see they have begun to board the plane for Rome. In a moment they will fly up as the others did, like a great expanding bird, starting out at our size, but growing too big for us. Behind this thick glass I hardly hear those Rome-bound engines begin, one by one, to scream out their expanding powers.

How nice it must be for all those people to enlarge themselves so. How condescendingly they must, sometimes, look down upon us here.

I have a ticket.

I am not unlike those others boarding their planes for

Chicago, Rome, Miami, and so soon to be transformed. And I am not unlike these who sit here waiting too. I am, in fact, quite a bit like them, for I have noticed that within my view there are actually three other coats of almost exactly the same brown as mine and I see two other little black hats. I have noticed myself in the ladies' room mirror, though not so that anyone knew I was watching myself. I only allowed myself to look as I combed my hair and put on my lipstick, but I did see how like them I am in my new clothes and from a certain distance. If I could just keep this in mind, for my looks, when I can remember them, influence my actions, and I am sure if I could see myself in some mirror behind the clerks, I would feel quite comfortable approaching them. But then there will be no more need of that.

But I know rest room mirrors are not quite trustworthy. They have a pinkish cast that flatters and, for all I know, a lengthening effect to make us all think of ourselves as closer to some long legged ideal. I must remember that and be careful. I mustn't fantasize about myself. I must remember I am not quite what the mirrors show me. They are, in a way, like subway windows where one sees oneself flashing by along the dark walls and one looks quite dashing and luminously handsome, needing, one thinks, only red earrings or a modish hat to be a quite extraordinary person, even standing out from the others.

There go those Rome people. Soon I will be off up there too. The thought is enough to make me feel dashingly handsome again, as handsome as all these clean-cut people so comfortable in themselves, so accustomed to their clothes and their bodies, and I feel young, almost too young, like a little girl on her first voyage alone (and it has been a long time since I went anywhere so it does seem like a first voyage).

That Rome plane looks slow from here, but I know how fast they're really going, and then, the larger you are, the slower you seem. I think they are already noticing how huge they are getting now. Once up, they may not be able to come down at all. They may sit looking out the windows, circling forever, dizzy at their own size compared to earth, unable to risk a landing.

But I'm going back. (I don't call it home anymore since I've been here so long.) I'm going back, but once I get up in that plane I don't think anything will matter. I'll see the world as it really is then and I won't mind not ever coming down at all.

I have a seat here by this wall of glass and I don't think anyone is noticing me. I have been here quite some time, but others come and go. They don't keep track of how long I've been sitting here. And, as I glance down at myself, I think again that I look quite as ordinary as anyone else. Why should they notice me with either criticism or admiration? I don't think it is at all evident that all my clothes are new.

I have a little black satchel on the floor beside me. In it I have my glasses, my newspaper, a cantaloupe, and a little bag of peanuts. The cantaloupe is certainly very ripe. I think I can smell it now and then, a sweet, good smell.

Just now I noticed a woman who came up near me and then moved away to take a seat farther on. I think I know why that was. It could have been the cantaloupe, that strange (to her) pungent sweetness, but I think not. In my haste to come here in time (it's true I arrived unnecessarily early) I put on all my new clothes without washing. I might say that washing in my apartment was never easy, and I may not really have washed very well for quite some time. I might as well have feet like a fat man, a very fat man, I should say. My feet are not fat, I mean, but they have a certain fat quality. That woman has found me out, and that is why she is sitting over across the way.

So I am not really at all like the others under all my nice clothes.

Yet is it a crime to be dirty? I can see very well that it is in a place like this though I never noticed back in my own room. Here it is certainly a crime, or certainly outstanding in one way or another, different, eccentric, extraordinary, and, I do think, a crime. Well, there's nothing to be done about it now, though it makes me feel quite shrunken, new clothes or not. How will it be in the plane, how will it be to be shrunken and expanded at the same time, for surely in the plane someone will have to sit next to me whether they like it or not. Perhaps the cantaloupe will help. Perhaps I will keep my satchel on my lap.

Think if I should drop it somehow up there and this elephantine cantaloupe, still swollen with altitude, should squash down on some tiny building, covering it with its cantaloupe-colored pulp, spreading its rich, sweet smell over everything, a cantaloupe large as the moon, ripe and ready, squashing them all in too much sweetness and too much juice. Too much, they would cry. It's too much.

Flight 350, Flight 321, Flight 235, Flight 216. I wonder if my feet together with my cantaloupe are capable of permeating the air of this whole interior as that voice does. Perhaps they already have and I am completely unaware of it. Wondering, I almost do not hear my own flight number, 216, even though I have memorized it, rechecked and rememorized it a dozen times. Flight 216 has been, the voice tells everyone in the whole airport without a tremble or change of quality, everyone, it tells, not seeking us, the passengers, out, to impart its private information, Flight 216 has been (I should have guessed) postponed.

Well, so that is the way it is, and now, immediately after, I'm not sure if the voice said just postponed or postponed indefinitely. I wonder if there's any sense in asking why or when. I wonder if there's any sense in waiting.

There goes another plane, I have not noticed where to this time. All the other people's planes are coming and going but I don't know why I ever thought mine would, even with my new clothes and my ticket.

Senseless or not, I am going to wait exactly as I waited before I knew my flight was postponed, but already I see there is a difference in my feelings as I watch the other planes rise. I am quite shrunken. I am shrinking as they rise up. I am growing too small for my new clothes. They will hang upon me in a most noticeable way, I am sure. I will be a spectacle. I will make a spectacle of myself just walking from here to the door. Everyone will notice.

But why am I disappointed in Flight 216? I have not even been sure I wanted to go back at all. In truth, I do not want to go back, not really. What did I want then? And the three hundred dollars? If I can get that back will it make up for what I wanted, whatever that was? I wonder if I *can* get it back for it certainly would be something to have. I wonder should I try now? But the flight was just postponed, not canceled.

I see a man at the desk who seems to be asking something. He is quite out of place there. He is wearing a homemade coat made out of an Army blanket, and he has a tangled, olive-drab beard. If he is asking about Flight 216, and he certainly must be, then I don't believe that I should at all. I don't believe that I should put myself in the company of such people. They might even think we were together, going off to the same destination. Still, I would like to have that money. Perhaps if I wait a half hour or so and ask then, they will not connect me with him.

So, here am I, a woman waiting. I wish I had some greater meaning at this time of disappointment. Were I a man, I could even be humanity waiting, all humanity, whose flight is indefinitely postponed, but I am woman waiting. Rather a cliché. It doesn't matter. Let her wait.

If I sit very still I feel a tiny sliding movement, a tiny, snaky motion of withdrawal inwards. My feet just barely touch the ground. Away goes another plane and I feel my heart lurch.

But the three hundred dollars. Has it been a half an hour yet? I forgot to check the clock at the start. I will have to wait for another to go by. My feet dangle. I am like a girl in woman's clothes. Anyone glancing this way will wonder who has dressed me in these woman-sized things and why. Have I lost my own clothes somewhere? they wonder. Was I in some sort of accident? Did I soil myself? Was I sick on myself and did I have to wear my mother's grown-up things? I do not think, if I went to the desk in my present condition, that they would give me the three hundred dollars at all. And even if I did have the money, would they serve me in the coffee shop? If I wait much longer I will have difficulty climbing up on their stools and it would be quite embarrassing for everyone if I continued to shrink right before their eyes as I sat there with my coffee and my sandwich. They would all know I wasn't a bit like them then. Just as we suspected when we first saw her sitting down and watching the planes, they would all say. Just as we suspected all along.

By now I don't even mean woman anymore. I am midget, waiting. I represent all midgets (there can't be so very many) waiting for their midget life to turn into real life, which is, of course, indefinitely postponed. (I am becoming quite sure that they did say "indefinitely" now.)

This slithering sensation, minute as it is, makes me itch, but, here in this huge, public place (there is room for quite a few airplanes in here, should they ever wish to pull away the glass walls and wheel them in upon these polished floors), here, I do not believe I should scratch myself.

My feet no longer dangle. I must slide off this chair before the drop becomes too steep. This I can manage easily within my clothes. By now people must think someone has just left a new brown coat on the chair. I squat, wrapped in a stocking, under the overhanging edge of it, and in a few minutes more I am small enough to step into my satchel. There it is comfortable and dark. I curl up next to the cantaloupe and newspaper and nibble on a peanut. I had not realized it, but I am quite exhausted. I roll my stocking into a pillow and lean back upon it. Smallness, I am thinking, must be quite as comfortable as largeness. They each have advantages. Here, snug as . . . as anyone might be in a soft and dark, black satchel, I fall asleep quickly.

How long I sleep, I have absolutely no idea, it may have been but a few minutes or the full clock around (and at my size time may seem different); at any rate, I wake, still within my satchel, to the movement of being carried, smoothly and with a rhythmic, wavy motion. I put my eye to the hole in the center of one of the grommets that hold on the handles. I see a sign, *Lost Articles Department.* Inside this large, shelved hallway, I am filed beside other satchels and suitcases of similar size and color. Well, I have my cantaloupe, my peanuts, and my newspaper. But I do see that the man here already wrinkles his nose as he comes by my shelf.

No one will be coming for me. That I am sure of. How long will they keep me here? Not long, for I see he has wrinkled his nose again. You don't suppose my feet, my tiny feet can still . . . ? What is that smell? he is thinking. I will have to search it out. Something is spoiling here in one of the packages, something just recently brought in. People just aren't careful, he thinks. They put perishables in their suitcases and then forget them for other people to clean up. Disgusting messes. They don't care. Perhaps, he thinks, perhaps I'll just throw it out without the disagreeable task of examining it. No one could want something spoiled anyway. I won't wait the allotted time (is it a week? a month?). Well, I just won't wait, he thinks. Out it will go by tomorrow, sure.

Perhaps, just at the last moment, I will call out to him and he will discover me here.

How will it be, finding a not very attractive, one-foot high, completely naked woman in the lost and found department? Not so young anymore, either. (But he is not so young, and quite completely bald.) How will it be finding a woman who was, to say the least, peculiar . . . different, even when she was of normal height?

Will he blush, seeing me? Would he take me home with

him secretly, hidden in the satchel? Keep me, perhaps, in a comfortable corner of his room with a little box for my bed and a cushion for my mattress? Of course sex will be impossible between us. . . .

But this is ludicrous.

No. No. I will not call out. I will not . . . I will never reveal myself. If I have to perish at the bottom of a garbage heap, I will not ever call out.

Old Foot Forgot

by R. A. Lafferty

"Dookh-Doctor, it is a sphairikos patient," Lay Sister Moira P.T. de C. cried happily. "It is a genuine spherical alien patient. You've never had one before, not in good faith. I believe it is what you need to distract you from the–ah–happy news about yourself. It is good for a Dookh-Doctor to have a different patient sometimes."

"Thank you, lay sister. Let it, him, her, fourth case, fifth case or whatever come in. No, I've never had a sphairikos in good faith. I doubt if this one is, but I will enjoy the encounter."

The sphairikos rolled or pushed itself in. It was a big one, either a blubbery kid or a full-grown one. It rolled itself along by extruding and withdrawing pseudopods. And it came to rest grinning, a large translucent rubbery ball of fleeting colors.

"Hello, Dookh-Doctor," it said pleasantly. "First I wish to extend my own sympathy and that of my friends who do not know how to speak to you for the happy news about yourself. And secondly I have an illness of which you may cure me."

"But the sphairikoi are never ill," Dookh-Doctor Drague said dutifully.

How did he know that the round creature was grinning at him? By the colors, of course; by the fleeting colors of it. They were grinning colors.

"My illness is not of the body but of the head," said the sphairikos.

"But the sphairikoi have no heads, my friend."

"Then it is of another place and another name, Dookh-Doctor. There is a thing in me suffering. I come to you as Dookh-Doctor. I have an illness in my Dookh."

"That is unlikely in a sphairikos. You are all perfectly balanced, each a cosmos unto yourself. And you have a central solution that solves everything. What is your name?"

"Krug Sixteen, which is to say that I am the sixteenth son of Krug; the sixteenth fifth case son, of course. Dookh-Doc, the pain is not in me entirely; it is in an old forgotten part of me."

"But, you sphairikoi have no parts, Krug Sixteen. You are total and indiscriminate entities. How would you have parts?"

"It is one of my pseudopods, extruded and then withdrawn in much less than a second long ago when I was a little boy. It protests, it cries, it wants to come back. It has always bothered me, but now it bothers me intolerably. It screams and moans constantly now."

"Do not the same ones ever come back?"

"No. Never. Never exactly the same ones. Will exactly the same water ever run past one point in a brook? No. We push them out and we draw them back. And we push them out again, millions of times. But the same one can never come back. There is no identity. But this one cries to come back, and now it becomes more urgent. Dookh-Doc, how can it be? There is not one same molecule in it as when I was a boy. There is nothing of that pseudopod that is left; but parts of it have come out as parts of other pseudopods, and now there can be no parts left. There is nothing remaining of that foot; it has all been absorbed a million times. But it cries out! And I have compassion on it."

"Krug Sixteen, it may possibly be a physical or mechanical difficulty, a pseudopod imperfectly withdrawn, a sort of rupture whose effects you interpret wrongly. In that case it would be better if you went to your own doctors, or doctor: I understand that there is one."

"That old fogey cannot help me, Dookh-Doc. And our pseudopods are always perfectly withdrawn. We are covered with the twinkling salve; it is one-third of our bulk.

And if we need more of it we can make more of it ourselves; or we can beg some of it from a class four who make it prodigiously. It is the solvent for everything. It eases every possible wound; it makes us round as balls; you should use it yourself, Dookh-Doc. But there is one small foot in me, dissolved long ago, that protests and protests. Oh, the shrieking! The horrible dreams!"

"But the sphairikoi do not sleep and do not dream."

"Right enough, Dookh-Doc. But there's an old dead foot of mine that sure does dream loud and woolly."

The sphairikos was not grinning now. He rolled about softly in apprehension. How did the Dookh-Doctor know that it was apprehension? By the fleeting colors. They were apprehension colors now.

"Krug Sixteen, I will have to study your case," said the Dookh-Doctor. "I will see if there are any references to it in the literature, though I don't believe that there are. I will seek for analogy. I will probe every possibility. Can you come back at the same hour tomorrow?"

"I will come back, Dookh-Doc," Krug Sixteen sighed. "I hate to feel that small vanished thing crying and trembling."

It rolled or pushed itself out of the clinic by extruding and then withdrawing pseudopods. The little pushers came out of the goopy surface of the sphairikos and then were withdrawn into it completely. A raindrop falling in a pond makes a much more lasting mark than does the disappearing pseudopod of a sphairikos.

But long ago, in his boyhood, one of the pseudopods of Krug Sixteen had not disappeared completely in every respect.

"There are several of the jokers waiting," Lay Sister Moira P.T. de C. announced a little later, "and perhaps some valid patients among them. It's hard to tell."

"Not another sphairikos?" the Dookh-Doctor asked in sudden anxiety.

"Of course not. The one this morning is the only sphairikos who has ever come. How could there be anything wrong with him? There is never anything wrong with a sphairikos. No, these are all of the other species. Just a regular morning bunch."

So, except for the visitation of the sphairikos, it was a regular morning at the clinic. There were about a dozen waiting, of the several species; and at least half of them would be jokers. It was always so.

There was a lean and giddy subula. One cannot tell the age or sex of them. But there was a tittering. In all human or inhuman expression, whether of sound, color, radioray or osmerhetor, the titter suggests itself. It is just around the corner, it is just outside, it is subliminal, but it is there somewhere.

"It is that my teeth hurt so terrible," the subula shrilled so high that the Dookh-Doctor had to go on instruments to hear it. "They are tromping pain. They are agony. I think I will cut my head off. Have you a head-off cutter, Dookh-Doctor?"

"Let me see your teeth," Dookh-Doctor Drague asked with the beginnings of irritation.

"There is one tooth jump up and down with spike boot," the subula shrilled. "There is one jag like poisoned needle. There is one cuts like coarse rough saw. There is one burns like little hot fires."

"Let me see your teeth," the Dookh-Doctor growled evenly.

"There is one drills holes and sets little blasting powder in them," the subula shrilled still more highly. "Then he sets them off. Ow! Good night!"

"Let me see your teeth!!"

"Peeef!" the subula shrilled. The teeth cascaded out, half a bushel of them, ten thousand of them, all over the floor of the clinic.

"Peeef," the subula screeched again, and ran out of the clinic.

Tittering? (But he should have remembered that the subula have no teeth.) Tittering? It was the laughing of demented horses. It was the jackhammer braying of the dolcus, it was the hysterical giggling of the ophis (they were a half bushel of shells of the little stink conches and they were already beginning to rot), it was the clown laughter of the arktos (the clinic would never be habitable again; never mind, he would burn it down and build another one tonight).

The jokers, the jokers, they did have their fun with him, and perhaps it did them some good.

"I have this trouble with me," said a young dolcus, "but it make me so nervous to tell it. Oh, it do make me nervous to tell it to the Dookh-Doc."

"Do not be nervous," said the Dookh-Doctor, fearing the worst. "Tell me your trouble in whatever way you can. I am here to serve every creature that is in any trouble or pain whatsoever. Tell it."

"Oh but it make me so nervous. I perish. I shrivel. I will have accident I am so nervous."

"Tell me your trouble, my friend. I am here to help."

"Whoops, whoops, I already have accident! I tell you I am nervous."

The dolcus urinated largely on the clinic floor. Then it ran out laughing.

The laughing, the shrilling, the braying, the shrill giggling that seemed to scrape the flesh from his bones. (He should have remembered that the dolcus do not urinate; everything comes from them hard and solid.) The hooting, the laughing! It was a bag of green water from the kolmula swamp. Even the aliens gagged at it, and their laughter was of a pungent green sort.

Oh well, there were several of the patients with real, though small, ailments, and there were more jokers. There was the arktos who—(Wait, wait, that particular jokerie cannot be told with human persons present; even the subula and the ophis blushed lavender at the rawness of it. A thing like that can only be told to arktos themselves.) And there was another dolcus who–

Jokers, jokers, it was a typical morning at the clinic.

One does whatever one can for the oneness that is greater than self. In the case of Dookh-Doctor Drague it meant considerable sacrifice. One who works with the strange species here must give up all hope of material reward or material sophistication in his surroundings. But the Dookh-Doctor was a dedicated man.

Oh, the Dookh-Doctor lived pleasantly and with a sort of artful simplicity and dynamic involvement in the small articles of life. He had an excited devotion and balanced intensity for corporate life.

He lived in small houses of giolach-weed, woven with careful double-rappel. He lived in each one for seven days only, and then burned it and scattered the ashes, taking always one bitter glob of them on his tongue for reminder of the fleetingness of temporal things and the wonderfulness of the returning. To live in one house for more than seven days is to become dull and habitual; but the giolach-weed will not burn well till it has been cut and plaited for seven days, so the houses set their own terms. One half day to build, seven days to inhabit, one half day to burn ritually and scatter, one renewal night under the speir-sky.

The Dookh-Doctor ate raibe, or he ate innuin or ull or piorra when they were in season. And for the nine days of each year when none of these were in season, he ate nothing at all.

His clothing he made himself of colg. His paper was of the pailme plant. His printer used buaf ink and shaved slinn stone. Everything that he needed he made for himself from things found wild in the hedgerows. He took nothing from the cultivated land or from the alien peoples. He was a poor and dedicated servant.

Now he stacked some of the needful things from the clinic, and Lay Sister Moira P.T. de C. took others of them to her own giolach house to keep till the next day. Then the Dookh-Doctor ritually set his clinic on fire, and a few moments later his house. This was all symbol of the great nostos, the returning. He recited the great rhapsodies, and other persons of the human kind came by and recited with him.

"That no least fiber of giolach die," he recited, "that all enter immediately the more glorious and undivided life. That the ashes are the doorway, and every ash is holy. That all become a part of the oneness that is greater than self.

"That no splinter of the giuis floorboards die, that no glob of the chinking clay die, that nc mite or louse in the plaiting die. That all become a part of the oneness that is greater than self."

He burned, he scattered, he recited, he took one glob of bitter ash on his tongue. He experienced vicariously the great synthesis. He ate holy innuin and holy ull. And when it was finished, both of the house and the clinic, when it had come on night and he was houseless, he slept that renewal night under the speir-sky.

And in the morning he began to build again, the clinic first, and then the house.

"It is the last of either that I shall ever build," he said. The happy news about himself was that he was a dying man and that he would be allowed to take the short way out. So he built most carefully with the Last Building Rites. He chinked both the buildings with special uir clay that would give a special bitterness to the ashes at the time of final burning.

Krug Sixteen rolled along while the Dookh-Doctor still built his final clinic, and the sphairikos helped him in the building while they consulted on the case of the screaming foot. Krug Sixteen could weave and plait and rappel amazingly with his pseudopods; he could bring out a dozen of them, a hundred, thick or thin, whatever was needed, and all of a wonderful dexterity. That globe could weave.

"Does the forgotten foot still suffer, Krug Sixteen?" Dookh-Doctor Drague asked it.

"It suffers, it's hysterical, it's in absolute terror. I don't know where it is; it does not know; and how I know about it at all is a mystery. Have you found any way to help me, to help it?"

"No. I am sorry, but I have not."

"There is nothing in the literature on this subject?"

"No. Nothing that I can identify as such."

"And you have not found analogy to it?"

"Yes, Krug Sixteen, ah–in a way I *have* discovered analogy. But it does not help you. Or me."

"That is too bad, Dookh-Doc. Well, I will live with it; and the little foot will finally die with it. Do I guess that your case is somewhat the same as mine?"

"No. My case is more similar to that of your lost foot than to you."

"Well, I will do what I can for myself, and for it. It's back to the old remedy then. But I am already covered deep with the twinkling salve."

"So am I, Krug Sixteen, in a like way."

"I was ashamed of my affliction before and did not mention it. Now, however, since I have spoken of it to you, I have spoken of it to others also. There is some slight help, I find. I should have shot off my big bazoo before."

"The sphairikoi have no bazoos."

"Folk-joke, Dookh-Doc. There is a special form of the twinkling salve. My own is insufficient, so I will try the other."

"A special form of it, Krug Sixteen? I am interested in this. My own salve seems to have lost its effect."

"There is a girlfriend person, Dookh-Doc, or a boyfriend person. How shall I say it? It is a case four person to my case five. This person, though promiscuous, is expert. And this person exudes the special stuff in abundance."

"Not quite my pot of ointment I'm afraid, Krug Sixteen; but it may be the answer for you. It is special? And it dissolves everything, including objections?"

"It is the most special of all the twinkling salves, Dookh-Doc, and it solves and dissolves everything. I believe it will reach my forgotten foot, wherever it is, and send it into kind and everlasting slumber. It will know that it is itself that slumbers, and that will be bearable."

"If I were not–ah–going out of business, Krug Sixteen, I'd get a bit of it and try to analyze it. What is the name of this special case four person?"

"Torchy Twelve is its name."

"Yes. I have heard of her."

Everybody now knew that it was the last week in the life of the Dookh-Doctor, and everyone tried to make his happiness still more happy. The morning jokers outdid themselves, especially the arktos. After all, he was dying of an arktos disease, one never fatal to the arktos themselves. They did have some merry and outrageous times around the clinic, and the Dookh-Doctor got the sneaky feeling that he would rather live than die.

He hadn't, it was plain to see, the right attitude. So Lay Priest Migma P.T. de C. tried to inculcate the right attitude in him.

"It is the great synthesis you go to, Dookh-Doctor," he said. "It is the happy oneness that is greater than self."

"Oh I know that, but you put it on a little too thick. I've been taught it from my babyhood. I'm resigned to it."

"Resigned to it? You should be ecstatic over it! The self must perish, of course, but it will live on as an integral atom of the evolving oneness, just as a drop lives on in the ocean."

"Aye, Migma, but the drop may hang onto the memory of the time when it was cloud, of the time when it was falling drop indeed, of the time when it was brook. It may say 'There's too damned much salt in this ocean. I'm lost here.' "

"Oh, but the drop will want to be lost, Dookh-Doctor. The only purpose of existence is to cease to exist. And there cannot be too much of salt in the evolving oneness. There cannot be too much of anything. All must be one in it. Salt and sulphur must be one, undifferentiated. Offal and soul must become one. Blessed be oblivion in the oneness that collapses on itself."

"Stuff it, lay priest. I'm weary of it."

"Stuff it, you say? I don't understand your phrase, but I'm sure it's apt. Yes, yes, Dookh-Doctor, stuff it all in: animals, people, rocks, grass, worlds, and wasps. Stuff it all in. That all may be obliterated into the great–may I not coin a word even as the master coined them?–into the great stuffiness!"

"I'm afraid your word is all too apt."

"It is the great quintessence, it is the happy death of all individuality and memory, it is the synthesis of all living and dead things into the great amorphism. It is the–"

"It is the old old salve, and it's lost its twinkle," the Dookh-Doctor said sadly. "How goes the old quotation? When the salve becomes sticky, how then will you come unstuck?"

No, the Dookh-Doctor did not have the right attitude, so it was necessary that many persons should harass him into it. Time was short. His death was due. And there was the general fear that the Dookh-Doctor might not be properly lost.

He surely came to his time of happiness in grumpy fashion.

The week was gone by. The last evening for him was come. The Dookh-Doctor ritually set his clinic on fire, and a few minutes later his house.

He burned, he scattered, he recited the special last-time

recital. He ate holy innuin and holy ull. He took one glob of most bitter ash on his tongue: and he lay down to sleep his last night under the speir-sky.

He wasn't afraid to die.

"I will cross that bridge gladly, but I want there to be another side to that bridge," he talked to himself. "And if there is no other side of it, I want it to be *me* who knows that there is not. They say 'Pray that you be happily lost forever. Pray for blessed obliteration.' I will *not* pray that I be happily lost forever. I would rather burn in a hell forever than suffer happy obliteration! I'll burn if it be *me* that burn. I want me to be me. I will refuse forever to surrender myself."

It was a restless night for him. Well, perhaps he could die the easier if he were wearied and sleepless at dawn.

"Other men don't make such a fuss about it," he told himself (the self he refused to give up). "Other men are truly happy in obliteration. Why am I suddenly different? Other men desire to be lost, lost, lost. How have I lost the faith of my childhood and my manhood? What is unique about me?"

There was no answer to that.

"Whatever is unique about me, I refuse to give it up. I will howl and moan against that extinction for billions of centuries. Ah, I will go sly! I will devise a sign so I will know me if I meet me again."

About an hour before dawn the Lay Priest Migma, P.T. de C., came to Dookh-Doctor Drague. The dolcus and the arktos had reported that the man was resting badly and was not properly disposed.

"I have an analogy that may ease your mind, Dookh-Doctor," the Lay Priest whispered softly, "–ease it into great easiness, salve it into great salving–"

"Begone, fellow, your salve has lost its twinkle."

"Consider that we have never lived, that we have only seemed to live. Consider that we do not die, but are only absorbed into great selfless self. Consider the odd sphairikoi of this world—"

"What about the sphairikoi? I consider them often."

"I believe that they are set here for our instruction. A sphairikos is a total globe, the type of the great oneness. Then consider that it sometimes ruffles its surface, extrudes a little false-foot from its soft surface. Would it not be odd if that false-foot, for its brief second, considered itself a person? Would you not laugh at that?"

"No, no. I do not laugh." And the Dookh-Doctor was on his feet.

"And in much less than a second, that pseudopod is withdrawn back into the sphere of the sphairikoi. So it is with our lives. Nothing dies. It is only a ripple on the surface of the oneness. Can you entertain so droll an idea as that the pseudopod should remember, or wish to remember?"

"Yes. I'll remember it a billion years for the billion who forget."

The Dookh-Doctor was running uphill in the dark. He crashed into trees and boles as though he wished to remember the crashing forever.

"I'll burn before I forget, but I must have something that says it's me who burns!"

Up, up by the spherical huts of the sphairikoi, bawling and stumbling in the dark. Up to a hut that had a certain fame he could never place, to the hut that had its own identity, that sparkled with identity.

"Open, open, help me!" the Dookh-Doctor cried out at the last hut on the hill.

"Go away, man!" the last voice protested. "All my clients are gone, and the night is almost over with. What has this person to do with a human man anyhow?"

It was a round twinkling voice out of the roweled dark. But there was enduring identity there. The twinkling, enduring-identity colors, coming from the chinks of the hut, had now reached the level of vision. There was even the flicker of the I-will-know-me-if-I-meet-me-again color.

"Torchy Twelve, help me. I am told that you have the special salve that solves the last problem, and makes it know that it is always itself that is solved."

"Why, it is the Dookh-Doc! Why have you come to Torchy?"

"I want something to send me into kind and everlasting slumber," he moaned. "But I want it to be *me* who slumbers. Cannot you help me in any way?"

"Come you in, the Dookh-Doc. This person, though promiscuous, is expert. I help you—"

Jim and Mary G

by James Sallis

Getting his little coat down off the hook, then his arms into it, not easy because he's so excited and he always turns the wrong way anyhow. And all the time he's looking up at you with those blue eyes. We go park Papa, he says. We go see gulls. Straining for the door. The gulls are a favorite; he discovered them on the boat coming across and can't understand, he keeps looking for them in the park.

Wrap the muffler around his neck. Yellow, white. (Notice how white the skin is there, how the veins show through.) They call them scarves here don't they. Stockingcap—he pulls it down over his eyes, going Haha. He hasn't learned to laugh yet. Red mittens. Now move the zipper up and he's packed away. The coat's green corduroy, with black elastic at the neck and cuffs and a round hood that goes down over the cap. It's November. In England. Thinking, the last time I'll do this. Is there still snow on the ground, I didn't look this morning.

Take his hand and go on out of the flat. Letting go at the door because it takes two hands to work the latch, Mary rattling dishes in the kitchen. (Good-bye, she says very softly as you shut the door.) He goes around you and beats you to the front door, waits there with his nose on the glass. The hall is full of white light. Go on down it to him. The milk's come, two bottles, with the *Guardian* leaning between them. Move the mat so we can open the door. We go park Papa, we seegulls. Frosty foggy air coming in. Back for galoshes, all the little brass-tongue buckles? No the snow's gone. Just some dirty slush. Careful. Down the steps.

Crunching down the sidewalk ahead of you, disappointed

because there's no snow but looking back, Haha. We go park? The sky is flat and white as a sheet of paper. Way off, a flock of birds goes whirling across it, circling inside themselves—black dots, like iron filings with a magnet under the paper. The block opposite is lined with trees. What kind? The leaves are all rippling together. It looks like green foil. Down the walk.

Asking, Why is everything so still. Why aren't there any cars. Or a mailtruck. Or milkcart, gliding along with bottles jangling. Where is everyone. It's ten in the morning, where is everyone.

But there is a car just around the corner, stuck on ice at the side of the road where it parked last night with the wheels spinning Whrrrrrr. Smile, you understand a man's problems. And walk the other way. His mitten keeps coming off in your hand. Haha.

She had broken down only once, at breakfast.

The same as every morning, the child had waked them. Standing in his bed in the next room and bouncing up and down till the springs were banging against the frame. Then he climbed out and came to their door, peeking around the frame, finally doing his tiptoe shyly across the floor in his white wool nightshirt. Up to their bed, where they pretended to be still asleep. Brekpust, brekpust, he would say, poking at them and tugging the covers, at last climbing onto the bed to bounce up and down between them until they rolled over: Hello. Morninggg. He is proud of his *g*'s. Then, Mary almost broke down, remembering what today was, what they had decided the night before.

She turned her face toward the window (they hadn't been able to afford curtains yet) and he heard her breathe deeply several times. But a moment later she was up—out of bed in her quilted robe and heading for the kitchen, with the child behind her.

He reached and got a cigarette off the trunk they were using as a night-table. It had a small wood lamp, a bra, some single cigarettes and a jarlid full of ashes and filters on it. Smoking, listening to water running, pans clatter, cupboards and drawers. Then the sounds stopped and he heard them together in the bathroom: the tap ran for a while, then the toilet flushed and he heard the child's pleased exclamations. They went back into the kitchen and the sounds resumed. Grease crackling, the child chattering about how good he had been. The fridge door opened and shut, opened again, Mary said something. He was trying to help.

He got out of bed and began dressing. How strange that she'd forgotten to take him to the bathroom first thing, she'd never done that before. Helpinggg, from the kitchen by way of explanation, as he walked to the bureau. It was square and ugly, with that shininess peculiar to cheap furniture, and it had been in the flat when they moved in, the only thing left behind. He opened a drawer and took out a shirt. All his shirts were white. Why, she had once asked him, years ago. He didn't know, then or now.

He went into the kitchen with the sweater over his head. "Mail?" Through the wool. Neither of them looked around, so he pulled it the rest of the way on, reaching down inside to tug the shirtcollar out. Then the sleeves.

"A letter from my parents. They're worried they haven't heard from us, they hope we're all right. Daddy's feeling better, why don't we write them."

The child was dragging his high-chair across the floor from the corner. Long ago they had decided he should take care of as many of his own needs as he could—a sense of responsibility, Mary had said—but this morning Jim helped him carry the chair to the table, slid the tray off, lifted him into it and pushed the chair up to the table. When he looked up, Mary turned quickly away, back to the stove.

Eggs, herring, toast and ham. "I thought it would be nice," Mary said. "To have a good breakfast." And that was the time she broke down.

The child had started scooping the food up in his fingers, so she got up again and went across the kitchen to get his spoon. It was heavy silver, with an ivory *K* set into the handle, and it had been her own. She turned and came back across the tile, holding the little spoon in front of her and staring at it. Moma cryinggg, the child said. Moma cryinggg. She ran out of the room. The child turned in his chair to watch her go, then turned back and went on eating with the spoon. The plastic padding squeaked as the child moved inside it. The chair was metal, the padding white with large blue asterisks all over it. They had bought it at a Woolworths. Twelve and six. Like the bureau, it somehow fit the flat.

A few minutes later Mary came back, poured coffee for both of them and sat down across from him.

"It's best this way," she said. "He won't have to suffer. It's the only answer."

He nodded, staring into the coffee. Then took off his glasses and cleaned them on his shirttail. The child was stirring the eggs and herring together in his bowl. Holding the spoon like a chisel in his hand and going round and round the edge of the bowl.

"Jim . . ."

He looked up. She seemed to him, then, very tired, very weak.

"We could take him to one of those places. Where they . . . take care of them . . . for you."

He shook his head, violently. "No, we've already discussed that, Mary. He wouldn't understand. It will be easier, my way. If I do it myself."

She went to the window and stood there watching it. It filled most of one wall. It was frosted over.

"How would you like to go for a walk after breakfast," he asked the child. He immediately shoved the bowl away and said, "Bafroom first?"

"You or me?" Mary said from the window.

Finally: "You."

He sat alone in the kitchen, thinking. Taps ran, the toilet flushed, he came out full of pride. "We go park," he said. "We go see gulls."

"Maybe." It was this, the lie, which came back to him later; this was what he remembered most vividly. He got up and walked into the hall with the child following him and put his coat on. "Where's his other muffler?"

"In the bureau drawer. The top one."

He got it, then began looking for the stockingcap and mittens. Walking through the rooms, opening drawers. There aren't any seagulls in London. When she brought the cap and mittens to him there was a hole in the top of the cap and he went off looking for the other one. Walking through rooms, again and again into the child's own.

"For God's sake go on," she finally said. "Please stop. O damn Jim, go on." And she turned and ran back into the kitchen.

Soon he heard her moving about. Clearing the table, running water, opening and shutting things. Silverware clicking.

"We go park?"

He began to dress the child. Getting his little coat down off the hook. Wrapping his neck in the muffler. There aren't any seagulls in London. Stockingcap, Haha.

Thinking, This is the last time I'll ever do this.

Now bump, bump, bump. Down the funny stairs.

When he returned, Mary was lying on the bed, still in the quilted robe, watching the ceiling. It seemed very dark, very cold in the room. He sat down beside her in his coat and put his hand on her arm. Cars moved past the window. The people upstairs had their radio on.

"Why did you move the bureau?" he asked after a while.

Without moving her head she looked down toward the foot of the bed. "After you left I was lying here and I noticed a traffic light or something like that out on the street was reflected in it. It was blinking on and off, I must have watched it for an hour. We've been here for weeks and I never saw that before. But once I did, I had to move it."

"You shouldn't be doing heavy work like that."

For a long while she was still, and when she finally moved, it was just to turn her head and look silently into his face.

He nodded, once, very slowly.

"It didn't . . ."

No.

She smiled, sadly, and he lay down beside her in the small bed. She seemed younger now, rested, herself again. There was warmth in her hand when she took his own and put them together on her stomach.

They lay quietly through the afternoon. Ice was re-forming on the streets; outside, they could hear wheels spinning, engines racing. The hall door opened, there was a jangle of milkbottles, the door closed. Then everything was quiet. The trees across the street drooped under the weight of the ice.

There was a sound in the flat. Very low and steady, like a ticking. He listened for hours before he realized it was the drip of a faucet in the bathroom.

Outside, slowly, obscuring the trees, the night came. And with it, snow. They lay together in the darkness, looking out the frosted window. Occasionally, lights moved across it.

"We'll get rid of his things tomorrow," she said after a while.

The Pressure of Time

by Thomas M. Disch

They were learning all about history, the holy martyrs and Rome burning down and if you didn't burn incense for Jupiter you had to go into the Colosseum while the pagans watched. Jupiter is a false god, but we believe in one god the Father Almighty. There was a little girl in the picture too, with a white dress for purity and white flowers in her hair, and Sister Augustine said the holy martyrs should be an inspiring example for every boy and girl.

They had waited all day, because the smallest children went last, but at last the Public Health man came and talked to Sister. He had a white dress with gold buttons, and his hair was gold, too, like tiny gold wires, because he was English. So they put on their sweaters and went outside to wait in line beside the medical unit in the wet gravel with puddles everywhere. Emma was the monitor. She stood at the end of the line in her red sweater and her little red polly boots, fingering the pink health card with her name on it. Her first name began with *E* and her second name began with an *R*, but she was slow in Reading—all the little letters looked the same. But if you don't learn to read, you won't know what the signs say on top of stores, you won't know what street you're on if you ever go to Dublin, and you can't make a shopping list.

She went in the door and the man with the gold beard took her card and jiggled it in his machine, and then Mary Ellen Poorlick screamed like a banshee. The man who stuck the needles in tried to talk to her, but with his funny accent you couldn't understand a word. Jamie Baro was next, then Emma, and she couldn't look away from the needle, as long as her own middle finger. If she had to be a holy martyr, she knew she'd have run away when the lions came out of their cages instead of singing along with the others, but the door was closed behind her now, and the man said, "Try and relax now, Emma." He was a fairy, because fairies have gold hair like that, and in any case all the English are bent as a pin. That's what Leonard said. He put something cold on her arm, while the needle filled up with more white stuff, and she clenched herself tight all over, and he stuck it right into her arm.

She knew the very next thing after that that she must have done something wrong then, because she was in the Principal's Office, and Sister Mary Margaret was putting water on her face, but worse than that her Cousin Bridie was there with one of the babies. Bridie was saying, "Oh, tension! Her mother is another great one for tensions."

She tried to sit up in the day-nap cot, but Sister Mary Margaret pushed her flat again. "You'd better rest a minute, my dear. You're not well."

Emma touched her arm where it hurt. There was a band-aid on it.

Cousin Bridie said, "We're taking up your time, Sister," and Sister Mary Margaret said, "Nonsense," and handed Emma a cone of water to drink.

"Say thank you," said Cousin Bridie. Emma said thank you.

"You see, it's all over now, and there wasn't anything to fuss about, was there? The pain is always in the waiting, not in the thing we've waited for."

Cousin Bridie sighed and rocked the baby. Her lips were unhappy, the way they got when she was cooking dinner, but when she listened to music her face was pretty, or when there was a funny show on the telly, and when she was like that you could talk to her and she was nicer than almost any other grown-up. But not when her lips were like that.

So she rested and then Sister Mary Margaret said, "Emma, your cousin is here to take you home with her for a little while. You have to promise to be very good. Sister

Augustine tells me you're one of her best-behaved children."

Emma looked down at the band-aid. "Did I do something then?"

"What do you mean, Emma?"

"Something wrong–out there?"

"Oh, this is nothing to do with the polio shot. We can't help things like that. It's because your grandfather–or rather your great-grandfather, I believe?"

"Yes," said Cousin Bridie.

"Your great-grandfather has finally passed on, as we all must, and you're to stay with your cousin during the wake. Only three or four days. We'll all have to say prayers for him to help him out of purgatory, though I'm sure he won't need many. He was a very good man."

"He was a patriot," Cousin Bridie said. She began to cry.

"Comfort yourself, Mrs. Anckers. I'm sure death came as a blessing. He was an old man and he suffered great pain. Pray to Our Lady. Think of the sorrow that must have been hers. We must all expect to lose our fathers and mothers, but *she* lost a child, her only child, so that He might pay the price for our sins."

Cousin Bridie stopped crying.

"Now, if Emma is feeling well enough, I must be getting back to my class. Your family is in my prayers." She touched a finger to Emma's arm, close to the hurt, and smiled and left.

Bridie put the baby in the pram that was standing in a puddle outside the door. The wheels made snaky tracks on the dry pavement. You could hear a classroom, inside, singing Old Black Joe. Emma loved Music best, taking after her father in that. Her father was dead.

Cousin Bridie took her hand crossing the street, though she didn't need to. Emma was six going on seven and walked home every day by herself or sometimes with the Kramer boy.

She asked, "How old is Granny?"

"Eighty-six."

"Is that old to die?"

"You might say so. In Ireland."

"But not in England?"

"Who's been talking to you about England?"

"Nobody."

"Your mother?"

"Sister Augustine says you don't have to die in England, because they're all heretics there."

"I'll bet your mother *has* been saying things to you." Cousin Bridie made one of her faces. She didn't get on with Emma's mother. The Anckers were poor and lived on O'Connell Street, while Emma and her mother lived with their grandfather above the flowershop, *Tauler's Ageless Flowers.* Mr. Tauler was a Jew, and handled the commercial end. Emma's grandfather made the flowers, but he was too fat to look after the shop, so Emma's mother did that now, and Emma washed the flowers with Fairy Liquid, first a capital *F,* then a capital *L.*

The Anckers lived in two rooms in the basement with the three babies, Florence, Christopher, and Angela. One whole wall was covered with the books, old books from before the Plague some of them. They were Leonard's books. Leonard was Cousin Bridie's tragedy. He had a degree from Trinity College and he was supposed to make houses except he didn't, so when you visited them you had to eat Public Health food from Unesco, and right before every meal Cousin Bridie would say, "I hope you don't mind the way we eat." It was better food most of the time than the food from stores.

After the babies' formula Cousin Bridie sat down by the telly, *Sunset Serenades.* Leonard was out at a Conservative meeting, and Emma, being careful, took out one of the tall books. A woman was laying down on a bed without any clothes and there was a fat nigger-woman behind her carrying flowers. Then there was a boy dressed up like an Irish National Security Agent and playing a flute. Then just some flowers. Then a sort of mess with a boat in it. Then the woman who looked so much like Emma's mother that they all agreed it was a miracle. She had a parrot too.

Leonard came home drunk and said he damn well did think it was a cause for celebration, and Cousin Bridie said he was disgusting and there are some things you shouldn't say.

And then Leonard said, "Well I say fuck him and fry him, the old bastard."

You should never say fuck.

And Cousin Bridie said, "Little pitchers."

And Leonard said, "Jesus Christ, why didn't you tell me we had company!"

Then they had dinner. Dinner was soup with cabbage and bones, then some fried protein and veg, then a nice fortified pudding, though Leonard took most of it on his own plate. Cousin Bridie said, "I hope you don't mind the way we eat" four different times.

After dinner you always have to watch the telly, first *Newsflash,* which never made much sense except about superstars, then *Looking Back,* about the First Famine a hundred years ago, and that was fun but it only lasted ten minutes, and then *This Emerald Isle.* Tonight it was only a panel discussion of teenagers about kissing. A month ago Sean Kramer had kissed her and she'd shown him her bottom and he showed her his bottom with the peewee on it. It was a secret. The discussion was moderated by the Right Reverend C. S. Marchesini, S. J., who was very much in the public eye lately and talked about. Sometimes kissing was a sin and sometimes it wasn't, and the best policy was to ask your confessor.

It was eight o'clock when Emma's mother came by; she was late. Cousin Bridie said, "Mary, you look just beautiful! Leonard, doesn't she look beautiful?"

Leonard said, "Yes."

Her mother said, "I dug it out of Ellen's trunk. It was the only thing I could find."

Cousin Bridie said, "It's just beautiful."

And it was, Emma thought, very beautiful. Her mother was always beautiful, more than anyone else she'd ever seen.

It was going to be a lovely funeral. People would be coming from Dublin to be there. The Council had voted a monument. Leonard had to laugh about that. He showed them the drawing *he'd* made, using the true and only limestone of Kilkenny that God put there. Leonard didn't believe in the new materials. Her mother said after all you can't tell the difference. Leonard said *he* could tell the difference. Her mother said she supposed a man in his line of work would have to, but it came to the question of money, didn't it? Cousin Bridie said she thought there were times when it wasn't a question of money. Some things are sacred. Her mother said, "Well, well, I suppose Bridie is right." Cousin Bridie made one of her faces.

They went for a walk, Emma and her mother, down O'Connell Street and up Cathedral Street and along the iron bars that fenced St. Stephen's Cathedral where Leonard wouldn't go, instead he went to Immaculate Conception on the other side of town, even on Christmas and Easter, and then in by the broken gate. Her mother explained about the wake and all the visitors and having to stay with the Anckers, because they were their only relatives now. You couldn't count the Almraths or the Smiths. But it wouldn't be for long.

"And then . . ."

"And then we'll go away?"

Her mother laughed the way she did when they were all living together and she lifted Emma up and hugged her into the chilly silk of Ellen's dress. Ellen died, and then Emma's father in the fight, and now Granny. They were Catholics and Catholics have to die. Someday Emma's mother would die, and someday Emma would die, too, and it can be a beautiful experience if you are in a state of grace.

"Yes, we'll go away. We *will* go away. But you mustn't talk about it, darling. Not even now. And if your Cousin Bridie tries to talk to you about England, or about me, you must say that you don't know anything about what I'm going to do with my share of the money. It's our secret. Do you promise?"

"Yes. But will you tell me about London?"

"London–oh, London is going to be wonderful, Emma. When you see it the first time you'll think you're in a dream. London is the most beautiful city in the world. Dublin is just a dustheap by comparison." She gave Emma one more squeeze and lowered her. The grass where they walked was so long that it tickled her legs over the tops of her boots and made them wet.

"There'll be music in the streets and sunlight all night long, or as good as sunlight. The buildings are all fresh and new, not scabby and full of mice, and there is a park there as big as all Clonmel that's filled with flowers, real flowers growing in dirt. And there are towers so high that on a cloudy day you can't see to the top, because the clouds get in the way. And the people will be different there. So much happier. The people are beautiful; they're young. No one is resentful or afraid. No one is poor. In London you can live your own life for its own sake. You don't have to lie to yourself or to anyone else. You can't understand what a difference it *will* make–to be beautiful . . . to be free."

"Will we have to be pagans, too, if we go there, and never die?"

Her mother stopped and squatted so her face was on a level with Emma's. She smiled with her mouth open, and her hair was blowing across her eyes. She looked beautiful.

"Darling! darling!" And she laughed. "It's not as simple as that. *They* can't help it that they don't die, and we can't help it that we do."

"Why?"

"If I could answer that question, Emma"–she brushed

her hair back, dark brown like Emma's, and stood up—"then Ireland would cease to exist."

They walked back to the gate on the path. A priest was standing by the second Station of the Cross, saying a rosary, swaying.

"Good evening, Mrs. Rosetti. So the end has come at last. He was a good man. The world will seem a little smaller now."

"Yes, a tragedy," Mrs. Rosetti mumbled, hurrying out the gate.

"Good evening, Emma," the priest called out.

"Good evening, Father."

She watched him flickering through the bars and holly prickles, as her mother hurried her along on the walk. How did he know her name was Emma? She'd never seen him before in her life.

His name was the Right Reverend C. S. Marchesini, S. J., from Dublin, and he gave the funeral sermon, Death, where is thy victory? St. Stephen's was filled almost like Sunday with just a few pews at the back empty. Emma sat between her mother and Mr. Tauler, the Jew who handled the commercial end, right at the front. St. Augustine said you shouldn't call them Jews if they were baptized, but everyone did anyhow.

Emma had a black dress too today, but the hem was only tacked because the babies were teething all night and Cousin Bridie got drunk. When her mother came in the car, there was a quarrel. Leonard said he'd be damned if he'd set his foot in that travesty, and her mother said it would come as no surprise to anyone if he was. Cousin Bridie started crying and kept it up all the way to the church.

Just before the last hymn everyone had to go look inside the coffin. Her mother lifted her up. He was wearing lipstick and smiling, and she thought he looked nice, because usually he didn't smile. He wasn't as fat either, and he didn't have his cane. Unless he was laying on top of it. He used to grab her with his cane, when she wasn't careful, slipping the crook around her neck. Her mother said that when she was a little girl he did the same thing to her. It was the sort of thing you had to put up with. Emma kissed him on the cheek. It was hard, like a doll's.

They rode in a car to the Rock, twenty miles, and when they got there the wind was incredible and the wreath almost blew off. There were fewer people out here, fuel being what it was. The Right Reverend C. S. Marchesini, S. J. The city fathers and the Archbishop. And of course all the relatives–Emma and her mother, Cousin Bridie with Florence, her oldest, and the Almraths from Dublin and the Smiths from Cork. Old Mrs. Almrath was Emma's great-aunt and sent her a holy card every Christmas that was blessed by the Pope. She had two, a Virgin and a Sacred Heart blessed by Innocent, and one, St. Peter, blessed by Leo. Someday, Mrs. Almrath said, she would get Emma an audience with Pope Leo.

They put the coffin with Granny in it in the hole and covered it up with dirt. Mr. Smith said, "He was a great man, a great man. They don't come in that size anymore." Her mother was holding Cousin Bridie around her waist, and Cousin Bridie was crying. The Anckers weren't getting any of the money, and that's what the fight had really been about. Bridie said she didn't care, but Leonard said *he* cared. He hadn't put up with the old bastard's shit all these years to have his nose rubbed in it now. Her mother said Leonard couldn't lose a game of draughts with any grace and everyone knew it. She was sorry for Bridie and the babies, but Bridie had made her mistake four years ago, and she'd said so at the time.

The last thing they did, they all gathered around the monument to admire it and to find a nice place to put their weather-sealed floral tributes. The monument was six feet tall and rather fat and there were hundreds of capital letters all over it.

It was dark and Emma was the ghost. She didn't know if she should run when she was bleeding, but she ran. Down the row of cattleyas, shimmering behind their curtain of air: no one. She glanced up at the holly, where the decorative soldiery of ancient Rome celebrated their eternal triumph. Of course they couldn't be hiding *there.* It was an illusion, something to do with light waves, she couldn't remember. She made a scary noise–Whoo! No one answered. Maybe they were all home safe. She went back, stood within the shadow of the vent, alone. Below and above Hampstead and the sky arranged themselves in geometries of white light. Each little star was a sun, far away, burning. She had seen them depart in cars like seashells, though she had not understood then where they were bound. Tau Ceti. All the stars have foreign names, and the planets are Roman gods. Her own name was foreign. So many languages, you'd never learn all of them.

Up the ramp then to the very top, past pots of planted palms, gray in the lamplight. Within the arcade there were no lights. She went *Whoo,* barely a whisper this time. Girls have more to be afraid of than boys, at night. The thin columns of seeming stone slanted up to the terminating darkness of the vault. Inside her weatherproof her clothes were damp with sweat. The newer ones had pores, like skin, but wouldn't that let the heat out too? The real solution was to live somewhere that was warm in the winter. Malaga. Hollywood. Carthage. Basking in the sun. Swimming in warm saltwater, though not if it was your period of course. Sharks can smell blood.

Unhealthy daydreams. Even if they weren't sinful, it was a bad habit to get into.

Four stars formed a rectangle within the arch's parabolic slice of sky: God's Door, her mother had said.

God closing his door
in the sky,
and all trace of its outline
disappears.

It was a famous poem before it was a song. Her voice squeaked nervously in the high arbors of the ziggurat, but the voice *she* heard, interiorly, was not her own but St. Theresa's.

Ecstasy—Emma wondered if she had any talent for that sort of thing. Though probably it was a sin. Probably.

She wiggled her right hand into the polly weatherproof and touched the larger breast. It had stopped hurting, but the left one was still painful, though not awfully. Another month, her mother had said, but it was already past that time.

She was too old, really, for games like this. Boring and juvenile. Daphne was only ten. She needed a friend more her own age, but there weren't any in this part of Hampstead. Even though they were so much better off now, she wished sometimes they were back on Lant Street.

Two grown-ups were making love in one of the caves. She walked past them quickly, embarrassed. The man called out her name.

It was Walt, and her mother was with him. She said, "Hello, Walt. How are you?" It had been a year or more since she'd seen him.

Her mother said, "We're both fine, sweetheart. Did you come up here looking for me?"

"No. I'm the ghost."

"Just haunting us, eh?" Walt said.

"It's a game they play," her mother said. "What time is it?"

Emma looked at the watch on her bracelet. "Seven-thirty."

Walt had sat up, but her mother was still laying in the mossy stuff. She sounded high. "Is King Arthur in?"

King Arthur was her name for Mr. Schiel, their benefactor.

"I don't think so," Emma said. "I don't know."

"Come and sit down with us a minute, Rose-Red." Walt patted the moss. His hair was changed from the way she remembered it, and his face was darker. He was a cook for Wimpy's and unbearably handsome.

"I can't. I have to look for the other kids. They're hiding."

"Emma?" Her mother rose to her knees in slow motion. Her mouth drooped open, like St. Theresa's. Emma had practiced the same expression when she was alone, but it didn't work for her. Her lower lip was too thin.

"Yes, Mother." She assumed a tone of tolerance.

"It would be better if you didn't say anything to Arthur about . . ."

"No, Mother, of course not."

"And if he asks–"

"I'll just say I've been playing on the roof since school and I don't know where you are."

"Neither do I, sweetheart. Neither do I." She chuckled, and Walt took hold of her hand. "I'm somewhere out in space, fitting all the links together."

"What?" Emma asked, though she knew better than to try and make sense of what her mother said at such times.

"The links–the links between the stars, the links of my armor, the links of the endless chain."

Emma nodded unhappily and backed off down the arcade. When she reached the ramp, she began running. Daphne, Ralph, and Ralph's little sister were all standing in the shadow of the vent, safe.

"Where are you going?" Daphne called to her.

She pressed the red button for the lift. She didn't know what to say. Her mother was supposed to have stopped taking that sort of thing. Arthur had spent all sorts of money to help her. "Home," she said, just as the lift opened its doors. She fed her house-tag into the slot.

The lift said, "Good evening, Miss Rosetti. I hope you've enjoyed yourself." But if you said anything back, it didn't understand. Arthur Schiel worked for a company and was rich, so they lived in a luxury building, but even though he'd been very good to Emma and her mother, he was a stupid snob and nobody really liked him.

Emma felt just sick.

He was waiting in the wool chair that had cost so much, undressed. The Volkswagen was parked by the sink, filling with water for his bath. Except for the splash of the water, the room was quiet. Arthur didn't like music.

"Where is your mother, Emma?" he asked.

"How should I know?" she said. She knew she should try to be nice to him, but it was so hard.

While she tucked her weatherproof away, he watched her with a sarcastic smile. She went to the back end of the telly, where he couldn't see her, and used the earphones while the flickering images smoothed her distress, like a hand that gently closed the lids of her eyes.

Arthur Schiel, sitting in the costly discomfort of the woolen chair, listened to the running water and stared at Emma's tapping feet with helpless, unassuageable rage.

That was the night they were thrown out and had to go to Lant Street to live, once again, with Walt.

The screen, an American-made holly, represented an interior of the Katsura Palace with a view onto a spring garden roseate with blossoms of apricot. Three feet by six (to match the tatami that they had always intended to buy), it rented from DER at £5 a month.

When slid aside, the screen discovered a nest of three desks and, above and below, a utility honeycomb housing a defunct dictionary, a wonky tape machine, and an Olivetti with a frayed, faint ribbon but still functioning, except for the tab. The remaining cells of this hive were given over now to Emma's collection of pebbles from the beaches of Brighton and Hastings: flint, shingle, sandstone, red and gray quartzite, shale, and chert.

Emmy—the Baby Bear of the household—had the smallest of the three desks. Her desk had its own drawer, which she always locked, keeping the key on her bracelet. Inside the drawer there were a diary for the year 2088 (never completed), a plastic daff, a small bottle of Lourdes water (a departing present from Sister Mary Margaret), a string of unmatched pearls salvaged from one of her mother's tirades, and an antique Suchard chocolate box. Inside the chocolate box, in a white envelope, were three photos, each two and a half by four inches.

The first showed three men and a cow standing before a large ochrous house. The shutters and the long wooden balcony railing above the first floor were painted moss-green. The cow, gravid with milk, stood in the foreground, interrupting a full view of two of the men. The third, drably dressed, faced away from the camera and seemed to be there, like the cow, for the sake of local color. The men smiling into the camera had somehow the air of tourists. Their faces were tanned with the same cheery gold as the walls of the house. The taller man wore a white suit embroidered with roses and a ruffled shirt; ringlets of red hair blew across his rather weak chin. The other man, bare-chested, in shorts, held a bottle of wine up, toasting the photographer. On the back of the picture, in purple ink, was written: "Reutte, July '52."

The second photograph showed the head and shoulders of a man resembling the taller of the two men in the first photograph, though now his hair was brown and his chin was strengthened by a van Dyke. He had put on some weight as well. His cheeks and lower lip seemed uncommonly red, his expression slack. Perhaps he had been drinking. His eyelids drooped, Buddha-like, over bright turquoise eyes that focused on the camera with an intensity out of keeping with his other features. Behind him an orange tree exhibited leaves and three small oranges. This photo was unlabeled.

The third bore an inscription across the cloud-haze in the upper third of the picture: "Walt and Me—Summer Holyday." The same man was once again redheaded. His beard was fuller, his face and body more lean. Except for a silver bracelet and a thick silver chain about his neck, he was naked, as was the little girl he held in the air. The skin of his torso, arms, and legs, shaved for competition and shining with oil, was perfectly smooth. His hands supported the girl's pelvic girdle, and she maintained a precarious balance by resting her forehead against his. They grinned, staring into each other's eyes. In the middle distance, part of the promiscuous mass of bathers, Emma's mother could be discerned resting in a beach chair, modestly bikinied, her eyes averted from the playful pair in the foreground to regard the gray-green sea.

Often when she found herself alone in their two-room flat, Emma would slide away the screen, unlock the drawer, and take out the Suchard box. When she had finished looking at the photographs, she would kiss each in turn, lips pressed tightly together, before replacing them in the envelope. She was in love with Walt.

"Are there," old Mr. Harness asked, "any in the class . . . who . . . ?" The dry lips crumbled in an unspoken apology. The quick eyes, yellow as the basins of the school lav, caught her embarrassed glance and shifted away.

Would I have been silent, if he had asked? Emma wondered. *Would I have faced the lions?*

After all, even if they did find out she was a Catholic, they couldn't do anything worse than tease her a bit, the way they had at the other school.

"Of course," he mumbled, "my account may differ significantly from the what-would-you-say . . . the official account of the Irish Church. It lacks the *nihil obstat.*

Events such as these, possessing still some flavor of controversy, resist our efforts to order them by simple schemes."

Charmian Levin, sitting behind Emma, touched a pencil-tip to a knob of her spine. Emma stiffened and tucked in her blouse.

"History is never simple, of course, until we cease to care too terribly much. One might liken the mechanism of tolerance to the painter's trick of aerial perspective: with distance, we lose the edge and color of things. We gain, perhaps, the vista."

Charmian, who at fifteen was the oldest girl at Inverness, swiveled ninety degrees on her stool and, with a schooled gesture, fluttered the white banner of her hair. "Oh, August–such blague!"

The yellow eyes lowered to regard the girl's glasslike sandals. The old man wondered, with a small sad spite, what part of his monthly salary they had cost.

"I *was* rather straying, wasn't I? To return, then, to the Papal Bull of 2034–"

Emma wrote in her notebook: "Papal Bull, 2034."

"–which was dubbed, almost immediately, the 'Mad Bull,' due to a short-lived effort, within the Roman hierarchy, to call the Pope's sanity into question. But, as the instigators of this plan were themselves immortal survivors of the Plague and, by this new pronouncement, excommunicate, their actions served only to hasten the schism that John was seeking to bring about."

Emma wrote in her notebook: "Heretics excommuinicated." Charmian's pencil traced a line along her lower rib.

"I think, in retrospect, that John acted in the best interests of his church, even though the immediate effect was an eighty percent reduction in its membership. That figure indicates how much, even then, the new sensibility had found itself at odds with the traditional outlook that the Church represented, for the ratio of mortals to immortals in the general population was then, as now, a mere fraction of one percent. In England and other more advanced nations, the falling-off had been much more drastic than that. In twenty thirty-two, two years before the Mad Bull, the Roman Catholic population of Britain had declined by fifty percent from its level at the turn of the century. And in other churches the decline was even more precipitate."

Emma wrote: "2032, 50%."

"The Church's real strength was in Central and South America, areas where disease and famine still maintained, if artificially, a sense of the mortal and a need to believe in an afterlife. But this could hardly be considered an enduring strength, founded as it was on ignorance and poverty. I think these considerations help to explain John's ruthlessness. The continued toleration of immortals within the Church could only have vitiated its potential as a what-shall-I-say . . . a rallying-point for the mortal element. And in this he was successful, as we know. We may judge it a small success, but possibly it was the only one that could have been wrested from the circumstances."

Emma wrote: "The Church victorious."

Mr. Harness asked: "Are there any questions? Charmian?"

"It still, you know, doesn't seem *fair.* I mean, most of that eighty percent that got booted out still believed all that stuff, didn't they? And then just to be told that it didn't make any *difference,* whether they believed. Could *they* help it they were born immortal?"

"On that point you would have to consult a Jesuit. The Church's position is that they could and can help it. We are all, or rather"—and again, and even more devastatingly, the lips crumbled—"*you* are all heretics. It's not essentially different from the notion of original sin."

"But, I *mean*! It's genetics."

"Yes—alas," said Mr. Harness.

Emma closed her notebook.

"Emma?"

"Please, I have to go to the lav."

Leaving Mr. Harness's room, Emma stepped squarely on Charmian Levin's splendid foot. She could almost feel, in her own foot, the pain she'd caused.

Once, in her first months at the Inverness School, Charmian had been Emma's best friend, but those days were gone forever. It was fruitless to suppose otherwise. Too much had been said on both sides, and there was no longer a basis for mutual respect.

Nevertheless, she did, bolted in the loo, open Charmian's note and read it, once, before flushing it down. It was an invitation to dinner that night with Charmian's family. Any reply was, of course, unthinkable. Mr. Levin was a business associate of Arthur Schiel, and if Emma's mother ever learned . . . It was bad enough (as Mrs. Rosetti had often pointed out) that Emma was finishing out the term at Inverness on the tuition provided by Arthur Schiel, but to visit the Levins *now,* to have to answer their well-meaning questions, to stand again in Mrs. Levin's proud salon, that perfect little temple of the New . . .

There was a knock on the door of the stall. "Emma, it's me, Charmian. I want to talk to you. Please."

"No."

"I *have* to talk to you. I told old Who-Shall-I-Say it was an urgent matter of feminine hygiene. Did you read my note?"

"No."

"You did read it. I can tell when you're lying, you know. Emma, I'm sorry for anything I said that might have offended you. I didn't mean it. I've been sick thinking about it, just sick. You *have* to come to dinner tonight."

"Do I?"

"I told my mother you were. She's always asking after you. She said she'd order a special cake from Wimpy's for us. We can be utter pigs about it."

Emma started to cry. It had not been a conscious cruelty

on Charmian's part, for Emma had never told her, or anyone else at Inverness, about Walt. Her new address was ignominy enough.

"Is it what I said about God? Is it that? I'm sorry, but I can't *help* what I believe, can I? I'd really like to believe in God, but I can't. I think it's a perfectly respectable idea, though, considered intellectually. I'd probably be happier if I did believe in him, but even then, I couldn't be a Catholic. They wouldn't let me. And I don't care *what* your church says–"

But Emma had never told Charmian she was a Catholic!

"–a person can't help the way he's born. *Will* you come to dinner?"

"It's impossible."

"Just this once. I can't *talk* to anybody anymore. Ellen is so basically stupid. You're younger than I am, but two years doesn't make that much difference. Emma, I need you–just desperately."

It was another ten minutes before Emma was persuaded. On their way to the tubes, Charmian said, "I have some tickets for Westminster Abbey. St. Theresa's going to be there."

"In person?"

Charmian arched a chalk-white brow. "Mm."

"Oh, wonderful!" She caught Charmian about the waist and kissed her cheek, leaving a scarlet smudge.

They are *more passionate,* Charmian thought with a somewhat grudging approval. She said: "You really *are* my best friend, you know."

Emma caught hold of the older girl's hand and smiled, but she could not bring herself to echo her words. It was not that she would, exactly, have been lying: Charmian was indeed her best–and her only–friend, as Charmian knew quite well. It was just that, even liking someone so awfully, it is unpleasant to be at their mercy.

Once you started burning their incense, they just didn't let you stop.

Noon, the First Friday of May. Along the High Street the shoppers offered to the vivid sun their English limbs, white for sacrifice. Like the very molecules of the air, flesh, warming, seemed to move at a quicker tempo. Mrs. Rosetti passed before the great moneyed pageant of shopfronts with a mild intoxication, as of amphetamine, scudding, a cloud. Dawdling, Emma followed.

The pavement divided right and left. Mrs. Rosetti would have preferred the mild self-surrender of the pedestrian belt that arced, at a temperate velocity of five mph, above and across the traffic stream, but Emma was able, with no stronger persuasion than a coaxing glance, to persuade her to take the left fork into the subway arcade. Fragments of advertising melodies lifted from sank into the ground bass of the ventilation, and at intervals the murmuring twilight opened into abrupt, bright recessions of holography. The hollies were crude things usually (for it had always been more dowdy, this side Thames)–book-vending machines, a shower of gold celebrating Ascot Day, odorless images of food that boded to be as flavorless in the eating, and everywhere dense crowds of mannikins in polly and paper dresses, and cheap copies of the new African masks. Often the shops proclaimed themselves with nothing more than a painted sign–

Buy Your
Wet Fish
Here

or, even more sparely–

Stuffs

–an austerity that had been smart a decade before but was now, once again, merely drab.

There was, however, one shop in this arcade that could equal, in a small way, the brilliances of Oxford Street or Piccadilly, and it was this that had lured both mother and daughter down from the daylight world. *The Bride Stripped Bare* was admittedly only an affiliate—one of the smallest—of the great Frisco-based couturier, but here, in Southwark, it was something quite out of the way. Already, this early, a crowd was gathered before the two long windows, and Emma, who was small for her thirteen years, had difficulty worming her way to a vantage point.

The model this week was a Madagascan, shorter even than Emma (a fashion house of any pretension had to employ mortals), with the piquant name of Baiba. The model's close-cropped head seemed grotesquely large, though considered as a thing apart it would have been judged a very pretty head indeed, with a ravishing pug nose and, when she grinned, deltas of deep-grained wrinkles about her dark eyes. She could easily have been as old as Emma's mother, though, of course, she carried the burden of her years with much more grace. Four attendants, two men and two women, dressed her and undressed her in Stripped Bare swimwear, Stripped Bare evening dresses, and Stripped Bare pollies and origami, but the last item—an elaborate ensemble of mourning clothes—Baiba put on without their assistance to a droll, rather honky-tonk version of *Death Shall Have No Dominion.*

"*Don't* they have lovely things there, Mother?" Emma asked, with what she thought a deceptive generality, as they continued down the arcade.

"Oh, yes," Mrs. Rosetti said, not taken in. "And very dear too."

"That little coral do-thingy was only twelve bob."

"That little coral doily would last about two days, *if* you were careful, and then it would be down the chute with it. Polly obsolesces fast enough."

"But I will need *something,* you know, for the party." Walt would be sixty-seven on the twelfth of May, and Emma was determined to shine for him.

Her mother was just as determined that she wouldn't—

not, at least, too brightly. "In any case, Emma, that dress is years too old for you."

"You say that about everything I like."

Mrs. Rosetti smiled vaguely. "Because everything you like *is* too old. Now *don't,* my darling, bring me down."

Emma, who had learned to read the signs of her mother's weathers, said no more, though she didn't, for all that, give up hope. Friday, when Walt was at work and her mother shopped, was a bad time to dig for favors. The disparity between the real and the ideal, between what the money had to go for and what one would simply *like,* was then too starkly defined.

They came out of the arcade in front of St. George the Martyr, another whited sepulcher of the C of E, which was nevertheless prettier, Emma had to admit, both inside and out, than St. George's Cathedral, where she went. Was it only that the Cathedral was made of yellow brick and lacked a proper steeple up front? The same architect, Pugin, had designed the cathedral in Killarney, which was *so* magnificent, but it only seemed stranger, then, that his London cathedral should be so . . . lacking. Emma would have liked, when she grew up, to become an architect, but for mortals that was out of the question. Leonard Ancker was the living proof of that.

"Come along then," her mother said. "It's only a church."

"Only!" she protested, but (Emma was in the state of grace) she obeyed. Almost at once the strength of this obedience was put to a second test. Passing Trinity Street, Emma wanted to turn off to look at the stalls of fresh flowers. Irises were selling at four and six the bunch, narcissi at three shillings. This time her mother would not be swerved.

"We don't have the time," she said. "Or the money."

"Only to look," Emma pleaded.

The fact was that Mrs. Rosetti, perhaps as a result of

years tending the shop, didn't appreciate flowers. "Emma!"

"Walt would like them. Walt loves flowers."

"Walt loves many things he can't afford, including us."

Sometimes her mother could be terribly coarse. Emma obeyed, though with a sense of having somewhat blemished, nonetheless, the immaculate Presence in the sanctuary of her breast.

At Maggy's on the Borough Road they stopped for a snack. Emma had a sixpenny cake from the machine, while her mother went to the counter for jellied eel. Maggy's was famous for its jellied eel. She ate them from the bag, four thick pale cylinders coated with quaking bits of gelatin. Now and again, chewing on one, she would wince, for her molars were getting worse.

Emma made a funny face. "I think those things are disgusting."

"That," her mother said, her mouth still full, "is half the pleasure of eating them. Would you like a taste?"

"Never!"

Her mother shrugged. "Never say never."

Which was, if you looked at it closely, a paradox.

They crossed St. George's Circus on the pedestrian belt. Emma's mother cursed the crowds of idlers and sightseers who rode the belt with no other purpose than to view the Vacancy at the center of the Circus. The Vacancy was a monumental sculptured hole, and Mr. Harness said it was one of the masterpieces of twentieth century art, but Emma, though she had looked at it and looked at it, could see nothing but a big, bumpy, black hole. There simply wasn't anything *there,* though now, because it was spring and people were flower-crazy, the lusterless plastic was strewn with flowers, irises and narcissi and even, here and there, the extravagance of a rose. The flowers were lovely, but the artist—Emma couldn't remember her name—could hardly be given credit for that. While she watched, a bunch of daffs, at two and six a dozen, hurtled from the north-south belt into the sculpture's maw, struck a ledge, and tumbled into the funereal heap in its farthest depth.

The drugstore on Lambeth Road was their last stop. Emma, as her conscience dictated, waited outside, almost within the shadow of St. George's Cathedral. From this simple, unkind juxtaposition, Emma had derived, some time before, her first conscious taste of irony. Her mother had not been to Mass for years. Just as everyone in Clonmel had foretold, Mrs. Rosetti had lost her faith. There was no use talking to her about it, you could only hope and pray.

Her eyes, when she came out, seemed much darker, black rather than brown. Her lower lip had slackened, become kind. She seemed, though in a way that Emma did not like, in some new way, more beautiful.

"Shall we go back now?" Emma asked, looking aside.

"As always," her mother said, with the barest hint, a wrinkle at the corner of her mouth, that this might be a joke. She leaned back against the garish mandala that was the trademark of the manufacturer of the shop's chief commodity.

"And did you go to Holy Communion today?" her mother asked.

Emma blushed, though it was certainly nothing to be ashamed of. "Yes. It's First Friday."

"Well, that's good." She closed her eyes.

After a long silence, she said, "The sun is very warm today."

"Yes," said a voice from behind Emma, "it will be summer before we know it."

Emma turned around. The speaker was an old woman in a dress of tattered black origami, an obvious piece of refuse. Sparse hair, dyed to a metallic silver, hung down over a face that was a witch's mask of sharp bones and pouchy skin.

She laid an arthritic hand on Emma's head. "She'll be a beautiful little lady, she will."

Mrs. Rosetti seemed to give this serious consideration before replying. "Probably. Probably she will."

The witch cackled. "You couldn't spare half a crown for an old woman, could you?"

"How old?"

"Old enough to know better." Another spasm of laughter, and the hand clenched, tangling itself in Emma's hair.

For no reason at all (since mortals no less decrepit than this woman were often to be seen in this part of the city) Emma felt terrified.

Mrs. Rosetti took a coin from her pocket and gave it to the old woman. Without a word of thanks, she pushed past Emma to the entrance of the drugstore.

Mrs. Rosetti put a hand on her shoulder. "*How* old?" she insisted.

It was hard to tell if the woman meant her smile to be as nasty as it looked to Emma. "Fifty-four. And how old are *you,* my lovely?"

Mrs. Rosetti closed her eyes tightly. Emma took her hand and tried to pull her away.

The woman followed them along the pavement. "*How* old?" she shrilled. "*How* old?"

"Thirty-seven," Mrs. Rosetti said in a whisper.

"It wasn't *you* I meant!" The old woman lifted her head, triumphant in her malice, then returned and entered the shop.

They walked back to Lant Street in silence, following a roundabout path along the least busy streets. Mrs. Rosetti did not notice her daughter's tears.

The bitterness that Emma felt was insupportable, and she could not, at last, stifle the cry of outrage: "How could you! How could you *do* it!"

Mrs. Rosetti regarded Emma with puzzlement, almost with fear. "Do what, Emma?"

"How could you give her that money? It was enough for a dozen daffs. And you just threw it away!"

She slapped Emma's face.

"I hate you!" Emma shouted at her. "And Walt hates you too!"

After the girl had run away, Mrs. Rosetti took another twenty grams. She sat down, not knowing where, not caring, and let the spring sun invade the vast vacancies of her flesh, a beauty that tumbled into her farthest depth.

The Island of Doctor Death and Other Stories

by Gene Wolfe

Winter comes to water as well as land, though there are no leaves to fall. The waves that were a bright, hard blue yesterday under a fading sky today are green, opaque, and cold. If you are a boy not wanted in the house you walk the beach for hours, feeling the winter that has come in the night; sand blowing across your shoes, spray wetting the legs of your corduroys. You turn your back to the sea, and with the sharp end of a stick found half buried write in the wet sand *Tackman Babcock.*

Then you go home, knowing that behind you the Atlantic is destroying your work.

Home is the big house on Settlers Island, but Settlers Island, so called, is not really an island and for that reason is not named or accurately delineated on maps. Smash a barnacle with a stone and you will see inside the shape from which the beautiful barnacle goose takes its name. There is a thin and flaccid organ which is the goose's neck and the mollusc's siphon, and a shapeless body with tiny wings. Settlers Island is like that.

The goose neck is a strip of land down which a county road runs. By whim, the mapmakers usually exaggerate the width of this and give no information to indicate that it is scarcely above the high tide. Thus Settlers Island appears to be a mere protuberance on the coast, not requiring a name—and since the village of eight or ten houses has none, nothing shows on the map but the spider line of road terminating at the sea.

The village has no name, but home has two: a near and a far designation. On the island, and on the mainland nearby, it is called the Seaview place because in the earliest years of the century it was operated as a resort hotel. Mama calls it The House of 31 February; and that is on her stationery and is presumably used by her friends in New York and Philadelphia when they do not simply say, "Mrs. Babcock's." Home is four floors high in some places, less in others, and is completely surrounded by a veranda; it was once painted yellow, but the paint–outside–is mostly gone now and The House of 31 February is grey.

Jason comes out the front door with the little curly hairs on his chin trembling in the wind and his thumbs hooked in the waistband of his Levi's. "Come on, you're going into town with me. Your mother wants to rest."

"Hey tough!" Into Jason's Jaguar, feeling the leather upholstery soft and smelly; you fall asleep.

Awake in town, bright lights flashing in the car windows. Jason is gone and the car is growing cold; you wait for what seems a long time, looking out at the shop windows, the big gun on the hip of the policeman who walks past, the lost dog who is afraid of everyone, even you when you tap the glass and call to him.

Then Jason is back with packages to put behind the seat. "Are we going home now?"

He nods without looking at you, arranging his bundles so they won't topple over, fastening his seatbelt.

"I want to get out of the car."

He looks at you.

"I want to go in a store. Come on, Jason."

Jason sighs. "All right, the drugstore over there, okay? Just for a minute."

The drugstore is as big as a supermarket, with long, bright aisles of glassware and notions and paper goods. Jason buys fluid for his lighter at the cigarette counter, and you bring him a book from a revolving wire rack. "Please, Jason?"

He takes it from you and replaces it in the rack, then when you are in the car again takes it from under his jacket and gives it to you.

It is a wonderful book, thick and heavy, with the edges of the pages tinted yellow. The covers are glossy stiff cardboard, and on the front is a picture of a man in rags fighting a thing partly like an ape and partly like a man, but much worse than either. The picture is in color, and there is real blood on the ape-thing; the man is muscular and handsome, with tawny hair lighter than Jason's and no beard.

"You like that?"

You are out of town already, and without the street lights it's too dark in the car, almost, to see the picture. You nod.

Jason laughs. "That's camp. Did you know that?"

You shrug, riffling the pages under your thumb, thinking of reading, alone, in your room tonight.

"You going to tell your mom how nice I was to you?"

"Uh-huh, sure. You want me to?"

"Tomorrow, not tonight. I think she'll be asleep when we get back. Don't you wake her up." Jason's voice says he will be angry if you do.

"Okay."

"Don't come in her room."

"Okay."

The Jaguar says "*Hutntntaaa . . .*" down the road, and you can see the whitecaps in the moonlight now, and the driftwood pushed just off the asphalt.

"You got a nice, soft mommy, you know that? When I climb on her it's just like being on a big pillow."

You nod, remembering the times when, lonely and frightened by dreams, you have crawled into her bed and snuggled against her soft warmth—but at the same time angry, knowing Jason is somehow deriding you both.

Home is silent and dark, and you leave Jason as soon as you can, bounding off down the hall and up the stairs ahead of him, up a second, narrow, twisted flight to your own room in the turret.

I had this story from a man who was breaking his word in telling it. How much it has suffered in his hands—I should say in his mouth, rather—I cannot say. In essentials it is true, and I give it to you as it was given to me. This is the story he told.

Captain Philip Ransom had been adrift, alone, for nine days when he saw the island. It was already late evening when it appeared like a thin line of purple on the horizon, but Ransom did not sleep that night. There was no feeble questioning in his wakeful mind concerning the reality of what he had seen; he had been given that one glimpse and he knew. Instead his brain teemed with facts and speculations. He knew he must be somewhere near New Guinea, and he reviewed mentally what he knew of the currents in these waters and what he had learned in the past nine days of the behavior of his raft. The island when he reached it—he did not allow himself to say *if*—would in all probability be solid jungle a few feet back from the water's edge. There might or might not be natives, but he brought to mind all he could of the Bazaar Malay and Tagalog he had acquired in his years as a pilot, plantation manager, white hunter, and professional fighting man in the Pacific.

In the morning he saw that purple shadow on the horizon again, a little nearer this time and almost precisely where his mental calculations had told him to expect it. For nine days there had been no reason to employ the inadequate paddles provided with the raft, but now he had something to row for. Ransom drank the last of his water and began stroking with a steady and powerful beat which was not interrupted until the prow of his rubber craft ground into beach sand.

Morning. You are slowly awake. Your eyes feel gummy, and the light over your bed is still on. Downstairs there is no one, so you get a bowl and milk and puffed, sugary cereal out for yourself and light the oven with a kitchen match so that you can eat and read by its open door. When the cereal is gone you drink the sweet milk and crumbs in the bottom of the bowl and start a pot of coffee, knowing that will please Mother. Jason comes down, dressed but not wanting to talk; drinks coffee and makes one piece of cinnamon toast in the oven. You listen to him leave, the stretched buzzing of his car on the road, then go up to Mother's room.

She is awake, her eyes open looking at the ceiling, but you know she isn't ready to get up yet. Very politely, because that minimizes the chances of being shouted at, you say, "How are you feeling this morning, Mama?"

She rolls her head to look. "Strung out. What time is it, Tackie?"

You look at the little folding clock on her dresser. "Seventeen minutes after eight."

"Jason go?"

"Yes, just now, Mama."

She is looking at the ceiling again. "You go back downstairs now, Tackie. I'll get you something when I feel better."

Downstairs you put on your sheepskin coat and go out on the veranda to look at the sea. There are gulls riding the icy wind, and very far off something orange bobbing in the waves, always closer.

A life raft. You run to the beach, jump up and down and wave your cap. "Over here. Over here."

The man from the raft has no shirt but the cold doesn't seem to bother him. He holds out his hand and says, "Captain Ransom," and you take it and are suddenly taller and older; not as tall as he is or as old as he is, but taller and older than yourself. "Tackman Babcock, Captain."

"Pleased to meet you. You were a friend in need there a minute ago."

"I guess I didn't do anything but welcome you ashore."

"The sound of your voice gave me something to steer for while my eyes were too busy watching that surf. Now you can tell me where I've landed and who you are."

You are walking back up to the house now, and you

explain to Ransom about you and Mother, and how she doesn't want to enroll you in the school here because she is trying to get you into the private school your father went to once. And after a time there is nothing more to say, and you show Ransom one of the empty rooms on the third floor where he can rest and do whatever he wants. Then you go back to your own room to read.

"Do you mean that you *made* these monsters?"

"*Made* them?" Dr. Death leaned forward, a cruel smile playing about his lips. "Did God *make* Eve, Captain, when he took her from Adam's rib? Or did Adam make the bone and God *alter* it to become what he wished? Look at it this way, Captain. I am God and Nature is Adam."

Ransom looked at the thing who grasped his right arm with hands that might have circled a utility pole as easily. "Do you mean that this thing is an animal?"

"Not animal," the monster said, wrenching his arm cruelly. "Man."

Dr. Death's smile broadened. "Yes, Captain, man. The question is, what are you? When I'm finished with you we'll see. Dulling your mind will be less of a problem than upgrading these poor brutes; but what about increasing the efficacy of your sense of smell? Not to mention rendering it impossible for you to walk erect."

"*Not* to walk all-four-on-ground," the beast-man holding Ransom muttered, "*that* is the *law.*"

Dr. Death turned and called to the shambling hunchback Ransom had seen earlier, "Golo, see to it that Captain Ransom is securely put away; then prepare the surgery."

A car. Not Jason's noisy Jaguar, but a quiet, large-sounding car. By heaving up the narrow, tight little window at the corner of the turret and sticking your head out into the cold wind you can see it: Dr. Black's big one, with the roof and hood all shiny with new wax.

Downstairs Dr. Black is hanging up an overcoat with a collar of fur, and you smell the old cigar smoke in his clothing before you see him; then Aunt May and Aunt Julie are there to keep you occupied so that he won't be reminded too vividly that marrying Mama means getting you as well. They talk to you: "How have you been, Tackie? What do you find to do out here all day?"

"Nothing."

"Nothing? Don't you ever go looking for shells on the beach?"

"I guess so."

"You're a handsome boy, do you know that?" Aunt May touches your nose with a scarlet-tipped finger and holds it there.

Aunt May is Mother's sister, but older and not as pretty. Aunt Julie is Papa's sister, a tall lady with a pulled-out, unhappy face, and makes you think of him even when you know she only wants Mama to get married again so that Papa won't have to send her any more money.

Mama herself is downstairs now in a clean new dress with long sleeves. She laughs at Dr. Black's jokes and holds onto his arm, and you think how nice her hair looks and that you will tell her so when you are alone. Dr. Black says, "How about it, Barbara, are you ready for the party?" and Mother, "Heavens no. You know what this place is like–yesterday I spent all day cleaning and today you can't even see what I did. But Julie and May will help me."

Dr. Black laughs. "After lunch."

You get into his big car with the others and go to a restaurant on the edge of a cliff, with a picture window to see the ocean. Dr. Black orders a sandwich for you that has turkey and bacon and three pieces of bread, but you are finished before the grown-ups have started, and when you try to talk to Mother, Aunt May sends you out to where there is a railing with wire to fill in the spaces like chicken wire only heavier, to look at the view.

It is really not much higher than the top window at home. Maybe a little higher. You put the toes of your shoes in the wire and bend out with your stomach against the rail to look down, but a grown-up pulls you down and tells you not to do it, then goes away. You do it again, and there are rocks at the bottom which the waves wash over in a neat way, covering them up and then pulling back. Someone touches your elbow, but you pay no attention for a minute, watching the water.

Then you get down, and the man standing beside you is Dr. Death.

He has a white scarf and black leather gloves and his hair is shiny black. His face is not tanned like Captain Ransom's but white, and handsome in a different way like the statue of a head that used to be in Papa's library when you and Mother used to live in town with him, and you think: Mama would say after he was gone how good looking he was. He smiles at you, but you are no older.

"Hi." What else can you say?

"Good afternoon, Mr. Babcock. I'm afraid I startled you."

You shrug. "A little bit. I didn't expect you to be here, I guess."

Dr. Death turns his back to the wind to light a cigarette he takes from a gold case. It is longer even than a 101 and has a red tip, and a gold dragon on the paper. "While you were looking down, I slipped from between the pages of the excellent novel you have in your coat pocket."

"I didn't know you could do that."

"Oh, yes. I'll be around from time to time."

"Captain Ransom is here already. He'll kill you."

Dr. Death smiles and shakes his head. "Hardly. You see, Tackman, Ransom and I are a bit like wrestlers; under various guises we put on our show again and again—but only under the spotlight." He flicks his cigarette over the rail and for a moment your eyes follow the bright spark out and down and see it vanish in the water. When you look back, Dr. Death is gone, and you are getting cold. You go back into the restaurant and get a free mint candy where the cash register is and then go to sit beside Aunt May again in time to have coconut cream pie and hot chocolate.

Aunt May drops out of the conversation long enough to ask, "Who was that man you were talking to, Tackie?"

"A man."

In the car Mama sits close to Dr. Black, with Aunt Julie on the other side of her so she will have to, and Aunt May sits way up on the edge of her seat with her head in between theirs so they can all talk. It is grey and cold outside; you think of how long it will be before you are home again, and take the book out.

Ransom heard them coming and flattened himself against the wall beside the door of his cell. There was no way out, he knew, save through that iron portal.

For the past four hours he had been testing every surface of the stone room for a possible exit, and there was none. Floor, walls, and ceiling were of cyclopean stone blocks; the windowless door of solid metal locked outside.

Nearer. He tensed every muscle and knotted his fists.

Nearer. The shambling steps halted. There was a rattle of keys and the door swung back. Like a thunderbolt of purpose he drove through the opening. A hideous face loomed above him and he sent his right fist crashing into it, knocking the lumbering beast-man to his knees. Two hairy arms pinioned him from behind, but he fought free and the monster reeled under his blows. The corridor stretched ahead of him with a dim glow of daylight at the end and he sprinted for it. Then–darkness!

When he recovered consciousness he found himself already erect, strapped to the wall of a brilliantly lit room which seemed to share the characters of a surgical theater and a chemical laboratory. Directly before his eyes stood a bulky object which he knew must be an operating table, and upon it, covered with a sheet, lay the unmistakable form of a human being.

He had hardly had time to comprehend the situation when Dr. Death entered, no longer in the elegant evening dress in which Ransom had beheld him last, but wearing white surgical clothing. Behind him limped the hideous Golo, carrying a tray of implements.

"Ah!" Seeing that his prisoner was conscious, Dr. Death strolled across the room and raised a hand as though to strike him in the face, but, when Ransom did not flinch, dropped it, smiling. "My dear Captain! You are with us again, I see."

"I hoped for a minute there," Ransom said levelly, "that I was away from you. Mind telling me what got me?"

"A thrown club, or so my slaves report. My baboon-man is quite good at it. But aren't you going to ask about this charming little tableau I've staged for you?"

"I wouldn't give you the pleasure."

"But you are curious." Dr. Death smiled his crooked smile. "I shall not keep you in suspense. Your own time, Captain, has not come yet; and before it does I am going to demonstrate my technique to you. It is so seldom that I have a really appreciative audience." With a calculated gesture he whipped away the sheet which had covered the prone form on the operating table.

Ransom could scarcely believe his eyes. Before him lay the unconscious body of a girl, a girl with skin as white as silk and hair like the sun seen through mist.

"You are interested now, I see," Dr. Death remarked drily, "and you consider her beautiful. Believe me, when I have completed my work you will flee screaming if she so much as turns what will no longer be a face toward you. This woman has been my implacable enemy since I came to this island, and the time has come for me to"–he halted in mid-sentence and looked at Ransom with an expression of mingled slyness and gloating–"for me to illustrate something of your own fate, shall we say."

While Dr. Death had been talking his deformed assistant had prepared a hypodermic. Ransom watched as the needle plunged into the girl's almost translucent flesh, and the liquid in the syringe–a fluid which by its very color suggested the vile perversion of medical technique–entered her bloodstream. Though still unconscious the girl sighed, and it seemed to Ransom that a cloud passed over her sleeping face as though she had already begun an evil dream. Roughly the hideous Golo turned her on her back and fastened in place straps of the same kind as those that held Ransom himself pinned to the wall.

"What are you reading, Tackie?" Aunt May asked.

"Nothing." He shut the book.

"Well, you shouldn't read in the car. It's bad for your eyes."

Dr. Black looked back at them for a moment, then asked Mama, "Have you gotten a costume for the little fellow yet?"

"For Tackie?" Mama shook her head, making her beautiful hair shine even in the dim light of the car. "No, nothing. It will be past his bedtime."

"Well, you'll have to let him see the guests anyway, Barbara; no boy should miss that."

And then the car was racing along the road out to Settlers Island. And then you were home.

Ransom watched as the loathsome creature edged toward him. Though not as large as some of the others its great teeth looked formidable indeed, and in one hand it grasped a heavy jungle knife with a razor edge.

For a moment he thought it would molest the unconscious girl, but it circled around her to stand before Ransom himself, never meeting his eyes.

Then, with a gesture as unexpected as it was frightening, it bent suddenly to press its hideous face against his pinioned right hand, and a great, shuddering gasp ran through the creature's twisted body.

Ransom waited, tense.

Again that deep inhalation, seeming almost a sob. Then the beast-man straightened up, looking into Ransom's face but avoiding his gaze. A thin, strangely familiar whine came from the monster's throat.

"Cut me loose," Ransom ordered.

"Yes. This I came to. Yes, Master." The huge head, wider than it was high, bobbed up and down. Then the sharp blade of the machete bit into the straps holding Ransom. As soon as he was free he took the blade from the willing hand of the beast-man and freed the limbs of the girl on the operating table. She was light in his arms, and for an instant he stood looking down at her tranquil face.

"Come, Master." The beast-man pulled at his sleeve. "Bruno knows a way out. Follow Bruno."

A hidden flight of steps led to a long and narrow corridor, almost pitch dark. "No one use this way," the beast-man said in his harsh voice. "They not find us here."

"Why did you free me?" Ransom asked.

There was a pause, then almost with an air of shame the great, twisted form replied, "You smell good. And Bruno does not like Dr. Death."

Ransom's conjectures were confirmed. Gently he asked, "You were a dog before Dr. Death worked on you, weren't you, Bruno?"

"Yes." The beast-man's voice held a sort of pride. "A St. Bernard. I have seen pictures."

"Dr. Death should have known better than to employ

his foul skills on such a noble animal," Ransom reflected aloud. "Dogs are too shrewd in judging character; but then the evil are always foolish in the final analysis."

Unexpectedly the dog-man halted in front of him, forcing Ransom to stop too. For a moment the massive head bent over the unconscious girl. Then there was a barely audible growl. "You say, Master, that I can judge. Then I tell you Bruno does not like this female Dr. Death calls Talar of the Long Eyes."

You put the open book face-down on the pillow and jump up, hugging yourself and skipping bare heels around the room. Marvelous! Wonderful!

But no more reading tonight. Save it, save it. Turn the light off, and in the delicious dark put the book reverently away under the bed, pushing aside pieces of the Tinker Toy set and the box with the filling station game cards. Tomorrow there will be more, and you can hardly wait for tomorrow. You lie on your back, hands under head, covers up to chin and when you close your eyes, you can see it all: the island, with jungle trees swaying in the sea wind; Dr. Death's castle lifting its big, cold greyness against the hot sky.

The whole house is still, only the wind and the Atlantic are out, the familiar sounds. Downstairs Mother is talking to Aunt May and Aunt Julie and you fall asleep.

You are awake! Listen! Late, it's very late, a strange time you have almost forgotten. Listen!

So quiet it hurts. Something. Something. Listen!

On the steps.

You get out of bed and find your flashlight. Not because you are brave, but because you cannot wait there in the dark.

There is nothing in the narrow, cold little stairwell outside your door. Nothing in the big hallway of the second floor. You shine your light quickly from end to end. Aunt Julie is breathing through her nose, but there is nothing frightening about that sound, you know what it is: only Aunt Julie, asleep, breathing loud through her nose.

Nothing on the stairs coming up.

You go back to your room, turn off your flashlight, and get into bed. When you are almost sleeping there is the scrabbling sound of hard claws on the floorboards and a rough tongue touching your fingertips. "Don't be afraid, Master, it is only Bruno." And you feel him, warm with his own warm and smelling of his own smell, lying beside your bed.

Then it is morning. The bedroom is cold, and there is no one in it but yourself. You go into the bathroom where there is a thing like a fan but with hot electric wires to dress.

Downstairs Mother is up already with a cloth thing tied over her hair, and so are Aunt May and Aunt Julie, sitting at the table with coffee and milk and big slices of fried ham. Aunt Julie says, "Hello, Tackie," and Mother smiles at you. There is a plate out for you already and you have ham and toast.

All day the three women are cleaning and putting up decorations–red and gold paper masks Aunt Julie made to hang on the wall, and funny lights that change color and go around–and you try to stay out of the way, and bring in wood for a fire in the big fireplace that almost never gets used. Jason comes, and Aunt May and Aunt Julie don't like him, but he helps some and goes into town in his car for things he forgot to buy before. He won't take you, this time. The wind comes in around the window, but they let you alone in your room and it's even quiet up there because they're all downstairs.

Ransom looked at the enigmatic girl incredulously.

"You do not believe me," she said. It was a simple statement of fact, without anger or accusation.

"You'll have to admit it's pretty hard to believe," he temporized. "A city older than civilization, buried in the jungle here on this little island."

Talar said tonelessly, "When you were as he"—she pointed at the dog-man—"is now, Lemuria was queen of this sea. All that is gone, except my city. Is not that enough to satisfy even Time?"

Bruno plucked at Ransom's sleeve. "Do not go, Master! Beast-men go sometimes, beast-men Dr. Death does not want, few come back. They are very evil at that place."

"You see?" A slight smile played about Talar's ripe lips. "Even your slave testifies for me. My city exists."

"How far?" Ransom asked curtly.

"Perhaps half a day's travel through the jungle." The girl paused, as though afraid to say more.

"What is it?" Ransom asked.

"You will lead us against Dr. Death? We wish to cleanse this island which is our home."

"Sure. I don't like him any more than your people do. Maybe less."

"Even if you do not like my people you will lead them?"

"If they'll have me. But you're hiding something. What is it?"

"You see me, and I might be a woman of your own people. Is that not so?" They were moving through the jungle again now, the dog-man reluctantly acting as rear guard.

"Very few girls of my people are as beautiful as you are, but otherwise yes."

"And for that reason I am high priestess to my people, for in me the ancient blood runs pure and sweet. But it is not so with all." Her voice sunk to a whisper. "When a tree is very old, and yet still lives, sometimes the limbs are strangely twisted. Do you understand?"

"Tackie? Tackie are you in there?"

"Uh-huh." You put the book inside your sweater.

"Well, come and open this door. Little boys ought not to lock their doors. Don't you want to see the company?"

You open, and Aunt May's a gypsy with long hair that isn't hers around her face and a mask that is only at her eyes.

Downstairs cars are stopping in front of the house and Mother is standing at the door dressed in Day-Glo robes that open way down the front but cover her arms almost to the ends of her fingers. She is talking to everyone as they come in, and you see her eyes are bright and strange the way they are sometimes when she dances by herself and talks when no one is listening.

A woman with a fish for a head and a shiny, silver dress is Aunt Julie. A doctor with a doctor's coat and listening things and a shiny thing on his head to look through is Dr. Black, and a soldier in a black uniform with a pirate thing on his hat and a whip is Jason. The big table has a punchbowl and cakes and little sandwiches and hot bean dip. You pull away when the gypsy is talking to someone and take some cakes and sit under the table watching legs.

There is music and some of the legs dance, and you stay under there a long time.

Then a man's and a girl's legs dance close to the table and there is suddenly a laughing face in front of you–Captain Ransom's. "What are you doing under there, Tack? Come out and join the party." And you crawl out, feeling very small instead of older, but older when you stand up. Captain Ransom is dressed like a castaway in a ragged shirt and pants torn off at the knees, but all clean and starched. His love beads are seeds and sea shells, and he has his arm around a girl with no clothes at all, just jewelry.

"Tack, this is Talar of the Long Eyes."

You smile and bow and kiss her hand, and are nearly as tall as she. All around people are dancing or talking, and no one seems to notice you. With Captain Ransom on one side of Talar and you on the other you thread your way through the room, avoiding the dancers and the little groups of people with drinks. In the room you and Mother use as a living room when there's no company, two men and two girls are making love with the television on, and in the little room past that a girl is sitting on the floor with her back to the wall, and men are standing in the corners. "Hello," the girl says. "Hello to you all." She is the first one to have noticed you, and you stop.

"Hello."

"I'm going to pretend you're real. Do you mind?"

"No." You look around for Ransom and Talar, but they are gone and you think that they are probably in the living room, kissing with the others.

"This is my third trip. Not a good trip, but not a bad trip. But I should have had a monitor–you know, someone to stay with me. Who are those men?"

The men in the corners stir, and you can hear the clinking of their armor and see light glinting on it and you look away. "I think they're from the City. They probably came to watch out for Talar," and somehow you know that this is the truth.

"Make them come out where I can see them."

Before you can answer Dr. Death says, "I don't really think you would want to," and you turn and find him standing just behind you wearing full evening dress and a cloak. He takes your arm. "Come on, Tackie, there's something I think you should see." You follow him to the back stairs and then up, and along the hall to the door of Mother's room.

Mother is inside on the bed, and Dr. Black is standing over her filling a hypodermic. As you watch, he pushes up her sleeve so that all the other injection marks show ugly and red on her arm, and all you can think of is Dr. Death bending over Talar on the operating table. You run downstairs looking for Ransom, but he is gone and there is nobody at the party at all except the real people and, in the cold shadows of the back stoop, Dr. Death's assistant Golo, who will not speak, but only stares at you in the moonlight with pale eyes.

The next house down the beach belongs to a woman you

have seen sometimes cutting down the dry fall remnant of her asparagus or hilling up her roses while you played. You pound at her door and try to explain, and after a while she calls the police.

. . . across the sky. The flames were licking at the roof timbers now. Ransom made a megaphone of his hands and shouted, "Give up! You'll all be burned to death if you stay in there!" but the only reply was a shot and he was not certain they had heard him. The Lemurian bowmen discharged another flight of arrows at the windows.

Talar grasped his arm: "Come back before they kill you."

Numbly he retreated with her, stepping across the massive body of the bull-man, which lay pierced by twenty or more shafts.

You fold back the corner of a page and put the book down. The waiting room is cold and bare, and although sometimes the people hurrying through smile at you, you feel lonely. After a long time a big man with grey hair and a woman in a blue uniform want to talk to you.

The woman's voice is friendly, but only the way teachers' voices are sometimes. "I'll bet you're sleepy, Tackman. Can you talk to us a little still before you go to bed?"

"Yes."

The grey-haired man says, "Do you know who gave your mother drugs?"

"I don't know. Dr. Black was going to do something to her."

He waves that aside. "Not that. You know, medicine. Your mother took a lot of medicine. Who gave it to her? Jason?"

"I don't know."

The woman says, "Your mother is going to be well, Tackman, but it will be a while—do you understand? For now you're going to have to live for a while in a big house with some other boys."

"All right."

The man: "Amphetamines. Does that mean anything to you? Did you ever hear that word?"

You shake your head.

The woman: "Dr. Black was only trying to help your mother, Tackman. I know you don't understand, but she used several medicines at once, mixed them, and that can be very bad."

They go away and you pick up the book and riffle the pages, but you do not read. At your elbow Dr. Death says, "What's the matter, Tackie?" He smells of scorched cloth and there is a streak of blood across his forehead, but he smiles and lights one of his cigarettes.

You hold up the book. "I don't want it to end. You'll be killed at the end."

"And you don't want to lose me? That's touching."

"You will, won't you? You'll burn up in the fire and Captain Ransom will go away and leave Talar."

Dr. Death smiles. "But if you start the book again we'll all be back. Even Golo and the bull-man."

"Honest?"

"Certainly." He stands up and tousles your hair. "It's the same with you, Tackie. You're too young to realize it yet, but it's the same with you."